# DOORMAKER

# ALSO BY JAMIE THORNTON

## DOORMAKER (Epic Fantasy)
*Rock Heaven: Book 1*
*Tower of Shadows: Book 2*
*Library of Souls: Book 3*
*The One Door: Book 4*

*Devil's Harvest: A Prequel*
*Torchlighters: A Short Novel*

## AFTER THE WORLD ENDS (Science Fiction)
*Run: Book 1*
*Hide: Book 2*
*Find: Book 3*
*Save: Book 4*
*Rage: Book 5*
*Raid: Book 6*
*Turn: Book 7*
*Live: Book 8*

## ZOMBIES ARE HUMAN (Science Fiction)
*Germination: Book 0*
*Contamination: Book 1*
*Infestation: Book 2*
*Eradication: Book 3*

**IGNEOUS**
BOOKS

PO Box 159
Roseville, CA 95678

*Rock Heaven: Book 1*

# DOORMAKER

# Jamie Thornton

IGNEOUS
BOOKS

To the readers who will never give up their search for answers.

# Chapter 1

BEFORE MAELLA'S FATHER LEFT, HE made her promise to never, ever open a door.

Maella still didn't understand why those were his last words to her.

She knew the family rule.

She had kept her promise even as her family had broken it again and again.

Her cousin had fixated on a medicine cabinet and opened it to a starry void that sucked him away. A car dashboard had mesmerized her aunt and she'd brushed it open to an angry swarm of wasps—and died from an allergic reaction after swelling to twice her size. Her great uncle had been in a depression while house-sitting for a neighbor, and he opened the fridge door. A tiger dragged him into a humid jungle, neither cat nor uncle seen again.

Two years after moving to their current house, her older brother, Esson, had disappeared through a door. He had only been fifteen years old.

She lived with her mother, her grandmother, and her little brother, Josa. They were all who remained of the family, but Maella didn't dwell on it. Well, she did, but only at night, when the darkness created its own form of privacy, since, after all, there was no door for her bedroom.

Her sixteenth birthday was in a few weeks, and the lack of privacy bothered her. A lot of things bothered her more than they used to. On days when Josa's noise and her mother's demands and her grandmother's guilting became too much, she escaped to the overgrown field behind the house. No one could see her there. It was the closest thing she had to a closed door.

She sat there now, on a decomposing oak log. The field backed up to a creek that ran dry most of the year—but not right now in the spring.

She always faced the door in the field, even on days like today when the grass had grown tall enough to hide it. The door was a black hole of decay and death and magic and magnetism.

"Maaayyy-eeellll-aaaaahh! Maaay-eell-aaahh!" Claritsa, her best friend, pronounced all three syllables of Maella's name with equal emphasis.

Maella stood on top of the log for a better look at the shifting stalks of grass. "Over here!"

Claritsa came crashing onto the flattened space around the log, stirring up lizards and pollen and mold. Out of the whole neighborhood, maybe this whole world, only Claritsa knew about her family's door problem. Two years ago, the same day Esson disappeared, she had discovered Maella's secret and they'd been inseparable ever since. She was the same age as Maella and liked to keep her hair in a pair of dark braids that whipped around her shoulders. Her thick bangs were just a little too long, but she had screamed bloody murder when her grandmother tried to cut them. "It's the latest style in Hollywood," Claritsa had said later to Maella.

Maella's mouse brown hair clung to her head in tight curls and made her look younger than she really was. She'd been born with hair like that—curly and tangled. She knew because her grandmother always brought up this troubling fact when Maella acted rudely.

Claritsa collapsed on the log and between gulping breaths said, "Cheyanne's got a new tricycle from the government… it's red and has a basket on front…and these bars on the back for someone to stand on…she's desperate to show it off and take us around."

Maybe Maella was too old for a lot of the things that used to entertain her as a kid, but any kind of bicycle meant freedom. Something Maella was desperate for. Normally, no one in their neighborhood could afford nice things. They bartered or salvaged or did without. She thrilled at the thought of seeing something new, even if it was just a tricycle.

"Then, let's go!" Maella leapt from the log, squished her shoes in the mud caused by a light rain the night before, and ran away laughing while Claritsa gasp-yelled for her to wait.

Bicycles were safe, and Cheyanne, even though she was much older, always wanted the two of them to come over. Everyone on the lane knew Cheyanne had brain problems that had kept her from graduating high school, getting a job, or moving into her own place, but her family had no money to name it, or do anything about it, and none of that mattered to Maella and Claritsa anyway. Cheyanne was one of the few people who never made Maella feel weird for not going to school with everyone else and for not having any doors in her house. Maella counted Cheyanne as her friend. She was pretty sure Cheyanne knew what it meant to feel like an outsider, just like her.

Maella raced through the grass, morning dew transferring from the stalks to her bare legs. Claritsa followed behind her, wearing Maella's worn-out skirt and her own shirt. Maella wore Claritsa's shabby khaki shorts, a thin t-shirt, and a jacket tied around her waist. Instead of two almost nonexistent wardrobes, the two of them pooled what they had into a single small one, infusing it with all the style two high school girls with no money, but lots of old fashion magazines, could muster.

They made it to the back end of the field, their socks soaked, their legs covered in flecks of mud. Maella took a path away from the part of the field where the grass hid the abandoned door. When she was six years old, Josa only three, and Esson eight, her family had escaped from their old home. They moved from place to place for years. But then the gold ran out and the servants left and her family moved into this ramshackle house. Her father hired someone to remove all the doors to the cabinets, drawer faces, bedrooms. They put up screen material as a front door. They replaced all the colored plates, cookware, and cups with glass and clear plastic versions. They lived without a fridge. They were really poor. Everyone on their poor country lane said so.

It was her mother who had found the front door.

It was like discovering a spot of quicksand, or hearing a rattler's telltale warning, or finding a mountain lion's den and not knowing if mom and cubs were still inside.

The workman had abandoned the door in the field without telling them. Maybe he'd had no room to haul it away, maybe he'd forgotten to take it, maybe he'd left it out of spite for the money Grandmother begrudgingly paid him from the last fold of damp, crumpled bills she kept tucked into her voluminous bra.

Once the door was laid to rest there, it settled in, besieged Maella's thoughts at night, taunted her with its solidness, its soiled permanence. The family couldn't move it. Mother was the only one of them who wasn't a doormaker. She could open doors without killing them all, but the door in the field was too heavy for her.

They were new to the neighborhood, known as the strange strangers who trashed all their doors, and they had no money to hire anyone else. They dared not burn it for fear it might spread and take out the field and grove and house and street.

Her father tried to destroy it. He used a sledgehammer and yet the door remained. He tried a saw, but her mother feared his fingers lifting the edge—it took so little—and she made him stop. So her father left the door to decay, and made Maella and both her brothers promise to never, ever go near it.

Sometimes Maella woke in the middle of the night, so late even the frogs and the crickets and night birds had gone to bed, and pictured the door. Its metal knob a chipped bronze. The wood a discolored, splintering gray.

This door should not have been there. This door haunted her. This door had taken her father.

After all his warnings and stories and promises, one day last summer her father had opened the door in the field. He'd lifted up its edge and vanished into the ground. Like it was nothing. Like it didn't matter to him what was on the other side. She'd screamed and run for her mother and found her sitting at the cracked metal breakfast table, crying over her eggs and coffee.

"He had to, Maella." Tears streamed down her red face and between her small breasts and behind her faded cotton dress.

"Why?" Maella demanded. She had turned fourteen years old by then and promised herself she wouldn't cry about Esson, about anything anymore. But her voice cracked from a mix of emotions she didn't know how to name. She felt outside herself, like the real Maella wasn't really standing at the table watching her mother fall apart and feeling her own insides break into pieces.

Her mother shook her head and lowered it.

Maella noticed a crumpled paper on the table. She smoothed it out but couldn't read the writing. Sometimes she could understand the words her mother and father spoke in the language from wherever they had all come from, but after arriving on Earth, her parents had refused to teach her and her brothers anything other than English. They swore it would help everyone better fit into their new permanent home.

The note was in her father's handwriting and their Botron family symbol marked the bottom of the page.

*A curved quarter moon, its points sharp like knives*—that's us, the doormakers, Grandmother explained once. *Three links, separate yet attached, pierced by the moon.* They are the —

But her father had caught them before Grandmother finished.

The only sound in the kitchen for a long minute was the drip from the kitchen faucet into dirty glass cereal bowls. A door wasn't dangerous to her family as long as you could see through it. Glass cups, glass plates, clear plastic everywhere.

"To keep us safe. Your father left to keep us safe," her mother finally said in answer to Maella's question. She would not utter another word of explanation.

That evening Maella took a broken golf club to all the windows on the first floor of their two-story house.

Josa watched with clenched fists and a blank look on his face, and her mother slapped her, but her grandmother folded her to her bosom, and then took in her mother and brother as well. All three of the women cried, and no one talked about fixing the windows because everyone knew there was no money. And her mother did not speak about blame.

They used the last of Grandmother's cash to buy extra firewood. There wouldn't be money to cool the house once the summer heat waves came.

Sometimes her mother still cried over her eggs, and this past winter's cold flowed effortlessly through the screens they hung up to keep out the bugs. It reminded Maella every day that her father had ignored all his promises and gone through a door. She would never forgive him for that, or herself for breaking the windows in a temper.

Maella hated that door in the field, how beautiful flowers had grown up around it, how it lay there rotting. How it taunted her. How even though she was almost sixteen, no one trusted her enough to explain what really happened when someone stepped through a door. How, as the days passed, it was like her mother and grandmother became more afraid, not less. How they never talked about what happened at all. How Maella could feel herself becoming desperate to know.

She wanted the truth. All of it.

But had no idea how to get it.

Claritsa caught up and cut in front, making Maella slip on the wet grass. Picking herself back up, Maella noticed green stains on her knees, and ran faster to escape the dark turn of her thoughts. She followed Claritsa through a grove of trees to their favorite path—a bridge of stepping-stones Claritsa had positioned so they could cross the creek without getting their feet wet.

Each stone was a potential door to Maella. Claritsa knew that and had placed the stones so that they wouldn't rock when stepped on. If the underside of one had a smooth enough surface to form a seal with whatever was underneath, then that was all it took. She could trip and accidentally lift up a stone with her hands and who knew what might come out.

It had to be her hands.

No other part of her body could open a door, only her hands. But Maella was always careful. Her family had made sure to tell her over and over again all the ways she could make a mistake—*that* truth had been drilled into her, relentless and thorough, over all the years she could remember. They had trained her—clasp your hands behind your back, focus on how your feet land so you won't trip.

Never lose that focus.

She ran behind Claritsa, eager for this day to turn into something other than pure boredom filled with feeling sorry for herself. Maella liked seeing Cheyanne have fun. It gave Maella hope that maybe she'd get lucky some day and figure out how to be happy, too.

Suddenly, on the last stone of their creek bridge, Claritsa froze.

Maella slammed into the back of her, sprawling them both forward onto the bank and shooting sand into the folds of her skin. Cold water gurgled into her shoes, but Maella was more concerned with where her hands had landed.

"Claritsa!" Maella said, fear making her heart pound so strongly it caught in her throat.

Claritsa knew about the doors and how careful Maella needed to be. But it was only sand. She was okay. No open doors. No starry voids.

Her heartbeat settled.

"Maella." There was a warning note in Claritsa's voice.

Maella looked up and into Barth's glittering stare. Daniel stood just behind him. Jack was on Barth's right.

Bartholemeau Hedrick—Barth, not Bart, for short unless you wanted a pounding—had dropped out of high school a couple of months ago at seventeen to help run his father's prescription drug business. Jack and Daniel had dropped out with him. Esson had been friends with Barth before disappearing through a door. Her mother made her promise to never go near him, but Grandmother dealt some sort of business with him every week.

Jack was Barth's shadow, but Daniel had been nice to Maella on occasion. He had even brought over a baked casserole from his mother after the lane gossiped about her father's abandonment.

"Well, look at this," Barth said. He sneered and wiped his nose on his arm. "Just who I was looking for."

Claritsa stood and water streamed off her skin, bringing up goosebumps. Maella stood up next to her.

Barth's plaid shirt was rolled at the sleeves and hung over a shredded pair of jean shorts. The other two boys matched him for shirts and shorts—Daniel's a muted green, Jack's a sickly yellow plaid. The boys looked burnt from too much sun, except they almost weren't boys anymore. Hair covered their legs, muscle roped their arms, their shoulders were broad.

"We're going to see Cheyanne," Maella said with a confidence she did not feel. "Let us through, Barth."

He laughed and shook away dirty blond hair from his eyes. "That retard? Why bother with her?"

Anger flushed Maella's cheeks. "Don't talk about her like that." She didn't understand how Esson could have ever been friends with someone so universally mean all the time.

"Seriously, Barth?" Claritsa said, rolling her eyes.

Barth was always going out of his way to prove he wasn't a loser by cutting everyone else down. But Maella wasn't going to let anyone make fun of Cheyanne, especially this jerk. "Maybe you should look in the mirror sometime. That way, you'll know what a real loser looks like."

Maella knew it was a stupid comeback as soon as the words left her mouth. She was too old for such childish insults—halfway through high school now, not that she'd ever stepped foot inside a real classroom. She blamed her lame insult game on not going to school like the rest of them had—how could she when every locker or book or classroom door might swallow her up?

Daniel shook his head, looking disappointed. Jack laughed.

"Yeah, oh, I'm sooo sorry." Barth rolled his eyes. "That cut so deep, you know. I feel terrible, just terrible. You've made me see the error of my ways. And I feel so bad about myself." He grabbed for Claritsa's arm.

Claritsa screamed and thrashed, but he was too strong. Maella launched herself at Barth, kicking and clawing. Sand flew into the air. His muscles did not budge until Maella sunk her teeth deep into his forearm.

Barth yelped, dropped Claritsa, shook off Maella, and swore. "You're going to pay for that."

"They're just kids, man, we've got better things to do," Daniel called out from a few yards away.

This offended Maella more than anything. The boys were barely two years older. But both Maella and Claritsa were tall and skinny and mostly flat. She might be almost sixteen, but her body had only begun to catch up and curve out. Her mother had been a late bloomer too. She tried not to care that she didn't yet look like how a woman was supposed to look, but that went as well as trying not to care about all the secrets her family still kept from her.

That is, she failed, miserably.

"Whose side are you on?" Barth demanded, narrowing his eyes at Daniel. "We came here for a reason. We're under a deadline."

"Yeah," Jack said. He crossed his arms, trying to look tough.

"A reason?" Daniel said, arching an eyebrow. "You can't be serious about all that stuff. I *know* you were making it all up, so just stop pretending."

Maella couldn't help herself. Her mother always warned her to stop running at the mouth, but Grandmother said she was too pigheaded to learn anyway but the hard way. "Jack Cord, you look like a clown in that shirt. Is that why you dropped out of school? To join the circus? Though I bet they wouldn't take you, would they?"

Better. She could live with that insult. At least it wasn't as embarrassing as her first one.

Jack's meaty hand snaked out and slapped her, sending stars across her eyes. Heat flashed across her cheek.

"Stop that!" Claritsa yelled and dragged Maella backwards into the creek.

Maella stumbled over a rock and they both fell. The creek water soaked their clothes and raised goose bumps. Maella's brain screamed at her in all of her family's voices—get your hands off the rocks! Don't open a door!

The boys stood in a line along the water's far edge, Barth with his arms crossed, Jack huffing and red in the face, Daniel frowning.

"Run?" Claritsa whispered into her ear.

Maella tensed her muscles.

Barth took one step into the water. "Come over here. There's no way you're getting out of a beating. And after that, there's business—"

"Run!" Maella screamed.

The girls scrambled backward across the rocks and the water. They made it to the other side of the creek and dashed through the grove of trees.

Claritsa pumped her thin legs next to Maella. The stomp of shoes sounded loud behind them. The boys were following and fanning out.

It wasn't long before the boys caught up. Barth began to take a path that would cut Maella and Claritsa off from the house. But if they could make it in time…Barth was afraid of Grandmother. Or at least he used to be. She could send the boys packing.

That's when Maella tripped.

There was a sickening sense of imbalance, and then all of a sudden, she found herself sprawled on the ground. Where were her hands? Panicked breaths erupted from her lungs until she could identify the burning sensation on her palms came from landing on some sticks in the grass. Her heart beat out of control. A loud wind filled her ears. Claritsa tumbled down a few feet away, a deep scratch on her cheek weeping blood.

Barth stood between them and the house. Daniel and Jack fanned out behind them, blocking the way back to the creek.

She forced herself to stand, but her knee buckled and blood welled out.

"Nice. Couldn't have picked the spot better my—" Barth began laughing. He pointed at Maella's chest. "Look at that."

She glanced down. The water and her fall into the grass had plastered her pale blue shirt to her skin. Her bra had been too soiled to wear today, and her jacket was still tied around her waist. Mother cleaned everything by bucket because they didn't dare own a washer and dryer with lids. Even she could see her nipples and her nonexistent breasts. For one split second, she imagined standing tall and fearless and with no shame. But no matter how desperately she wanted to be that person—she wasn't.

No, she wanted to die, just die, from embarrassment.

Barth's expression narrowed as his gaze returned to Maella's face. Everything about him turned cold, calculating, and business-like. "Your brother gave my father a lot of trouble, and it's time to collect on what's due."

Maella folded her arms over her chest. "Josa can't—"

"*Eddy* cost my dad a lot of business and money," Barth said, taking a step forward as he raised one hand into a punching fist.

The name sounded strange until Maella remembered— Esson had said his name sounded too weird, like someone not from around here, because they weren't from around here. He hadn't liked being different, so he'd told people to call him Eddy.

"He said only *he* knew how, but I'm pretty sure that's a lie." Barth took a step forward. "He lied about a lot of things and I'm gonna test one of those lies right now."

Maella had no idea what he was talking about, but her older brother had a special talent for getting himself into trouble. Whatever had gone on between Esson and Barth, she figured it had to do with prescription drugs and it must have been bad.

Claritsa huddled against Maella. No one could see them, not with the tall grass stalks in the way. When Maella looked to Daniel for help, he avoided her eyes. Jack seemed to be enjoying the whole spectacle, a big smile splitting his face. Maella wanted to wring his neck like Grandmother did to the chickens they ate for holiday dinners.

Barth took another step.

Claritsa made a furious dash away.

"Grab her," Barth said as he went for Maella, catching her by the ankle, which tripped her to the ground again.

Scrambling away, she felt a hard edge underneath her hands. Splinters of wood shot burning pain into her palms.

The door in the field.

Maella drew in a sharp breath as she pictured how Barth had moved through the field. Had he been herding them to this spot? She had thought he meant to cut them off from the house, but what if—

A cold sweat broke out across her skin.

But what if he had been trying to bring them—here?

The smells of wet mud and broken grass and sweaty skin filled their punched-down section of weeds. Claritsa was pushed down next to Maella. Jack and Barth stood over them as two dark shadows, the sun behind their backs. Daniel was nowhere in sight. He'd probably been tasked to guard their rear against escape.

Maella had never been this close to the door. Had never dared touch it before. Her stomach flipped in fear, but she dared not let any of her feelings show.

She scrambled to her feet, keeping as much of herself away from the wood as possible. "Do you think we would have *any* money when we don't even have windows?"

Barth motioned at Jack. "Get over here and pick up the—"

"Idiot," Claritsa said between clenched teeth.

Barth's fist snaked out and punched Maella in the stomach. "Keep talking, Claritsa, and I'll just keep hurting your friend over here."

Maella lost her breath and fell onto her hands and knees, onto the door's rough, splintering wood. It felt like she was drowning and couldn't get her lungs to work.

"Go ahead," Barth said, eyes flicking over to Claritsa. "Call me an idiot again."

Maella took gulping breaths and forced herself to look up at Barth. He stood over her, face dark with the shadows the sun made. Anger made blood rush by her ears. A feeling of recklessness began to fill her. The same recklessness that had filled her when she broke all the windows with a golf club, and it mixed with her fear and her anger until she couldn't separate them anymore.

"Idiot."

The word escaped her lips at the same time as Claritsa's. Maella's heart soared. *This* was why they were best friends.

Claritsa rested a hand on her shoulder and stood rigid, her expression fierce. Her twin braids fell straight down her back. Maella promised herself to tell Claritsa later about how good her bangs looked—like a really tough movie star in an action movie.

Barth's expression turned ugly. "Hold them."

Jack came and grabbed Maella and Claritsa by their necks. He squeezed until Maella thought he would cut off the blood to her brain. She clawed at Jack's hands and her head spun. The sunlight brought tears to Maella's eyes.

Barth advanced, except—

He walked right past them and headed for the rotting door.

Panic fluttered in Dessa's stomach. No. There was no way he could know—

A blur of motion sent Barth flying through the air with a grunt. Daniel. He tackled Barth and they both fell onto the grass with a thump.

Jack's grip faltered. "What the hell, Daniel?"

Taking advantage of Jack's lack of attention, Maella yanked herself away. Claritsa did the same, rubbing at her throat and falling to her knees.

Maella tried to drag Claritsa. "Get up, get up."

Claritsa coughed—hacking, gulping coughs.

Daniel jumped off Barth, hopping from foot to foot. "This is stupid. Just stupid. Leave them alone. Eddy isn't worth this."

Barth swept his leg around, taking Daniel to the ground. He jumped up and delivered a savage kick to Daniel's belly, making him grunt in pain.

"You don't know *anything*. You know what my father will do?" Barth kicked Daniel again and brushed dirt off his shirt like this was all no big deal. "You shouldn't have done that."

As Maella got Claritsa up, Jack came back to himself. He herded them until they stood right on top of the door.

Dizziness overtook Maella. She never wanted to touch this thing. She never wanted to come near the door that had taken her father. Panicking, she searched for an escape. Barth and Jack stood in front of them. The house was behind them. Daniel lay on the ground, gasping for air. Maella thought about the safety of her grandmother's arms and attitude and wished for it with all her strength. But that sick feeling in her stomach told her they wouldn't make it to the house in time. She could still feel the violence in Barth's fist where he punched her, and the way her lungs still stuttered, like they weren't sure of this whole breathing thing, and the things he had said—

What did Barth know?

Maella grabbed Claritsa's hand.

Claritsa tore her tear-streaked gaze away from Barth and focused on Maella. There was a coldness in her eyes that made Maella shiver, and she was glad Claritsa's anger wasn't meant for her.

As Daniel lay huddled on the ground, Barth joined Jack.

Claritsa glanced down at the door and then stared at Maella, a question in her eyes. Like she was asking permission for something. All it would take was for Maella's hands to be touching the door, even if someone else opened it. There was no way Claritsa could think *that* was a good idea —

Maella shook her head. They would run for Grandmother. They would have to make it. They would *have* to.

Something in Claritsa's face shuttered close.

"Run!" Maella yelled as she leapt into the grass, the dew soaking her socks with a shock of coldness again. She expected to hear Claritsa's stomp next to her.

But there was nothing.

Maella stopped and turned back. Claritsa had grabbed the edge of the door and was pulling up.

Barth laughed. "I love it when people do my work for me."

For a split second, the whole world went silent. Maella wanted to shout into that silence for Claritsa to let go of the door. Let go. Let go—

—And then Barth shoved Maella at the door.

She flailed, trying to keep track of her hands, trying to avoid Claritsa and the door that was heavy, almost unmovable. But Claritsa *had* moved the door. Most of it still touched the ground, but the closer edge showed a dark strip.

A gap.

Maella fell against that gap and became wedged. The air smelled like wet soil and Josa's musty socks. Her hands touched the door, even as she tried not to, even as everything in her screamed to keep her hands away from it, even as her bare legs pressed against the cold, slimy ground, even as wood dug splinters into the flesh of her bare arm.

Her hands touched the door as Claritsa was opening it. All her training told her it was enough.

It was more than enough.

Her stomach exploded with butterflies even as she held her breath and waited for something to happen—a wave of water, an explosion of fire, a pile of snakes, her father and Esson waiting on the other side, laughing at the joke they'd played on her all these years.

The adults in her life had made her promise never to open a door because she was too young to understand the dangers, even as they turned the knob and invited themselves into danger's living room.

Darkness and silence greeted her.

That confused Maella even more.

She tried to slither out, the wood scratching her skin, and the mud soaking its coldness into her clothes and getting underneath her fingernails.

She was pinned.

Out of sight, somewhere behind her, Barth, Daniel, and Jack shouted at each other. In front of her, from out of the darkness of the door's gap, a cool, humid breeze brushed her face.

"Come on, Maella." Claritsa groaned and the door moved just enough to let Maella take in a deeper breath. But she was still stuck, her hands were numb, and nothing at all like she'd been warned would happen, had happened.

There was nothing. Worse than nothing. Only numbness.

Maella clawed at the ground underneath the door as relief and fear washed over her at the same time. That's all she could find—dirt and darkness and bugs.

All the lessons, all the warnings, all the training.

This was everything she had ever been warned against. But nothing had happened.

Maybe there was something wrong with her. Maybe the terrible thing the rest of her family could do—maybe it was broken inside of her.

Maybe she was broken.

The door's weight vanished as it was lifted off her back.

"Maella," Claritsa whispered, frantic.

Maella looked up. Barth and Jack each held a side of the door just high enough to release Maella from being pinched in place. The sun framed Barth's outline so brightly it hurt Maella's eyes.

"Higher," Barth said, cursing, but with a desperate note. "Lift it higher. I have to see—"

She turned back to see for herself what lay underneath the door. But the darkness was thick, so she used her hands to feel around, desperate for something other than dirt and dampness and slimy worms.

What was wrong with her? Had she been avoiding opening doors all these years for nothing? Could she have gone to school and—

Wait—

Where there should have been slimy, cold dirt, she found the edge of something else. Pushing her hand out over the lip, she felt only empty space.

An opening that shouldn't be there. A doorway.

"There," Maella breathed out the word like a sigh.

"What is it?" Barth said. "What's down there?"

She didn't let herself think about the dangers yet. Instead, she focused everything she had on one goal—closing this door before whatever was on the other side of that cavernous hole could kill them.

She wormed her way backward across the grass, thinking fast. All Barth and Jack had to do was drop the door. Once it sealed with the ground again, that would be it. The door would close. Everything would go back to normal.

A part of Maella hiccuped at the thought.

Normal. Where everything about the doors remained a secret. Where her family walked on eggshells around her and it was getting worse every day. Where she was promised *the truth* some far off day that never seemed to come.

But none of that changed the danger of *this* moment. So Maella attempted to stand on shaky legs as Claritsa grabbed her hand and helped her up.

Maella turned to face Barth. "You have to drop—"

Barth, still holding the corner of the door, aimed a kick at Maella's stomach.

She lost the ability to breathe and fell backwards. Where there should have been ground—wasn't. The pain from the kick made her want to vomit. Claritsa's grip on her hand was like iron.

Claritsa was falling with her—

Before Maella could feel afraid, before the doorway her hands had made consumed them, she saw the look of surprised relief on Barth's face.

Why would Barth be relieved?

Then Maella fell over the edge, breaking the promise she had made to her father.

# Chapter 2

MAELLA HIT SOMETHING COLD, WET, and soft.

The cold of it shocked her into breathing again. When she and Claritsa had tipped over the edge, she thought they would fall for ages, but it had felt like only a few feet.

The darkness was so thick and complete it was like she had been buried underground. Her heart raced. She didn't want Barth to close the door and lock her down here to die in the darkness. Her hands dug into damp, gritty, squishiness, exploring, trying to find something to hold on to. It all smelled like a weird coldness. Part of her brain recognized she was touching mud, but another larger part of her brain didn't recognize anything at all except that she had opened a door and that door had buried her alive.

"Maella?"

Claritsa's voice stilled Maella's hands, but more importantly, broke the panicked race of her thoughts.

"I'm here," Maella said. Her voice echoed strangely in the darkness, like they were in a large, cavernous space.

"Why did you lift up the door..." Maella started. "We could have made it to Grandmother, but you made me—"

"Maella—"

"We could have—"

"Maella." Claritsa's voice was scratchy, panicked.

Maella felt Claritsa paw at her arm and then grab her hand with a strength that made her wince.

Then Maella remembered.

Claritsa did not do well in the dark, not since Maella had found her locked in a small shed two years ago when Esson had vanished. Claritsa had been yelling—Maella didn't know for how long before she found her, but—long enough that Claritsa's voice had turned scratchy and dull. Maella had feared she'd lost Claritsa through the door with Esson.

It's how come Claritsa knew. It's how come they could be friends. Two years ago Claritsa had seen Esson open a door and then been locked in a shed. Maella had broken the shed lock with a pry-bar rusting in the grass. It took five minutes of coaxing to get Claritsa to actually open the door since Maella could not. Ever since, Claritsa fell into a stony, dangerous silence whenever Maella mentioned anything about that day.

Maella squeezed Claritsa's hand. "It'll be okay." She looked around for any hint of light that would show a way out. Her eyes constantly searched for anything to lock onto, making her dizzy. Finally she closed them and the spinning stilled.

"Where are we?" Claritsa's voice floated away and bounced back.

"I don't know." A part of her didn't even care. They were alive. The door hadn't killed them. And Barth somehow had known about the doors—it was the only thing that made the relief on his face make sense. The way she'd been herded to the door, the way he had kicked her through.

He had known about the doors.

Or, he had at least suspected, and today had proved the truth of that suspicion.

And when would *she* find out the truth?

Mud suctioned at her knees. A faint clash of metal echoed from somewhere far off. She opened her eyes, searching for the sound, but that just made her dizzy again.

"Did you hear that?" Maella whispered. Talking loudly didn't feel right. She decided they must actually be underground somewhere because she couldn't see any stars, if stars existed here. The air felt so still, like it hadn't moved in years, but the way the sounds moved around made her think of a tunnel.

Claritsa whispered, her voice shaky. "I heard it."

"I think maybe we should follow it."

"I can't tell where it's coming from." Claritsa almost wailed these words.

Maella bit her lip to keep from telling her to shut up. It felt wrong to be loud. Claritsa's entire body shook against her.

One time, after Father had left, after Claritsa had caught her crying, she'd taken Maella over to her house. They'd leaned up against the side of Claritsa's washing machine during the spin cycle. Claritsa talked about roller coasters and car races, things Maella had never experienced, and it had felt dangerous, being that close to the machine's lid, imagining what would happen if she lifted it—would she see the clothes spin into a vortex that would suck her inside?

But she didn't open it.

Instead, she let its shaking take over and control the way her insides shook so that she wouldn't fall to pieces.

Claritsa was falling into pieces in the dark. Maella couldn't let herself do the same, no matter how strongly fear twisted her insides. She had to help Claritsa and get them out.

Maella tugged on Claritsa's hand and forced them to stumble through the ankle-deep muck. She hoped they were going in the right direction. The cold brought out goosebumps on her skin. They were dressed for spring weather and were now wet with icy mud. They were like blind people feeling their way through the unknown bowels of a monster.

Claritsa hiccuped beside her. Maella's free hand hit against something rough, something that finally wasn't mud. It felt like rock, like the inside of a cave. "I think I found a wall."

She followed its ragged edge. The clanging started up again, and this time Maella swore she heard a man yell. She stumbled on a stick of some sort. The sounds seemed closer, like maybe they were going the right direction after all.

She tugged at Claritsa's hand while keeping one hand on the wall. The space began to lighten. Suddenly she could see the cragged rock wall they followed, the dark iron color of the wet mud they stumbled through, the mud-covered sticks strewn around them in piles. They were inside a rocky tunnel, just like she'd suspected.

Then her straining eyes caught a pinprick of impossibly bright light ahead. "Do you see the light?" Maella said, forgetting to whisper. "Do you see it there? It must be the way out."

A noise sounded from behind them.

Not metal. A muffle, like an animal sniffing. Maella turned but only saw the barest glint of Claritsa's shining eyes.

"I see it!" Claritsa moved ahead, tugging on Maella's hand.

Maella followed Claritsa's lead now.

Another snuffle, or maybe just a rush of wind, sounded above and behind her. The wind felt hot and humid. Claritsa dropped Maella's hand, rushing ahead.

"Wait," Maella said. She tried to run, but stumbled instead. Forcing herself up, she heard the suctioning steps of something big moving behind her. Bigger than a bear, bigger than an elephant, bigger than anything she knew could exist.

"There's something following us," Maella said. "There's something—"

Claritsa looked over her shoulder. Even though she was back lit with the light outside the tunnel's entrance, Maella saw her eyes travel up, as if scanning something huge, and then widen with fear.

"Run, Maella! Run!"

Maella put all her muscle into lifting each leg out of the mud. Each step achingly slow. The hot wind of the monster seemed right on top of her.

The light grew, revealing more details of the long rocky tunnel, like the largest worm in the universe had burrowed through it. Some of the sticks that had tripped her were cracked in half, others not yet covered in mud were almost white.

There was a click, like the sound a neighbor's dog had made with its teeth the time it missed Grandmother's chickens by an inch.

The monster snorted and something brushed the top of her head. Before the monster blocked the light, Maella saw it took up almost the entire space. It wasn't a worm, it was something with wings and a tail.

She fell and cold mud covered her face. The light disappeared. Fear made it a struggle to breathe. The mud grabbed at her clothes and held her down. Grit crunched between her teeth. She wiped at her eyes, scratching her skin. The light came back, but it seemed so impossibly far away.

The monster's step caught the edge of her jacket. The weight of its step sunk the surrounding mud, turning it into a kind of quicksand. A loud pop hurt her ears when the mud released.

Claritsa screamed.

Maella struggled to wipe away the mud from her face and mouth so that she could breathe, so that she could yell at Claritsa to run, to hide, to draw the monster's attention so that Claritsa would be safe. All she managed was a coughing sound lost in the suctioning steps of the monster.

Claritsa screamed again.

Another sickening click of the jaw.

Claritsa stopped screaming.

The steps continued, warping the surrounding air.

Maella fought off the mud and stumbled forward through the tunnel. At least she hoped it was forward. The light was gone.

She felt the rocky wall in front of her. Cold, unforgiving. She took a deep breath and picked a direction. She would keep her hand on the rocky wall and follow it out and find Claritsa safe, oh please, let it be the right way.

It was so hard to hear anything over the pounding in her ears. Her eyes tried to focus on something, anything. One step, another step. She wanted to puke. She couldn't let herself.

Light burst out, but it came from the corner of her eye, from behind her.

She had chosen the wrong direction.

Maella cried out in frustration and panic. She faced the light and ran as fast as she could, each step dragging in the mud.

There.

Against a small crevasse in the wall was a crumpled shape. Beyond that, the tunnel's opening.

A pile of sticks lay next to the shape.

Not sticks.

Bones.

The sticks were bones.

Maella ran to the crumpled shape as fast as the mud would let her. She cursed like she heard her dad curse when he had discovered the door in the field.

She crept within inches, but Claritsa wasn't moving.

Maella began to shake. She couldn't hear anything except for the pounding blood in her ears. What if she reached out and touched her friend and—

Claritsa hiccuped.

Maella fell onto Claritsa, hugging her fiercely.

"I heard the snap," Claritsa whispered between hiccups. "I thought it must have got you. And then I felt its breath and it must be huge. But then I pressed myself into the wall and it kept going. I think it's too big to turn around. I think it has to go all the way out and—"

As if to confirm the truth of her words, the light ahead of them winked off again.

A trumpet sound blasted down the length of the tunnel. Maella clapped her hands over her ears from the pain. She held her breath, waiting for the monster to return. Instead, the light reappeared.

Outside the tunnel somewhere, people screamed so loud she could hear it over her ringing ears.

The monster no longer blocked the exit.

She tugged Claritsa away from the wall and through the last section of the tunnel. They burst through the ring of light at the tunnel opening like they were jumping into a pool.

Instead of finding wet mud on the other side, the ground was firm beneath their feet. Light seared Maella's eyes—the sun hot and big in the sky, hanging bigger than Maella could ever remember. A sound, like a shot, came from behind— from the tunnel's darkness. Maella whirled around. Down the tunnel, somewhere in its ceiling, was the doorway back home. But there was no time to go back for it now. Not if they didn't want to get eaten.

She blinked and felt hot tears streak down her cheeks from the pain of going from dark to light and back to dark. "Did you hear that, Claritsa? There's something else—"

"Maella, it's eating them!"

Maella turned away from the cave's darkness. Her eyes took long seconds to bring the world into focus. She saw only a few yards ahead at first, enough to know they had come out on the ledge of a hillside covered in a forest of a type of tree she didn't recognize, not that she knew her trees very well. Grandma always wanted her to pay attention to plants, but she never did, other than to make sure she knew poison oak when she saw it.

They stood above a small valley with an open meadow in its center. Trees rimmed the meadow, forming a thick forest that sloped up to their ledge and covered the surrounding hills. Shapes in the small valley below moved and one shape flew around.

At first, it looked like some of the people were fighting each other. Horses, spears, swords, bodies in the grass that didn't move. But then the fighting just seemed to stop as they realized a dragon-like monster flew above them. Many ran for the trees, but weren't fast enough.

In spite of the sunlight, the monster was dark, like the cave. Its feet were tucked underneath. Its body was as big as a whale, its tail long and lashing about like a whip, its ears triangular and pointed. Its snout was long, and even from their ledge, large white teeth glinted in the sunlight as it flew around, trumpeting, and scooping up people in great gulps.

People were dying right in front of her. The monster had almost killed her and Claritsa, but instead was killing these people.

Maella felt sick to her stomach. Was this her fault?

"Maella, we need to get out of here."

A part of Maella detached. This part saw Claritsa covered from head to toe in drying mud, hiccups rippling her body like a series of small earthquakes, her eyes wide and shining with tears.

But the other part of Maella, the bigger part, couldn't think about anything, except—the monster had been sleeping and her door woke it up and you weren't supposed to open doors because someone always died.

"Come away from there!" A woman's voice yelled from behind them. "Don't you know better than to go near the Klylup's home?"

A hand roughly grabbed Maella's arm, slipped off the mud that caked Maella like it did Claritsa, then renewed the grip, digging claw-like fingers into her flesh, yanking her up from the ground.

"Hey!" Claritsa said. "Let her go!"

Maella didn't fight the way the hand seemed ready to tear her arm from her shoulder. What did the pain matter stacked up against the pain she witnessed below?

The woman sucked in her breath. "Covered in the Klylup's mud…You went inside? You woke it?"

"We didn't do anything," Claritsa said. "We were being attacked and we—"

"You've got its mud all over you, girl. It only comes from one place in these mountains. Everyone knows better than to disturb the Klylup—"

Maella tore her eyes away from the massacre to really look at the woman. She was middle-aged, squat, stout, wearing some sort of beige-colored wrap for clothing like out of a history book. Her face was lined with wrinkles. Piercing blue eyes frowned at Maella. The woman's other hand shook Claritsa's arm, almost lifting her from the ground.

"I did it," Maella said. "I woke the Klylup."

"What did you say, girl?"

Maella returned her gaze to the valley. Some of the fighters had made it safely to the trees. The last one in the meadow dashed for safety. She held her breath and prayed he would make it. Please. Make it to the trees.

He was only a few yards away, jumping over dead horses and dead soldiers. The monster trumpeted and dived. It snapped its mouth and beat its wings to return to the sky.

"I opened the door," Maella said, staring at the spot where the man had been gulped up.

"Maella!" Claritsa shook her head, warning her to shut up. But she couldn't. She wouldn't.

"I shouldn't have done it. But I did. I opened the door."

"You opened a door? What fool talk is that?" The woman scrunched up her face, her eyes disappearing into folds of skin.

"I opened a door and we were in one place and now we're in another. And my father told me to never open the door, especially the door in the field. He told me never to open the door—" Maella repeated the words until she was crying. He had told her and she had tried not to disobey, and now those people in the valley were dead because of her and—

She felt a swat on her head. Claritsa yelped a second later. As the stars cleared from her vision, she felt another blow, harder.

"The last doormaker came through two years ago. There's none left, you hear?"

Maella's mind stuttered over the woman's words, unable to process them. "I opened the door and I shouldn't have, but I did." Maella waited for another blow.

The woman did not disappoint and slapped her upside the head. "Stop lying, girl."

"She's not lying," Claritsa said fiercely.

The woman looked at each of them in turn. "Filthy, Klylup-covered, disobedient, wretched young women." She grabbed great handfuls of their hair.

Pain erupted on Maella's scalp and she gritted her teeth to keep from yelling out. She deserved this pain. She deserved so much more than this.

The woman dragged them along the hillside on a small little dirt trail that overlooked the valley. "Foster will deal with you. Figure out who your kin is and beat you until you're bloody for these lies and for waking up the Klylup." She began mumbling to herself. "No sense in it, no sense in all the fighting they done, but not right either to mess with the Klylup. Not right at all."

Claritsa stared holes into Maella's skull, trying to get her to look. Maella couldn't bear it right then. No matter how hard her scalp hurt, her heart hurt worse. Instead, she focused on keeping in step with the woman's gait so her hair wasn't torn out of her head.

They stayed high up, along the edge of the hills, before dropping down to the valley, avoiding the battle that was no longer a battle. The Klylup had flown off, maybe to guard its tunnel, and the door to home. The surviving people had all fled into the trees. Silence made Maella's ears ring.

They walked for what seemed ages, Maella and Claritsa stumbling along on tiptoe. She tried to keep track of the cave that contained the door, but lost all sense of direction as the path through the forest became flat and wide. Trees changed from forest to orchard. Neat ordered lines of trees so unlike Mr. Tarry's overgrown mandarin forest at home. Maella and Claritsa liked to run around in it when the limbs were almost ready to break from the weight of the fruit and talk about boys and big houses and swimming pools and room service. But if Mr. Tarry caught you, he wasn't against firing a rifle shot or two just to scare you off.

The last line of orchard trees opened to the edge of a small stonework village set in a circular pattern. A dozen or more single-story buildings were carefully laid out to face the open space in the center.

Claritsa had stopped trying to catch her attention. She purposefully looked away now. Maella had probably just helped kill people, and she didn't know how to act, except that she felt sick and like she didn't want to speak another word for the rest of her life.

The trail beneath their feet became smooth, hard-packed, and once it hit the outer edge of the buildings, stone. It looked like one of those fancy brick neighborhoods Maella had only seen from the bus window that one day over five years ago when she'd been ten and had disobeyed and went to school in spite of the danger—just to see what it was like. She hadn't made it even a step inside the building before her mother arrived to scoop her up. Then CPS had come for a visit and they'd needed to move towns soon after.

A few women wearing clothes similar to their hair-dragging escort hurried with purpose in and out of buildings, carrying baskets and jars. Cooking smells made Maella's stomach cramp. People spoke in languages she didn't understand and couldn't even place. Even through her horror, she wondered how the woman had known to speak English to them. But then Maella overheard people rounding a corner who were speaking English. Something about boiling rice and bandages.

The woman dragged them across the center of the open space.

Another woman carrying a basket heaped with cloth strips stopped to watch them. "Linn Weavey, let go of their hair before you draw blood."

Their escort bobbed her head at the speaker. She clenched her hands more firmly into Maella's scalp. "Sorry, ma'am, but this is business for Foster, they—"

"They are two young women who you are causing a great deal of pain—"

"But Samay—the Klylup." Linn stopped and brought Maella and Claritsa up short, not letting go.

Samay approached. She looked Maella's mother's age, but there were barely any lines around her eyes, whereas her mother had plenty.

Samay turned her gaze back to Linn. "Did you see?"

Linn nodded. "It's over."

"So, they'll be back soon with the wounded. Foster is already back."

"It's the Klylup that ended it." Linn Weavey said. "These girls woke it."

"Yes, I can see the mud shows where they've—"

"They woke it."

"Linn, you need to stop interrupting me."

Maella felt Linn crouch a few inches. "Yes, ma'am."

"Whether it was them or the battle those men decided to fight over territory…" Samay lapsed into silence and her expression became troubled. She cleared her face into blankness. "…take them to Foster in one piece!"

Maella held her breath, wondering who would win this and why it even mattered to Samay. Finally, Linn loosened her grip and then let go of Maella and Claritsa's hair altogether.

"Better," Samay said.

Maella rubbed her scalp and felt the blood return to her head.

"Girls, look at me."

Maella did as Samay asked. Samay's eyes were brown and looked at Maella as if she could see into her soul.

"I don't know whose kin you are under all that Klylup filth, but once Foster is done with you, I expect your help with these bandages, and once the wounded—" her voice broke on that word and Maella knew there must be someone she cared about fighting in the valley. She hoped it wasn't someone the Klylup ate—hoped it with all her might to not be responsible for killing someone this woman loved.

"Once they return, we need everyone here and helping." Samay tilted her head toward Linn. "Everyone." Without another word, she hurried into the shadow of a building and called out an order that made everyone pick up speed with their tasks.

Maella felt a push on her back that almost sent her sprawling on the stone.

"Get going." Linn pushed them until they stood before a wood door carved full with symbols. She shoved Maella at the door latch and raised her hand as if to strike. "Open it."

"So you don't actually want to bring us to Foster?" Claritsa said.

"What foolish talk is that? This is Foster's place."

Maella stepped a few inches away and folded her arms across her chest. "I will not open that door." She planted her legs into the stone like she'd seen her mother do to her father when he pushed her too far on something. It didn't work so well since her legs still shook.

"Fool girl. Open the damn door."

"You're the fool," Claritsa said. Mud covered her from head to toe, the scratch on her cheek no longer bleeding. Maella barely recognized her except for her flashing eyes and the flip of her bangs. "She says she can open doors to other worlds and get people killed, but you want her to open this door?"

Linn's hand froze in mid-strike. Fear flitted across her face.

"Idiot." Claritsa stepped to the door, ready to open it for the both of them like she'd done for the last two years.

"Wait." Linn said in a panicked voice, as if she thought better of Claritsa opening the door, but it was too late.

The door opened to a stone room with a stone floor and a couple of chairs. Light streamed from wood blinds mounted between the beams of the ceiling. Several men surrounded a large desk covered in papers in the middle of the room. The men wore thick leather that covered their bodies like shields. Swords were strapped to their waists. Beards covered their faces. Dust and blood covered them from head to toe. They talked in hushed, urgent whispers, gesturing at the papers.

"Mr. Foster," Linn said, her voice suddenly high-pitched.

Three sets of bloodshot eyes turned onto Maella, Claritsa, and Linn.

Maella stood strong, her feet planted on the floor, and moved to clasp her hands behind her back like Grandmother had taught her. She was used to being scrutinized, laughed at, ignored, looked down upon. They could go jump in the creek for all she cared.

"Sorry to interrupt," Linn said. "It's just...I was on the ridge...I was..."

"Spit it out, now," said the man Maella supposed must be Foster. Shadows obscured all but his outline. He was a large, muscular man who swallowed the chair he sat in.

"I saw these two come out of the Klylup's cave. They're covered in its filth. They disturbed the Klylup!"

Foster rose from his chair. A slant of light illuminated his face, strong-boned with a well-kept beard. His hair was matted with dried blood. Then the shadows obscured his features again. He approached, and though Maella could not see his eyes, she could feel his examination.

"Whose kin are you?" Foster asked, looming over them.

Maella looked up but did not answer.

"She says—"

"I opened the door," Maella said, interrupting Linn. "I opened the door and we came through it and I woke the Klylup."

"What childish games are you trying to play, girl?" Foster said, quietly. "We have plans to make and men to save. We've fought a battle and been driven back and we have not yet accounted for all our wounded and you talk about doors and Klylups—do you have a death wish? Did someone you love fall in battle and now you wish to join him?"

Maella had never even held hands with a boy, let alone kissed or fallen in love with one. Claritsa would tell her stories sometimes of her own crushes and kisses—stories that made Maella long for a day she feared would never come. Who could ever love her when she didn't understand, let alone control, what was broken inside her?

Foster took a step back and looked at the three other men. "You recognize these girls?"

"Maybe if they were cleaned up," one said. His leg was slashed from knee to ankle, the leather pants hanging open like a flap, blood running down his skin in a thin line that formed a puddle on the stone floor at his feet.

The other man said something in a language Maella thought could be French and shrugged his shoulders.

Foster didn't bother looking at Linn, as if she was beneath his notice. "Men are dying, spilling their blood to protect this place, our crops, our home. And you bring two young women with a lovesick death wish to interrupt me?"

"But I thought—"

"I did it," Maella said, becoming angry that he didn't believe her, angry that she wasn't being held responsible for unleashing the monster. If they didn't punish her, she would never be able to live with herself. "We were in some place different and I opened the door and now we're here."

It happened so fast Maella didn't register his movement at first.

Foster dragged her over to his small, flimsy desk, took her hand in his, and pressed it roughly against a drawer handle. He smelled like blood and scared animals and sweat and something else she couldn't name at first—a terrible dead smell that choked her.

Claritsa yelled and rushed up, clawing at Foster's grip, but he brushed her off and two of the men pulled her away, holding her back.

"Leave her alone! Don't hurt her," Claritsa said.

"I don't like liars," Foster said. "And I don't tolerate door-makers to live. Open the drawer, girl."

Maella's hand trembled inside Foster's grip. She wasn't supposed to touch drawers, or closet doors, or refrigerator doors, or cabinets, or—

"Please, don't."

If he made her open the drawer, who would die as punishment for opening the door this time?

"Open it, and we shall see a drawer of pencils and knick-knacks," Foster said.

"Sir," the man with the slashed leg said. "What if she *is* a doormaker? Let us bring in more men, let us—"

"Silence," Foster said. "I killed the last one by my own hand. There are no more. Only impostors and lying women who are old enough to know better."

Maella tried to make sense of his words, but it was all too much and her brain couldn't process any of it, except Foster was crushing her hand and making her reach for the desk drawer.

"Don't!" Claritsa cried out. "She's telling the truth."

Maella's hand numbed under his grip. The smooth metal of the drawer handle felt cold on her skin. She did not at all feel it when he forced her to pull open the drawer an inch.

Orange flames erupted.

The flames from nowhere shot out and lapped at Foster's hand covering hers. His grip was so tight she barely felt the heat. Foster's skin began to bubble on his fingers. There was shouting and the smell of burning flesh and the room turned into chaos.

Foster jumped backward, tumbling to the floor while cradling his hand. The flames sputtered for a moment, then came back stronger, two feet higher than the drawer. Smoke curled at the ceiling as the desk itself caught fire. Maella sat stunned on the floor where Foster had thrown her.

Linn was nowhere to be seen, but the two men edged around the desk to the door. The flames made it easy to see their sweating faces, rolling, bloodshot eyes, fear in every line of their battle-weary muscles. They must have lost their hold on Claritsa because she appeared on her knees at Maella's side.

"Get up, Maella. Get up! We've got to get out."

Maella couldn't tear her gaze away from the desk. The flames reached higher and black smoke filled the room. Soon, the drawer would disintegrate altogether and no one would be able to close the door.

Maella pictured the flames filling the room, and then expanding from it, eating the other buildings and the crops and the nearby orchard.

Because she'd opened another door. Because she'd broken the one family rule.

She wished desperately for Grandmother to appear and fix this. To tell her what to do to make it right, or at least make it stop. And then, as if Grandmother stood next to her, as if she had walked into the room and come upon the scene of this mess like she had done when Maella had broken the windows—she heard her grandmother's voice.

*Close the damn door, Maella. Just close the damn thing.*

Maella pried off Claritsa's hands, jumped up, and ran to the inferno that used to be the desk. The drawer was still intact, its edges smoking, its metal handle red with heat.

Maella wrapped her hand in her shirt. She held her breath and dove toward the drawer, hand and arm extended. She hit the metal straight on with her palm, felt a dull burning as the heat transferred through the cloth, and only realized once pain bloomed harsh across her hand that she could have just used her shoe to kick the damn door closed.

The drawer shut and the wood desk exploded into a shower of sparks. Burning splinters grazed Maella's face before she stumbled away to collapse next to Claritsa on the cool, stone floor.

Within seconds, the desk turned into a pile of softly glowing coals. The door burst open and men charged in with water buckets, shouting at each other as they doused the last of the embers. At Foster's command, Maella and Claritsa were tied up with their hands behind their backs.

The last thing Maella saw before a hood came down was a roomful of men, horror etched across their faces, all staring at her.

# Chapter 3

"MAELLA?"

Maella sniffed. The hood over her head smelled like wet wool. They were alone somewhere, inside a different building than the one that had contained the burned desk.

"Are you crying?" Claritsa said.

"I'm sorry, Claritsa. I'm sorry I did this to you." All of Maella's questions burned her up inside. Her family had kept the truth, the full truth, from her for her entire life. There must have been a good reason, but she couldn't see it. Not now, not here, when she was like a baby in the face of Foster's hatred and Linn's disgust and even Samay's anxious handling of Maella like she was a wild animal about to bite.

"I'm not sorry."

"But Foster said they're going to kill us. That they don't allow people like me, like my family, to live."

Claritsa didn't respond.

A part of Maella knew she was too dangerous, she deserved to die. Hadn't she been trained her whole life to avoid opening any doors because of the terrible things that would happen? Then, just like that, she'd broken the one family rule. Part of Maella knew she was in shock, but knowing that didn't stop her thoughts from spinning out of control. "What if flames had come out of the door in the field? We would have been killed."

"But it didn't, Maella, and you saved us instead."

"Only to get us executed now."

"Stop it. You didn't know."

"But I did know! It was the one rule. I will never, ever open a door again. I would rather die first."

Silence filled the dark space between them.

"Then you really will kill us," Claritsa said finally.

Maella's mind stilled and her body went cold. "What are you talking about?"

"I'm sorry, Maella. I'm sorry I made you open the door. I…this is my fault. If I hadn't lifted the door in the field—but if they're going to kill us—then you've got to open another door. You've got to get us out—"

"Don't you remember the flames?" Maella interrupted.

"Don't be an idiot. What can we do but take our chances?"

"No." Fear rose up inside Maella's chest and clawed at her throat. All her family's warnings, all her training, all the stories of death and destruction, all the people she watched die in that valley, scooped up by the Klylup her opened door had awakened. This was her fault. "I'm not going to do it. Better to die than open another door."

"Maella." Claritsa's voice sounded soft and strangled. "I don't want to die."

Maella didn't respond. What was there to say? That she'd gotten her best friend involved in her family's mess and now was willing to let her die because of it?

A scratching sound drew Maella's attention to the side of the room. The hood over her head made it impossible to see anything, but she strained her ears, trying to understand the sound. She couldn't figure out how far away it was, or what size creature made it. Was there a guard in the room with them? Had he heard everything they just said?

Then a familiar masculine voice whispered their names, shocking Maella into a rigid, upright position.

"Maella? Claritsa?"

Maella could feel someone so close hot breath tickled her skin beneath the cloth covering her face. "Who's there?"

"Shhh, keep your voice down."

Daniel.

Strong arms reached around and embraced her, fumbling to untie the bindings at her wrists. She felt cloth against the cloth covering her face, the warmth of a body, the beating of a heart, the smell of grass and sunshine and their creek. It comforted her and made her feel weird all at the same time.

The ties fell from her wrists. All at once, the cloth lifted from her face. And then suddenly she was inches away from large brown eyes, a scruffy, familiar expression, a green plaid shirt, clothes and skin smudged with dried Klylup mud.

"What are you doing here?" Claritsa exclaimed when Daniel uncovered her head next.

"Shut up. They're right outside."

Claritsa lowered her voice. "What are you doing here?"

"Where's here? Where the hell is here?" Daniel looked between Claritsa and Maella and then settled an accusing stare onto Maella.

They weren't in the same world anymore. Or if they were, it was a different time period, or—she really had no clue, except they spoke lots of different languages and used swords and spears to fight flying monsters.

"I don't know," Maella said finally. Her family had only ever trained her not to open any doors. They had promised her the truth in some distant future when she was old enough that never seemed to arrive. They had not prepared her for any of this.

"Then do you know how to get back?" He asked, staring holes into her like he could see inside her soul. His body seemed stretched like a string about to snap. Daniel was on the verge of panic. And why wouldn't he be? Daniel had tumbled into a monstrous world far from home with no idea any of this had existed before now.

Maella bit her lip and slowly shook her head.

"Answer my question," Claritsa said, almost hissing. "Why are you here?"

He shrugged, stood up, and went to the window. His movements were stiff and somehow forced. Maella imagined him having stood on something on the other side of the window to pull himself through. It looked too high and small otherwise. Maella and Claritsa wouldn't get through it without help.

"You both fell away into the dark and Barth pushed me after you," Daniel said, still facing the window. "I guess because I tried to help you. He pushed me in to punish me and now I'm here. But where is here? What the hell *is* all this?"

Once a doormaker opened a door, the portal stayed open until someone—it didn't have to be a doormaker—closed it. Barth had somehow known about her family's door problem. Esson must have revealed enough to make Barth wonder, and then finally act.

"Did Barth follow?" Maella said, her voice raising a notch.

Daniel paused for a long second before answering. "No."

Maella released a breath. They were in enough danger without adding Barth to this mess. If they could just find a way back to the Klylup's cave, back to the door to home—a flicker of hope rose inside Maella. Maybe she could undo some of the damage she'd caused. Maybe she could at least get them all back home. Maybe—

"How do you know?" Claritsa demanded.

"I know," Daniel said as he looked down at his shoes and scuffed the floor with one.

"But *how* do you know?" Claritsa said, eyes boring into him.

He looked up, frowning, then turned away again. "They used the door to push me down. They closed it on me. *That's* how I know."

That small, flickering hope inside Maella blew out.

Once a door closed, it became a regular door again. Dangerous for her family to open, but nothing special to anyone else. And doors, once closed, didn't always open to the same place. Not that it mattered. What had been a door in the field on their side was probably now just a seamless, rocky wall on this side—impossible for her to open.

Making it impossible for them to use it to return home.

She pushed aside the rising panic that threatened to take over at that thought. Instead, she told herself to be glad that of the three boys who could have fallen through with them, at least it was Daniel, and not Barth or Jack. Even though Daniel was friends with the others, and part of whatever business Grandmother had with Barth, he'd tried to stop the other two at least.

She didn't trust him, but she didn't not trust him either.

"Anyway," Daniel said, sounding like he was trying to force his voice to relax, and failing. "I thought you should know everyone's running around like crazy trying to take care of the wounded. They're calling you a doormaker and saying there'll be an execution in the morning, no matter the wounded, and whether Madame Heller likes it or not— whoever she is."

Maella brushed off the name. She had no idea who Madame Heller was. "You have to help us. You have to—"

"All I want to know…" He jittered from foot to foot, nervous, glancing at the open window and then locking eyes with Maella, "…is if you know how to get us home. You did it, didn't you? You made that door in the field into—I don't know. Do you have any idea how to get us back?"

Maella shook her head as she tried to force down the panic threatening to swallow her up again. "I have no idea."

"Can't you just open another door?" Claritsa said, the words sounding choked. "Maybe the next one will take us home."

"Did you already forget what happened when I opened the drawer?"

"What are you talking about?" Daniel asked.

"Foster made her open the desk drawer," Claritsa said, her voice carefully neutral. "There was a fire."

Daniel looked at Maella like she had some sort of contagious disease. "That was you? What's wrong with you?"

"I…" It seemed like Claritsa had always known and Maella had kept it a secret for so long that she didn't know how to explain it now. "We've always—my whole family—has always opened doors and had horrible things happen."

"So you weren't just too poor to get new doors. You did all that on purpose?"

Maella nodded. "It happens when we open any kind of door, like a drawer, or a cupboard, or…" But she stopped because she could hear the litany in her head, her grandmother and mother making her repeat all the things she wasn't allowed to touch or move or open. Just in case. Just in case whatever this thing was that was wrong with her brothers and her father and her grandmother was wrong with her, too.

She hadn't been allowed to keep the locket Claritsa had given her last year for her fifteenth birthday. She wasn't allowed to use toothpaste that came from a tube. She wasn't allowed to go to school. But she didn't want Daniel to know all that—all the ways she was handicapped, disabled, all the things wrong with her.

Daniel bit his lip and glanced at the window like he was speaking to it instead of them. His body trembled, like he was barely containing panic of his own. "Then I'm out."

Claritsa locked her eyes onto him. "What are you talking about?"

"If you can't get me home… then I don't want to be saddled with you two. There are people fighting out there, and… and animals I haven't seen before."

"You can't leave us!" Claritsa said.

"I untied you, uncovered your heads, and unlocked the window. They're all busy with their stupid battle and all the people dying. I think I've done more than enough for two people who got me sent to who-the-hell-knows-where!"

Claritsa took a step closer, unafraid. "You jerk. You plaid-shirted jerk. You have to help us. You have to get us out of here. If your friends, your disgusting, horrible monsters for friends, had let us cross the creek, none of this—"

"You're the one who lifted the door for her—"

"Because you trapped us!"

Daniel and Claritsa raised their voices even as they stepped toward each other. Claritsa's head barely reached Daniel's shoulder.

"If her brother—"

"This is your fault—"

Maella heard noises outside the locked door. "Shut up! There's someone coming!"

They froze mid-yell.

There were stomping feet and someone yelled, "Get the key, open it up!"

Daniel jumped and pulled himself up through the window, disappearing.

Maella despaired at the window's height. She waited for Daniel to come back, poke his head up, reach a hand over, jump back through, boost them out.

Nothing.

She tried jumping for the window, anyway. Claritsa grabbed her legs, lifting her up.

The door burst open and three men with swords came in, surrounding a woman—Samay.

The guards didn't look happy to see Maella and Claritsa unbound and uncovered. They moved the girls to another room. This time a room without a window.

As the guards retied their bonds, sending dried bits of mud from their clothes to the floor like brown snowflakes, Samay promised to get them a stay of execution.

Maella had hid this thing about herself for so long—now all these people had found out. They confirmed what she already knew.

She would never be normal. And she would pay for it for the rest of her life—however long that lasted.

# Chapter 4

WHEN MAELLA ASKED ABOUT FOOD the next morning for their rumbling stomachs, one of the guards replied that they did not waste food on those about to die. A female guard made sure no mistakes were made as the girls used the bathroom—that is, the bucket. There wasn't even a privacy curtain, because, Maella knew, and they must know too, even a curtain could act as a door under the right circumstances.

At least the woman gave them the courtesy of facing away.

The girls washed in a cold basin of water locked to the floor, like the toilet bucket had been locked down—so that neither could be turned over and used as a door.

It felt like a different season here than at home, so Maella shook off as much of the dried mud from her jacket as possible before putting it over her shirt. It only helped a little bit. She was wearing shorts, after all. Claritsa didn't even have long sleeves.

The guards pushed the two girls out into the town square. The bright light shocked Maella's eyes and she squinted since she couldn't use her tied-up hands to block the sun. A set of gallows had been erected overnight in the middle of the town square. It was made of rough, unfinished wood, and the ropes dangled from it, swinging slightly in the wind.

It seemed as if the whole town was there. Linn, smiling in a self-satisfied way. Foster, at the steps of the gallows, arms folded, a grim set to his features, no more blood in his hair. Women holding children or propping up injured men.

Claritsa forced out a half-sob. "This must be a joke."

"Quiet!" One of the guards poked Claritsa in the back, which made her stumble a step.

She whirled around. "Do you get off on hurting girls? Is that your thing?"

The guard she directed the insult at paled, embarrassed. "I..."

Maella searched the crowd, the gallows, the outer ring of buildings. There had to be a way out of this. She just needed to find it. Maybe Daniel was having second thoughts about abandoning them. But a scan of the crowd revealed no familiar faces. Expressions ranged from angry to eager. Everyone a stranger. They couldn't die here in some unknown world, in some unknown place. Could they?

A little voice inside Maella said they very much could. Didn't she remember all her family members who had come to their own bad end because of doors?

"Pick up the pace," Foster called out.

The embarrassed guard dropped back. Another one took his place.

Claritsa stood her ground.

"I'll not touch you unless you force me to do so. Please turn around and continue."

The anger and confidence in Claritsa vanished. She became like a lost, frightened fawn, like the one the girls had stumbled across near their creek once.

"Please, Maella. Do something."

Maella swallowed, but couldn't get past the huge lump in her throat.

The crowd was thick with weary, bandaged, angry faces. Men with spears and swords, some on crutches, others with bandages that seeped blood, stood on guard. Maella did not doubt they were ready to use their weapons. She scanned all of it again, searching for a chance, for any way out of this—but she couldn't see it.

The guard motioned them forward.

Claritsa trudged to the gallows steps.

They were going to die, and it was Maella's fault.

Suddenly, like being struck by lightning—all her shock, the guilt, the fear—all of it vanished.

So what if opening another door led to something terrible? Maella and Claritsa were about to be executed.

She didn't care about any of the dangers her family had spent her entire life warning her about. She didn't care about the rules.

If opening another door could save them—of course, she would do it.

Maella trembled under that new conviction as Foster stood her and Claritsa on the step stools underneath their separate ropes. The stools sat upon a trapdoor of some kind. A sliver of excitement rose and then vanished just as quickly.

Her hands had to open the door—that she knew. It wouldn't work if she used her feet or any other part of her body. But they had tied her hands. Her burned fingers throbbed as proof of how tightly they were bound. The noose already rested upon her neck. There was no way to open the trapdoor, not before it killed her and her best friend.

Foster stepped to the edge of the gallows platform. He held hoods in one hand and crumpled them as he spoke. His other was wrapped with bandages—the hand he had burned while forcing her to open the drawer.

"We do not allow doormakers to live!"

A few of the onlookers shouted agreement. Many nodded.

He spoke in another language. Maella guessed he repeated his words. He switched to a third language that sent tendrils of familiarity through her. She swore she could almost recognize some of the words, but then he switched back again to English.

"Our laws have been in place for generations to care for our way of life, to protect us from those who would take that away from us. I have tested and proved this doormaker, as I tested and proved the one who came before her."

Shock coursed through Maella, remembering now.

The doormaker before her. How long ago had he said?

"Who was it?" Maella shouted, straining forward even as the rope's rough fibers bit into her skin. She had to know if her brother or father had somehow come this way.

Foster ignored her.

She shouted her question again, and again, and again. People became restless, a few of them shouted back at her to be quiet.

Foster stopped talking, turned, and walked up to Maella. Standing on the step stool made her the same height as him. He backhanded her across the face with his good hand.

She almost fell off, except Foster caught and steadied her. The sting of his blow numbed her cheek. It felt like the slap her mother had given her the day she broke the windows.

She deserved it then, but not now.

"I won't stop until you tell me!" She tried to enunciate her words through the numbness. She wanted to cry because her brother or her father might have been here, maybe on this very spot, maybe with ropes around their necks. "Just tell me what he looked like. Just tell me that."

Foster let his arm fall to his side. His eyes were hard and bloodshot. "He looked like you."

For a long, stunned moment, Maella couldn't process his words. But then a cold knowledge entered her belly.

Someone who looked like her?

*Esson.* He had to be talking about Esson.

They'd killed Esson because he didn't know any better than her what it meant to be a doormaker. Tears spilled down her cheeks. Snot dripped from her nose. It was like it was yesterday when she had found Claritsa in the shed, and her brother might as well have died that day. She didn't know she had been hoping to still find him alive.

"Fire!"

The word came as a shout from far away. Foster turned back to the crowd.

Maella looked out and saw smoke drifted in a thick column from behind the circle of houses that surrounded the town's open space.

A woman shouted. "The hay barn. The feed!"

People began running.

Foster jumped off the gallows.

She couldn't move for what seemed like an eternity. Her older brother had been here. Foster had killed him.

"Can you get loose?" Claritsa asked.

Maella shook her head, trying to bring herself back to the present. This was their chance. She tried to force her hands out of the ropes, but they were too tight. The stool underneath her feet shifted.

She looked around. There had to be—

Someone jumped onto the boards and raised a shining knife to her face. She screamed as the blade came down, but it missed, and began sawing at the rope that bound her hands.

And then she saw the attacker's face.

Daniel.

Rope fell away from her hands. He removed the noose around her neck.

"Thank you," she said, breathless, unable to stop herself from admiring the broadness of his shoulders and the fierce strength in his arms, even as she wondered *why* he was helping them now. Daniel had left them to their fate and made clear he wanted nothing to do with them. Why was he back?

"Open a door, Maella," Daniel said, voice hoarse with intensity. "Whatever's behind the next door, it can't be worse than this place, and maybe it will take us home."

Maella bit her lip. Whatever calculations he'd made in his head overnight, the conclusion led to Maella, and what she could do, as his best chance at getting home. Even though she hated being used and hated being seen as little more than a tool—she also understood it.

What choice did he have? What choice did any of them have except do everything they could to stay alive?

Daniel went to release Claritsa from the ropes.

Maella jumped off the step stool, making it tumble onto the stone. She crouched onto the rough-hewn wood next to the trapdoor that had a small ring attached that could be used to pull it up—

To open it.

Her palms were sweaty and her heart beat wildly. What if —

Foster's shouts cut through. She looked up, locking eyes with him. His mouth contorted in a snarl, in a look of determination and hate so complete, she shivered from its impact. He sprinted across the cobblestone as he drew the sword strapped to his waist.

Maella shut off her doubts, wrapped her hands around the cold metal ring, and pulled. This time, opening a door was no

accident. Her legs quaked but held. The wood creaked, the
door released.

She waited for the flames, or a dark Klylup cave, or just the
ground underneath, but what appeared wasn't any of those
things.

Her eyes couldn't understand the picture, but it was too
late. Before she could move of her own free will, someone
pushed her and she tumbled through the door.

# Chapter 5

MAELLA FELL FOR WHAT SEEMED like forever through empty clear blue sky, toward a deeper blue ground.

She fell into the deeper blue ground, and the shock of the cold water took her breath away, and she sank.

Her lungs constricted. She clawed for the surface. When she broke through, she gulped down air, and salty, icy water that sent her into a coughing fit. She choked on wind spray. The white-capped waves pushed and pulled at her body, driving her near a dark, tall rock that loomed overheard.

She'd never been to the ocean. It might as well have been on another planet for how little her family could afford to go on trips to other places. Too many requirements, too many potential questions and accidents.

The water tossed her around like a doll and she wasn't a good swimmer. She struck out with all four limbs and managed to avoid the sharpest-looking rocks. A drowsiness descended, warming her. Her brain couldn't decide whether she should kick or float.

Floating sounded easier. She could stop fighting the waves and let them take her wherever they wished. Maybe the rocks wouldn't hurt so much.

*Maybe you should stop acting like a child, and start acting like a young woman worth something,* said a voice in her head that sounded awfully like Grandmother's voice again.

She wanted to ignore the words, then she pictured Esson's face and how he looked the last time—though she didn't know it was the last time. He hadn't confided in her. He had joined up with Barth by then and stopped talking to her, to any of them. His skin had taken on this strange purple tint. He would disappear for hours when he was supposed to be at home with her and Josa doing lessons with Mother.

She forced her eyes open and stared at a clear blue sky while the water lapped at her body. She didn't want to think about Esson. It hurt too much. Twisting in the water, she used her legs like mini-propellers. Sharp, mean-looking rocks were only feet away. One more wave would do the job Foster had failed at if she didn't—

She kicked out with all her strength. A wave swamped her, pulling her back underneath its icy grip. It was dark and not at all blue, but an opaque green. She grazed the edge of something that left a new, sharp pain across her right side.

The water parted and exposed a flat space. She kicked out again and again and used up what little strength remained in her arms to edge herself over, if she could just—

The next wave hit and finished what Maella could not. The water deposited her onto the stone, battering her knees and scraping the palms of her hands. She froze in that position, relishing the solidness of the rock beneath her.

After another wave almost took her back out, she scrambled further up and lay down again, allowing herself to feel the cold. Even though it was wet, she untied her jacket from her waist and put it on. At least it was clean now. Everything smelled like seafood. Part of her wondered if a Klylup would appear and finish her off.

"Maella?" Claritsa's voice, faint and lost sounding.

Claritsa and Daniel stumbling along the rocky coastline. Daniel caught Claritsa before she fell into a wave. Both looked as miserable as Maella felt.

She had opened a door and they were the only ones here and they were all still alive.

She let go of the anxiety she hadn't known she held—that one of them would pay the price because she'd opened a door. But they were both alive and there was no Klylup.

Claritsa and Maella tumbled into each other, hugging fiercely.

"I'm so cold," Claritsa said, teeth chattering against Maella's ear.

"We have to get warm," Daniel said, a blue tinge to his lips, a scowl on his face, and a dark smudge of ash staining his cheek. "We'll die of hypothermia. Or lose a few body parts to it. That's what happened to my uncle."

"But we're alive," Maella said, voice full of wonder. She didn't understand it. She needed to understand it. Her family had always warned her about doors, and they were right about the doors, but they had also lied. Why had they lied?

Suddenly, another person jogged into view, torn jean shorts and plaid shirt soaked, straggly blond hair plastered down, an even deeper scowl on his face than on Daniel's.

*Barth.*

Maella couldn't move. "What's he doing here?"

Claritsa let go of Maella and turned around.

"He pushed me, right?" Daniel said, a hint of apology in his voice for the half-truth he had told. "Well, he pushed too hard and fell through himself."

Maella didn't buy that excuse for a second. Barth knew enough about the doors that he'd decided to test whether Maella could open one. And then he had pushed Daniel through—that Maella could believe. But no way did he accidentally fall through himself. He came on purpose. Whatever he believed about the doors—whatever Esson had told him—there was something Barth wanted from them.

Claritsa frowned. "But you said—"

"He didn't want you to know," Daniel said. "I didn't see —"

"He was on the other side of the window," Maella said, the pieces clicking into place as she spoke the words out loud. "You were both there. Maybe Barth pushed you through against your will, but he came through on purpose. And you were both there. You could have saved us then."

Daniel looked cold, wet, and miserable. "But he—"

"Saved you when I was good and ready to save you," Barth said, having approached within earshot now. The sneer on his face was less impressive since the rest of him looked like a drowned rat. "And if Jack, the idiot, had followed instructions, we'd have our own secret portal back home." Barth cursed. "But Jack messed things up and now it's Plan B."

Daniel at least had the decency to look miserable at being caught out on all his lies. "The door back home really is closed. When that monster did its trumpeting thing, I think Jack got scared. I saw the door slip from his fingers and close and just disappear like it was never there."

Maella's skin crawled. She believed Daniel. At least, she believed this part of what Daniel was saying. But Barth was dangerous. Barth was somehow connected to losing Esson and had orchestrated this, not knowing what he was getting them all into. Because of Esson. She thought Esson had died when he opened the door, but that wasn't true. And now Esson really was dead—

Claritsa was there, a pile of rocks collected in her shirt. She held one out because Maella could not pick one up herself.

Maella threw the rock as hard as she could at Barth. He yelled and jumped out of the way, but not fast enough. The rock glanced off his cheek.

"Don't you come closer!" Maella screamed. "Not unless you want a concussion!"

They both threw the rocks. It felt like breaking the windows. Fury and clarity. No time to think, only do, only defend, only react, only prove to herself she wasn't helpless.

Barth kept his distance, hiding behind an outcropping, yelling obscenities in their direction.

"He's the one who saved you two," Daniel said simply. "The fire was his idea."

Barth shouted, threatening stuff about what his father would do to their families, but then his voice trailed off, maybe because he realized how ridiculous his threat sounded here—wherever here actually was. He poked his head above the boulder.

Maella cocked back her hand for another throw.

"What's that?" Claritsa said in a strangled voice.

They all looked up to where Claritsa pointed, straight into the blue, perfectly clear sky, except for a perfectly rectangular cloud that was too dark to be a cloud. It was mottled brown, rough-looking, like wood, and smoke drifted lazily out and floated up around it, further into the sky, as if it were a trap-door hung a few hundred yards above them.

Maella thought she saw a pale face, flushed red with anger —and then the rectangle went black, as if someone had covered the opening with a rug.

"Is that the door?" Daniel asked.

"I think so," Maella whispered.

"Can they follow us?" Daniel asked. "Those men trying to kill you?"

"I don't know."

Barth cursed. "You don't know. Course you don't." He stepped away from the boulder, warding up his hands in case another rock went flying. "It's called reconnaissance, by the way—that's why we didn't help you at first. We knew as soon as we did they'd all go crazy looking for you. Like they're doing right now." Barth crossed his arms. "I told you." He looked at Daniel, acting like they had been having an argument Barth had just won.

Daniel looked at the ground and bit his lip, as if ashamed.

Maella didn't know whether to believe Barth or not, but her mind couldn't stay on that thought. She puzzled through the rectangle in the sky. "I don't think they can open it again, not if they closed it, but…"

But Maella didn't really know. All the warnings and stories and rules were about not actually opening the door, and all the bad things that could happen to her if she did, but none of her family had explained exactly how the doors worked, other than if a door was opened, it could be closed by anyone, not just a doormaker.

But what if someone didn't want to close the door? What if they kept it open? Could they use it again later?

No one would be stupid enough to risk themselves over something like that.

"It's not possible," she said with more confidence. "They can't come through once it's closed."

Barth looked ready to challenge Maella.

Before he could get out another word, she said, "You knew. You knew about my family." It wasn't a question. "All this time. Since Esson—"

"Eddy never could keep a secret for long," Barth said, smug.

Maella narrowed her eyes, examining him. He acted too full of himself. This bravado didn't match the relief on his face when she'd tumbled through that first door.

Maybe he had known something about the doors. Maybe Esson had told him, or shown him something, but that didn't mean he knew any more than her, or even as much as her.

Barth pointed down the rocky beach. "So here's what you're going to do—"

"We should check out the lighthouse," Daniel interrupted. "Figure out where we are and what this place is."

"What lighthouse?" Maella asked.

"We saw it when we came out of the water," Claritsa said, teeth chattering again.

Maella decided she and Claritsa should try to ditch the boys at the first opportunity. At home, they could have lost them through the trees along the creek, or in the overgrown fields, or hid out in a building on one of the foreclosed farms. Here, she didn't know the terrain, or the hideouts, or the dangers. Except that Barth was definitely on the list of dangerous things to avoid. And Daniel—she didn't really know whose side he was on.

"Fine," Barth said. "That's what I was planning to do, anyway. Daniel walks first, then you two are next. I'll take up the rear. Consider it for your protection. But if you really want to know the truth, you're too easy to read. You'll take off first chance you get, even though we saved you back there. You took us here and you'd leave us to rot without a regret. You see it too, don't you, Daniel."

It wasn't really a question, but a statement designed to manipulate Daniel into a certain way of thinking and Maella could tell that it worked. Also, she had just been thinking about ditching them, and no, she wouldn't have regretted it. Well, maybe in Daniel's case, but not in Barth's.

Claritsa gave her a helpless look that said, *what else can we do*? Then she ran to catch up to Daniel.

Maella's limbs felt stiff and she didn't know if she could bear Barth walking behind her, dogging her steps, able to mess with her, and she wouldn't see it coming.

"Ladies first," Barth said, standing back a few yards.

Maella still held a rock in her hand. She thought about throwing it at him. "You think I'm turning my back on *you*? There's no way I'm trusting you—"

"I can't be trusted? We don't even know what you are," Barth said, deadpan.

She looked up at him in surprise.

"A demon? A servant to Satan?" Barth continued. "Maybe just a monster escaped from its master who knows a few special tricks. Whatever you are, I don't think you're human, and I'm not letting you out of my sight."

Maella wanted to protest. Of course, she was human. But deep down inside, sometimes, just at night since her father had left, she thought maybe she wasn't quite human either.

She scuttled after Claritsa. Not human? She tried to think of all the ways she was. She bled, she cried, she laughed. Claritsa would know. Claritsa would be able to tell. With Barth forgotten for the moment, she pocketed the rock and caught up to Claritsa.

"You don't think I'm some sort of monster, do you? You know I'm human, right?"

Claritsa hugged her arms around her chest. She squinted at Maella, stumbled on a rock and then caught herself.

"Don't be stupid."

"But Barth said—"

Claritsa turned piercing eyes onto Maella, her teeth still chattering. "You're really listening to Barth—"

"He said this thing I can do, maybe it means I'm possessed, or—"

"Takes one to know one," Claritsa laughed, but Maella was in no mood to joke.

"Claritsa, please."

Claritsa sighed. She picked her way around a group of unstable looking rocks. "You're human, Maella. You can do something that makes you special, though most of the time I think it makes your life much harder. If opening doors meant you were a demon or something, wouldn't it be less dangerous, or at least less life-threatening for you? I'm trying not to hold all this against you, but seriously, Maella, get over yourself. You're human, just like me, and if you don't get it together, either Barth is going to get us or something else will!"

Maella dropped back a step under the waves of emotion coming off Claritsa.

"I'm sorry."

Claritsa sighed again. "Don't be sorry." She stopped and looked at Maella, then picked up her steps again. "You're the only one who can get us out of this."

"But I don't know how!"

"I know you don't know how. I know it. But you're still the only one who can. That's the way it is. You're the only one of us who can open doors. But if you start believing even one word that comes out of Barth's mouth—"

"But—"

"Even one word, Maella. Then, you know what? He'll have won and I bet then that we'll never make it out of here."

They were wet and cold and there was nothing around that looked like shelter except for the lighthouse, which was an impossibly tall white tower of stone that pierced the sky ahead of them. Maella wrapped her arms around her chest and thought over what Claritsa had said, forcing herself not to think about Barth creeping along behind her. Well, she did think about it, but it was no longer the most pressing thing on her mind.

Claritsa was right. She'd never let Barth mess with her head at home. Why would she let him start now?

They stopped at the edge of the long shadow the lighthouse threw across the ground. Her muscles spasmed because the shivering wasn't enough to keep her warm under her wet layers. The sky was clear, but it didn't share much warmth, or cover up the black little rectangle. It disturbed Maella, this rectangle. She thought it should disappear if the door had actually been closed. Just like Daniel had said happened to the doorway in the Klylup's cave when Jack let it close. But she didn't know for certain if this was true.

The door to the lighthouse was a white rectangle inserted into the circular stone base of the tower. The whole thing looked both old and new, and also solid, like out of pictures she'd seen of Roman ruins. They stood in a semi circle around the entrance, Maella in the back.

"I'll open it," Daniel said.

But before he could, the door swung inward and disappeared into the shadows.

A voice boomed, low and full. "You're late."

# Chapter 6

THE MAN WAS A LITTLE taller than Maella. Gray hair, uncombed, fell past his earlobes. Gray eyebrows framed brown eyes that pierced each one of them as he turned them first onto Barth, then Daniel, then Claritsa, and finally Maella. He wore loose, light linen clothing that contrasted with his darker skin and looked older than her father but younger than her grandmother.

He held open the door in one hand and his other hand held both a cane and a flame-lit lantern. "Please come in."

Maella exchanged a look with Claritsa.

Claritsa shrugged her shoulders.

He closed and locked the door behind them. The sound of the door's thud and latch echoed up the tower for what seemed like minutes. The smell of salt grew faint inside. Stone steps with no railing curled along the wall, disappearing into the upper stories of the place. The only light came from glass-paned windows that followed the staircase and the lantern.

"Who are you?" Barth demanded.

"I am Keeper Shaul. You may call me by my occupation—Keeper."

"And just what do you keep?" Barth said, unable to keep the sneer out of his voice.

"What is this place?" Maella said.

"Where are we?" Claritsa said.

"The pattern," Keeper Shaul said simply, ignoring the girls.

Maella stepped forward. Her hands were clasped behind her back like she'd been taught, but she unclasped them now, gesturing. "Where are we? Why are we late?"

Keeper Shaul glanced at Maella's hands. The hand Foster had forced to open the drawer showed a few blisters, but the adrenaline and then the cold water had numbed the pain—and the burns were nothing like what Foster had earned.

"You are cold and wet and likely hungry and tired. And that needs attention. Follow me." He hobbled around the foot of the staircase, disappearing behind it. Maella wondered how he managed to make it up the steps and how often he needed to climb it and why whoever had put him here didn't send someone with two good legs, or install an elevator, or—

"Come on." Claritsa tugged at Maella's arm.

Daniel had already followed the old man, but Barth stared at her with his arms crossed, waiting for her to go first.

All the stonework only accentuated the severity of the place. The air felt cold and damp as she followed. Her heart sank, wondering if she would ever feel warm again, but then a warm gust brushed her face and bare arms. The air began to smell like smoke from a fireplace.

They were drawn to the warmth like a magnet. The hallway led them to a kitchen. A wood island sat in the middle where Keeper Shaul was laying out cheeses, bread, nuts, and fruit. Another wave of warmth blasted her and her muscles stopped trembling. The fire cast shifting orange light across the wooden cabinets, their faces, and made shadows dance on the walls. The sight of food made Maella's mouth water. The four of them surrounded the island, and without another word, began tearing into the food.

Maella chose an apple, a piece of crusty bread, and a thick chunk of stinky cheese. She finished eating these and just as she began to think about her thirst, Keeper Shaul set out four glass cups of water.

She could drink out of a glass cup. There were no worries about opening a door when you could see through it. She wondered if Keeper Shaul knew that.

Keeper Shaul's eyes kept drifting over Barth and Daniel, but always back to Barth.

After a while, Barth noticed and stood straighter. He kept a mild scowl on his face, but continued eating everything in sight.

Keeper Shaul brought out more food from a pantry area. There were dishes, plates, cookware, utensils, but no stove, no refrigerator. The cabinets had no doors and looked like someone had purposefully built them that way. A huge pot was strung over the fire. A sort of soup bubbled in it.

Then her attention was drawn back to the odd sort of staring contest happening between Barth and Keeper Shaul.

"Thank you," Maella said finally to break the silence, because she thought Barth was ready to blow. He'd lashed out a fist at someone accidentally calling him Bart instead of Barth once, and Keeper Shaul had been looking at him wrong for a very long time now.

Keeper Shaul narrowed his eyes and flicked them toward Maella. "It is my job. I keep this place ready for when doormakers are called here. The pattern still holds, here, for now. And so I am here to keep the pattern."

Maella looked down at the island. In the midst of her hunger and feeling warm again, she had forgotten why they were there. Because of her.

She had a million questions, and Keeper Shaul knew she was a doormaker without her having to prove it. That meant he had to have some answers.

She looked up. "How did you know about me? And what's the pattern? Why are doormakers called here?"

Keeper Shaul's hand stilled on his cane. He froze like she'd delivered the punch Barth's body language threatened.

She shivered at his look—like the light had gone out of him.

"No." Keeper Shaul said the word stiffly, in denial. He pointed his cane at Barth. "He is supposed to be the doormaker. The pattern proclaimed it."

Claritsa moved closer to Maella. The long tail of her braids brushed Maella's arm.

Now Maella understood Keeper Shaul's fixation on Barth. Maella felt almost nauseated from the food. She had disappointed him, but it was more than that. His friendly, grandfather-like approach was gone, replaced with something much colder. He looked at her like he knew who she was and what she'd done, and he hated her for it.

Barth looked from Maella to Daniel and back. "She's the freak, not me. I should bust your lip for even thinking it was me." Barth relaxed against the island to prove he didn't care about any of it now. He grabbed another piece of cheese and stuffed it into his mouth.

The old man's eyes flicked back to Barth for a brief second, then closed. "All doormakers end up here," he said, his voice cracking. He did not look at Maella as he spoke, but just past her, as if he were looking at someone over her shoulder.

"Why did you think it was Barth?" Claritsa asked.

Keeper Shaul waved his hand at Claritsa. "It is nothing to concern you. The legends speak of a boy. The pattern said there would be a boy…" He mumbled to himself, the words too low to understand.

"Well, she's a girl and a doormaker," Claritsa said.

"She is not the one we've been searching for," Keeper Shaul said, dismissive. Like now that he knew Barth wasn't a doormaker, no one in the room mattered to him.

Maella's stomach flipped. She was all wrong and Keeper Shaul knew it.

Claritsa caught Maella's attention and rolled her eyes as if to make light of Keeper Shaul's words. *Boys are stupid. Don't listen to him*, she seemed to say. But Claritsa's face was troubled. Claritsa's parents had all but abandoned her with her grandmother. They'd taken her brothers, but not her. They were boys. Claritsa was a girl. That was how things went in her family.

"Crazy old man," Barth said quietly to Daniel. Then louder, "Just tell us where we are and how to get out of here."

"This is your seventh door, is it not?" Keeper Shaul's voice was steady now. The wood tip of his cane struck the stone with a sharp report when he said seventh.

"No," Maella said, shaking her head. "No, I never opened a door until yesterday."

Firelight flickered in his eyes. Maella began to sweat under the intensity of both the fire and his stare.

"How many doors have you opened since yesterday?"

"The first one in the field—" Maella began.

"And then the drawer," Claritsa interrupted.

"And then the trapdoor to here," Maella finished. "Three."

"The pattern is not as broken as that… yet. It means there were four more doors you opened sometime in the past."

Maella shook her head. "No, I never did." She surveyed each person around the island. Claritsa on her left, a look of concern on her face. Keeper Shaul, not much taller than Claritsa, calling her all but a liar, Barth looking like he thought about something else altogether, and Daniel, who looked at her with a bit of fear.

Keeper Shaul drew in a sharp breath. "It is *always* the seventh door that brings a doormaker here. It has always been so, since we keepers have kept the pattern, and even as the pattern has begun breaking."

He looked over Maella's tight brown curls, the curve of her jaw, the shape of her nose, the way she hung her arms at her sides, her hands clasped behind her back as her mother and father had taught her. It's how the people in town had looked at her when she dared going with Claritsa for an ice cream cone once during the summer fair. They had looked at her the way Keeper Shaul looked at her now—as being from 'that family.'

"I know you," Keeper Shaul said.

Maella shook her head. "I've never—"

"You're from the Botron family. You look like them. I should have seen it. I *would* have seen it, but I had hoped…" Keeper Shaul shuddered, as if bringing himself back to the present. "You may not remember it, but you *must* have opened four doors before now."

Maella thought back to before. Her mother told her she had been six when they'd fled. They had moved around for five years until the gold ran out and the servants left. She had met Claritsa when they'd moved into her current doorless house near when she turned eleven. She was now almost sixteen. During all those years, she had never opened a door. She knew she hadn't. Her parents and grandmother had always made her be so careful.

But she could not remember anything before she was six years old except for the smell of smoke.

"Maybe," Maella said, finally. "I don't know."

"Your blood is tainted."

"What?"

"Your father betrayed the pattern. He—"

"None of this matters," Barth interrupted. "Who cares who she is? Who cares who she isn't?"

"What are you talking about?" Maella imagined the door in the field, the way her father had cursed, discovering it, the way he had disappeared through it, leaving them. She felt the rising panic of that day when she had cried out for him to stop, but he hadn't.

There must have been a good reason. She needed to believe there was a good reason for this gaping wound he'd left inside her.

"What did my father do?" Maella said, her voice cutting through the room. If she could, she would have pinned Keeper Shaul to the wall with her words.

He looked like he couldn't believe he had to deal with her. "He was not supposed to marry your mother. Her blood is diluted."

Barth laughed. "So this is about who her father banged? Oh, that's classic."

Keeper Shaul rapped Barth sharply on the leg with his cane.

Barth almost snarled. Maella didn't care. Her thoughts whirled inside her head. She couldn't make sense out of any of it and didn't really want to—her mother couldn't open doors. It was why they could manage to live in a house still at all. She wasn't a doormaker like the rest of them. That ability had been inherited from her father. But diluted or not, why should that matter? Unless—

"Is she why something bad happens when I open a door? Is it because she—"

Keeper Shaul looked puzzled at Maella's words. "What is this nonsense? Your mother's blood interrupts the pattern the keepers set. Doormakers are only betrothed to other doormakers. She makes no difference to the doors you open —though she and Doormaker Botron are guilty of keeping you in terrible ignorance. This is not how it's done!"

"Just get us back to where we're supposed to be, old man," Barth said. "Get us back home."

Keeper Shaul burned a hole into Barth's face with his stare until Barth finally looked away. All the air left the room, at least it felt like it did. Keeper Shaul straightened and blinked, as if unable to believe he had to utter something so obvious.

"There is no way back home."

# Chapter 7

BARTH CURSED AT MAELLA. CLARITSA shouted at Barth. Maella demanded to know what Keeper Shaul meant. Daniel stared hard into the flames.

Keeper Shaul swept food crumbs from the wood island onto the floor. "There was a war," Keeper Shaul said, silencing the room.

He collapsed in on himself, like the way her mother and father and grandmother did whenever she asked them about the past.

"We lost."

He swept out of the room. His linen clothing flapped around him, his gray hair pushed back as if by a breeze. He moved more gracefully with a cane than Maella thought possible, and she realized now—didn't know how she had missed it before—that he walked barefoot on the cold stone.

Maella could hear her heart beating in her ears. It whispered that this was all her fault somehow.

She could see it in their eyes, too.

She had broken the rules. They were paying for her mistakes.

"He's lying," Daniel said.

"He has to be lying," Claritsa said.

Barth didn't say anything.

Maella followed after Keeper Shaul, determined to get more answers. But even though he was old and walked with a cane, by the time she had caught up, he had stopped between two hallways. At the entrance to each hallway was an empty chair. Each side led to rooms with open doors that revealed a series of cots.

"This used to be a place of learning," Keeper Shaul said. "But that was before the pattern began breaking. You will stay here tonight. Tend to your wounds. Rest."

Something in Maella's chest squeezed. Keeper Shaul knew things. "You have to tell me. You have to—"

"I must rest," Keeper Shaul said sharply.

"You can't just say something like that and expect us to be able to sleep!" Maella said.

He leaned heavily on his cane. His feet were calloused and red from the cold. "The open door stirs the beast. It is too dangerous to risk anything more tonight. And I must research first. I must review the pattern. I must have missed something, but it has to be there…" He locked eyes on Maella. "They did you great harm, keeping you in ignorance like this. And yet, and yet..."

Maella stepped forward and a pleading note entered her voice. "Please."

Keeper Shaul looked at her again, really looked at her.

His eyebrows drew together and his lips thinned. "No Botron bastard will move me. Your family is the enemy of what I stand for in all but name. You should graciously accept that I will allow you to sleep here tonight."

Maella opened her mouth to protest.

He left her standing there in between the two hallways.

Claritsa, Barth, and Daniel rushed up.

"Where is he?" Barth demanded.

"Maella?" Claritsa said. "What did he say?"

Maella shook her head. "He's gone. He said this used to be a school for doormakers. He said there's a beast." She didn't need to say Klylup out loud for them all to think it.

"He'll pay for this," Barth said, but he shook a little as he said it, unable to hide that even he was unsettled and scared by it all.

Daniel stood behind Barth, almost using him as a shield from everything that had happened.

"Shut up, Barth," Claritsa said, flipping her braids behind her shoulders. "There's no point in fighting about this now. Keeper Shaul is gone."

"Then we'll go after him," Barth said.

Maella shook her head. "I think he's worried. He said something about research and—"

"I'm going to bed. Do what you want," Daniel said and left down the opposite hallway.

Barth opened and closed his mouth like a fish and then followed after Daniel. "This isn't finished." He tossed the words over his shoulder as he disappeared down the hallway.

Maella stood there with her hands fisted at her sides. She was exhausted, suddenly needed to pee, scared of Barth, but more scared of Keeper Shaul and his cryptic words.

Claritsa placed a hand on her arm. "Come on. We'll never find Keeper Shaul in the dark like this. Daniel's right."

Maella let Claritsa tug her down the opposite hallway. They were all in shock. Different worlds? No going back? Maella couldn't even begin to wrap her mind around the not-so-subtle accusations Keeper Shaul had made about her family.

She let Claritsa lead her down the hallway to a closed door opposite from the cots.

"I hope this is a bathroom," Claritsa said.

Maella waited in front of the door, hands clasped behind her back. Claritsa reached for the knob. The only sounds were their soft footsteps on the stone and trickling water.

"Wait," Maella said, realizing. "I can open this one." The top half of the door was open and the bottom half did not seal with the frame. It was a tall door, so keeping the top part open still kept everything private, but also safe for doormakers.

"It's okay." Claritsa said and opened the door.

The trickling water sound grew louder. Stone walls, stone floors, stone ceiling. The lights were already on. No, that wasn't right. Light came from a little bit of the remaining sunlight from the ceiling. From a skylight. Water trickled down the surface of one wall. A clever ledge of stone created a mini-waterfall that fell into a sink. It almost felt peaceful. Maella tracked the water's path. It flowed down and into a trough that disappeared underneath several stone benches with holes in the middle.

At first, Maella didn't understand, but then—

"Those are toilets," Maella said.

They both stepped into the bathroom and closed the door behind them.

Claritsa peered into one of the holes. "You've got to be kidding."

"And these are the sinks," Maella said. "To wash up." She noticed off-white cotton towels in a stack on the floor. She reached for one. It was rough, and her hand came away dusty. They had been sitting there, unused, for a long time. She didn't know how she knew what everything was, only that it somehow felt familiar and strange at the same time.

"What is this place?" Claritsa said.

"Another world?" Maella responded. Her attempt at being lighthearted sounded forced even to her own ears.

"Yeah." Claritsa said, subdued. She went to the sink and put her hands under the waterfall. "Oh! It's like ice."

"There has to be something to make the water run," Maella said.

"Let's just do what he said," Claritsa said. "Let's just. I don't know. Let's just go to sleep and think about everything in the morning."

The food Maella had eaten tugged at her now, making her feel sluggish. This was the first moment since everything started that she seemed not to be running or fighting or panicking. She ran her hands through the water and it did feel cold, like ice, but it also shocked her awake enough to brave the toilet.

They washed up in silence and ventured into the other room to check out the cots. This room had a skylight, too. It bathed everything in a soft white light. Ten wooden cots with thick blankets folded and stacked on each cot, waiting for students who didn't exist. Lumpy things next to the blankets she suspected were supposed to be pillows. Everything was covered with a fine layer of dust.

"It's weird," Claritsa said. "There's no electricity. There's no wiring. But there's running water and I'm not even cold."

Maella hadn't noticed any of that until Claritsa said it. She guessed it would feel odd—except, that's pretty much how she had been living with Josa, her mom, and grandmother for a long time now. This was all normal to her—except for the whole doormaker-you're-not-The-One stuff.

Yeah, except for that.

"Claritsa," Maella said.

Claritsa turned bloodshot eyes onto Maella. She shook her head. "Tomorrow."

Her bangs had dried perfect. Her braids had picked up some dust and hair flew out in all directions. The scratch on her cheek was an angry, thin red line. She looked tired and on the verge of tears.

"Okay," Maella whispered.

This room had a door like the bathroom that they could close—half-open on the top—a door that a doormaker could open. There was even a lock, but both of them wanted to stay ready for anything, so they kicked off their shoes but kept on their clothes.

The floor was warm under Maella's feet, like it was heated. Claritsa was right. This place was a strange mix of rough technology.

She climbed into the cot next to Claritsa's and nestled into the blankets. The wood slats groaned under her before settling. The skylight faded to nothing and pitched the room into a darkness so complete she couldn't see her own hands. She shivered in spite of the blankets. She wished they'd gotten a lantern from Keeper Shaul.

"I didn't mean to make you," Claritsa said into the darkness.

"What?" Maella said, sitting up in the cot. Not that she could see anything.

"With the door."

Maella eased back under the blankets. In the chaos of the Klylup, Foster, and now Keeper Shaul, she had forgotten. "Oh."

"You asked me why—but Maella, I don't know why. I just, I just saw them and I got so angry for you. They were there that day, with your brother—"

"Esson?"

"With Esson. They were there. At least Barth was, I think, at least at first—"

"How much does Barth even know?"

"I…I don't know."

Barth had pushed Maella through the door in the field. Not only had he looked surprised, but he had also looked relieved. Like he'd figured he was crazy to think whatever he saw with Esson and the doors could be real, and now he had proven that at least he wasn't crazy. He couldn't have known that she could do it, too. He had guessed. But he had guessed right. A headache scrambled her thoughts. Maybe her thoughts scrambled the headache. It was too much.

"Wait...what happened to Esson?" Maella said finally, her thoughts catching up with Claritsa's words. "What did you see? You never said—"

"Esson locked me up, Maella." Claritsa's voice rose in pitch. "I don't remember anything. All I can remember is he made me promise to ask you about the doors. He repeated it over and over. Or that's what it felt like. I don't know. I don't..." Claritsa broke into sobs.

That shocked Maella. Claritsa was the strong one who always launched herself into fights on Maella's behalf.

"Forget it. Don't worry about it." But it was the opposite of what Maella really wanted to say. She wanted to scream— what happened? But Claritsa didn't have an answer. If Claritsa could remember anything, she would've shared it.

In her mind, Esson had died when he went through the door. She'd spent two years believing he was dead. Now she found out he had lived long enough for Foster to kill him. It turned her heart inside out. But it wasn't only that. It was about what happened to her father, and her aunt, and her cousin, and why her family had fled, and from where they had fled, and why did they have gold and servants, and why did everyone on this side of the door want to kill her?

"I am sorry, Maella. I wanted to prove to them they couldn't hurt us and I think...I think part of me wanted to see if it was all real. I was afraid I had imagined it that day. But now...this is my fault."

Maella reached over a hand. She felt the rough fiber of the wool blanket and felt for Claritsa's shoulder. "This is not your fault."

Claritsa clasped her hand. "I will never do that again. I promise, Maella, that I will help you never open a door again."

"It's not your fault. It's not." Maella didn't know how long they were like that until Claritsa stopped crying. Maella's arm fell asleep. A few tears may have leaked out of her own eyes.

Claritsa's hand dropped away. Maella flexed her arm to bring the feeling back.

She listened to the darkness and sought out the bathroom's trickle of water. It never stopped. If she listened hard enough, she heard the waves from the ocean outside. If she brought her focus back to the room, she heard Claritsa's breathing, a steady, calm, sleeping sound.

Maella didn't feel so calm. Her heart beat in her chest like it was ready to jump out.

Claritsa, Barth, and Daniel were stuck with her—because of this terrible thing she could do. Foster had killed Esson. Her heart skirted away from that knowledge. She wasn't ready to open that grief right now, maybe never.

She knew so much more than she did a day ago—but she still knew so little.

All her life she had asked questions, but her family had never answered them. They'd kept her in the same kind of darkness she lay in now.

Just asking questions about their past had brought her family so much pain. So she had stopped asking.

Something shifted inside of Maella. Her family was mixed up in something so much bigger than she had ever imagined.

She needed to understand.

She needed to ask questions and get answers.

She needed to learn why her family was so hated.

She needed to prove Foster wrong—her family wasn't a bunch of monsters.

It was too late to go anywhere but forward. But going forward meant going backward—to the past, to figure out what happened.

She would prove Keeper Shaul wrong, too. She couldn't care less about the pattern and his legends, but she knew this —her family didn't betray the pattern, whatever the pattern was.

Or if they did, it was for a reason.

Purpose filled her and steadied her frantic thoughts.

She came to a decision in the dark.

It wasn't Claritsa's fault.

It wasn't Maella's fault.

And Maella knew, somehow, no matter what Keeper Shaul believed, it couldn't be her family's fault either.

She would find the reason for all of this and she would prove all of them wrong about her family.

# Chapter 8

KEEPER SHAUL CALLED THEM TO breakfast. They ate around the kitchen island like the night before. He said there was no point bothering with the school dining room. Too much of a mess. The fire made the room warm enough in spite of the morning chill. A breakfast of bread, dried fruit, and nuts were filling, even though Keeper Shaul's expression was cold.

Daniel and Barth didn't look as mean this morning with their tousled hair and out-of-place plaid shirts and scruffy shorts. They ignored each other, like they'd been arguing. That was all fine with Maella because she had a million questions for Keeper Shaul and started in on them at once.

She began by asking about being a doormaker and getting back home.

Silence.

She asked about the pattern and the legends next.

More silence.

She launched into questions about her family.

Keeper Shaul struck the stone with his cane. "Enough. Be quiet."

Anger flushed her with heat. "I am tired of not knowing. You said—"

"I am trying to show you," Keeper Shaul said. "I thought you might desire breakfast first."

"I don't," Maella said.

"Very well." Keeper Shaul left the kitchen.

Maella followed at his heels. Daniel and Barth stuffed food in their pockets before following. Claritsa stayed close to Maella.

Keeper Shaul took them to the lighthouse entrance, around the column of stairs, and onto a landing that fell away to the darkness below. More stairs, but these went into the ground instead of the sky. He mumbled to himself, and Maella wondered if he remembered that they followed.

Maella followed down after Keeper Shaul. The stone steps beneath her shoes felt slippery. Her fingers dug into the dirt walls and came away with cold mud crusting her hands. She shivered. The mud reminded her of the Klylup cave.

"You okay?" Claritsa whispered behind her.

"Yeah," Maella said.

Faint light illuminated the next stair down. Light enough to not make Claritsa freak out. Maella reached above her and immediately hit the ceiling, then brushed something sticky. She yelped and snatched her hand away.

"What's wrong?" Daniel's voice floated down.

"I…it's nothing. I felt a spider web." Maella told her heart to calm down. She clamped her arms against her sides and clasped her hands behind her back to leave as much space between her and the walls and ceiling as possible.

The stairs became the never-ending downward spiral. She wondered if this was why Keeper was so short, or if his height was a lucky accident.

It became a never-ending downward spiral. Maella didn't realize the waves crashing against the shore had been in the background until their sound disappeared. All she heard now was the earth sucking up her breath and deadening the sound of their steps.

"How much longer?" Barth shouted.

Maella flinched. Talking loudly didn't seem right down here—like you were just asking to wake up some terrible monster.

Keeper Shaul did not respond. The hair on the back of Maella's neck stood up. He was still ahead of her, wasn't he?

"We are here," Keeper Shaul said.

Maella slipped on the last stone step and fell on her tail-bone. Pain shot up her spine and she gasped.

Keeper Shaul stared down at her with a grim set to his lips. "I know that pain well." He tapped his cane against his bad leg. "I only have this one stick. It's why I go barefoot. Watch your step."

Maella gulped down a cry of pain as she stood. She wished she were in Grandmother's arms, back at home, safe in her bed.

Keeper Shaul turned away.

They faced a door. A monstrous metal door coated green from time and water and salt. Intricate workings in the metal had almost been eaten away.

Maella's heartbeat ramped up. "No. I won't open it."

Keeper Shaul wrestled with the handle. The door stuck at first, then swung open with a screech. He turned, barely able to hold back a sneer. "This room is not for doormakers to open. Doors can also keep doormakers out of places we don't want you in." He said this like it was common knowledge, something every child should have learned. Pointing his cane at a light that flickered in the distance, he said, "Through here. The lighthouse has always been a focus point for the pattern. There are certain risks that this brings. We must be quiet."

Daniel and Barth crowded behind her and Claritsa. Daniel's face was a mask of anxiety. It was there in Barth's expression too, though he tried his best to look cool and like none of this insanity could phase him.

"Where are we?" Claritsa whispered.

"Near the center of the earth. Muahahahaha," Barth said, but there was a hitch of fear in his voice that no amount of forced bravado could cover up.

Keeper Shaul's gray robes and hair twirled. He whacked Barth upside the head with his cane.

Barth yelped, and held his ear, bravado gone, replaced with the look of a little boy in shock. But in a flash, like he knew he had exposed himself, he turned his expression into a scowl and a mean look appeared in his eyes. "You're going to pay for that."

"Be silent if you value your life," Keeper Shaul said, ignoring Barth's threat. "Do you not know?"

The four of them looked at Keeper Shaul with confusion.

He sighed. "No, of course you do not."

Maella braced herself for another family insult. Instead, Keeper Shaul said simply, "Doors disturb more than worlds. You may talk again when we reach the light."

Without further explanation, Keeper Shaul led them across a narrow path. A rough stone wall rose steeply to their left. A lagoon of water lit underneath with purple light, gurgled to their right. Keeper Shaul disappeared around a corner. Claritsa and the others followed, Barth's scowl set firmly in place. Maella hung back.

A large, dark shape moved underneath the water. Two triangle-shaped ears broke the surface without a sound. Something that looked an awful lot like a long tail lashed underneath the water without a ripple.

Maella drew in a sharp, silent breath, and hurried to catch up to the others. The pathway continued along the water. It all glowed purple, almost lavender, and the water was so clear it showed the rocky bottom of the basin.

Maella searched for the light source and for the moving shadow. "What's in the water?"

Keeper Shaul hobbled along. He glanced once over his shoulder and picked up the pace in spite of his cane. "Klylup," he whispered. "This way. Quickly now."

Maella's heartbeat choked her throat. They stayed silent because it was clear now that their lives depended on it.

When they left the lagoon, everyone breathed easier, but Keeper Shaul continued with a grueling pace until they reached another massive, deteriorating door. A door with no lock, but sturdy enough to keep out a Klylup, Maella realized. He opened it and they entered a small, cave-like room.

Keeper Shaul used his torch to light more torches around the room. They created a flickering, smoky ring of light that clogged Maella's lungs.

"Why is there a Klylup here?" Maella asked. "Is it because of the doors?"

But Keeper Shaul did not answer, and her attention was soon drawn elsewhere.

Someone had pushed a large wooden table against one rocky wall. An open book sat on this table—one of those books normally only seen in museums under glass. Thick, huge, with worked leather covers, and pages that, as she approached the book, seemed as fragile as dry leaves in autumn, but when she brushed a finger against one, found it unyielding to her touch.

"Don't touch that," Keeper Shaul said sharply.

Maella drew back her hand as if bitten by a snake.

"What is it?" Claritsa asked.

Claritsa and Daniel crowded around Maella.

"This," Keeper Shaul said, his voice holding a note of tenderness. "This is the pattern."

In the silence, water gurgled and their sharp breaths created an irregular beat—and something else. Echoing voices and scraping metal. Everyone crowded the book and stared at it like it was some video game about to turn on.

Maybe it would start playing music.

She almost giggled at the thought. Not because it was funny. No, none of this was funny. They had walked past a Klylup lagoon and it was all insane and she knew somehow it was only going to get worse.

"It's a bunch of stupid numbers," Barth said.

"No," Daniel interrupted. He hovered his fingers over the page. "May I?"

"You may," Keeper Shaul said.

Maella bit her lip. Daniel was allowed, but not her?

"You know how it works," Claritsa said, astonished.

Daniel shook his head, but his eyes never left the paper. "No. It's just...there *is* a pattern to it." He let his fingers brush the text.

It looked like a jumble of numbers and letters to Maella. There probably was a pattern to it, but not one she could see.

"These are dates?" Daniel said.

"Yes," Keeper Shaul said.

"And these..." Daniel's finger skimmed a line of numbers and symbols. "Location markers. Identification symbols."

"Yes," Keeper Shaul said again.

Barth pushed Daniel aside. He peered at the pages, his eyes never locking onto the text. He rifled through the pages, bending the corner of one, tearing the edge of another, flipping faster, his frustration mounting.

Keeper Shaul's cane snaked out and hit Barth on the head, but it was like Barth was ready for it, expecting it, because he grabbed the end of the cane with both hands and ripped it away. Keeper Shaul's robes swirled into the air and his body made a thudding sound as he hit the ground.

Barth stood over him, the cane held like a bat in his hands.

Maella rushed to Keeper Shaul's side. "Don't you dare, Barth. Don't you dare."

Barth laughed, but it sounded hysterical, like how she might have sounded if she allowed her panicked giggle to escape. Like the sound of someone cracking under pressure.

"The door-freak speaks for her own freak-kind," Barth said, a strangled note in his voice. "How nice, how fun-freakin'-tastic."

Daniel went to his knees. The book had tumbled to the floor, and he picked it up, cradling it like a baby. Maella had no idea he cared about stuff like that. He'd dropped out of school at the same time Barth did.

Claritsa stood behind Barth. Her hands were locked into fists and she looked ready to launch herself at him.

Daniel set the book gently back on its table.

"She is not my kind," Keeper Shaul said quietly.

His words drove an icy knife into Maella. "Why do you blame me for something I didn't do? I don't know about any of this! You won't let me touch the book. You hate me because of my family. You won't answer my questions—"

"The worlds are falling apart," Keeper Shaul said, still on the ground. "They have been for a long time. And for a long time, the pattern held, but it also is changing." Keeper Shaul groaned as he pushed himself to sitting.

"You don't get it," Barth said, bringing the cane up higher. "I. Don't. Care. I want to go home." The cane in his hand wavered, like he realized how small and petulant those words made him sound—like a child calling for his mother. His eyes flashed in anger. He flexed his grip on the cane. "Tell us how to get home, old man, or you're going to regret it."

Maella swore she heard voices again, the stomp of feet, metal grating on metal.

"Barth, you're crazy," Maella said. "You're being stupid—"

"I am telling you exactly what you need to hear," Keeper Shaul said, "but you are too foolish to hear it."

"Let him speak," Daniel said. "It's a code. It tells you which doors have been opened, who opened them, and where they went. It tells you, if you study it long enough and look for the patterns, the likelihood a door will open to a certain place—" he pointed his finger at Keeper Shaul and then Maella. "Barth, if you hurt him, he can't tell her which door to open to get us home."

Barth looked between Daniel and Keeper Shaul. "Is that true?"

Keeper Shaul sighed and stared at Daniel. "My boy, you would have made an excellent student. It's a shame for all of us that you are not a doormaker." He glanced at Barth. "Your friend is mostly correct."

Barth lowered the cane.

"Give it back to him," Maella said, putting some venom in her words.

Barth held out the cane.

Maella wanted answers from Keeper Shaul, no matter how much she also wanted to tell him off. She helped him to his feet even as he shrugged her away, hissing something under his breath that she didn't understand.

Keeper Shaul took back the cane and shuffled to the book, smoothing its pages and mumbling under his breath. "All the doors a doormaker opened used to go exactly where the doormaker wished. But that was long ago. Doors no longer do a doormaker's bidding. Even the same doormaker opening and closing *the same door* will reach a different place each time. The worlds are falling apart now. We don't know what held them together at the beginning, though people have a few ideas. I have spent my life studying The Pattern. I am one of the few remaining pattern-keepers."

Maella had so many questions she didn't know where to begin. Keeper Shaul turned what seemed like a hundred pages and scanned the text with his fingers. He couldn't possibly be reading the book that fast, more like he was using it for comfort. "It is said there is the One Door that can still control the worlds. The One Door will take a doormaker anywhere he wishes—"

"Where is it?" Hope rose inside Maella like an ocean wave about to crash on the beach. "Is that the door I need to open to take us back home?" She stepped closer to the book, eager to decipher its strange marks and numbers. She would find the One Door, use it, and get them all back home safely.

Keeper Shaul hissed and closed the book. "No one knows where it is. It's said that only The One doormaker can find it and repair the worlds." He looked strangely at Maella. "You are not The One."

Anger flared in Maella. "I know I've disappointed you, turning out to be from the Botron family and a girl and all, but this is getting stupid. How can I make things right if you won't let me try? So I'm not The One you've been looking for. Got it. Just tell me what I need to know to get my friends back home."

And to understand why her family fled and why everyone hated them so much. But she didn't add those last bits. She didn't think Keeper Shaul would care much about any of that.

"I have researched your family for a long time." Keeper Shaul's hands remained on the book, keeping it closed. "It is my job to understand the patterns left for doormakers to follow. I reviewed everything last night—to be sure—though I *was* already sure. While it is not always clear which family opened each door, while it is not always clear where doors open or when they are opened, what remains clear is this: Your father and your brother have done more damage to our worlds over this last year than—"

"Wait." The word caught in Maella's throat. "What about my father and brother? This last year?"

Keeper Shaul flipped the book to the most recent pages. Almost every entry showed gaps that looked like they should have been filled in with letters, numbers, or symbols. He ran his finger down the page and rattled off a date and time she didn't recognize, but there was something she did—

Her family's symbol.

*A curved quarter moon, its points sharp like knives—that's us, the doormakers. Three links, separate yet attached, pierced by the moon. They are the—*

"Earth to Rathe. Transversal inversion. Door on Shed."

What? She had been expecting to hear about the door in the field. "Who was that? Who went through the shed door?"

"Esson." Claritsa and Barth said in unison. They stared at each other and then looked away.

"But it wasn't the shed," Claritsa said, looking sick to her stomach. "I was in the shed."

"It was a fridge," Barth said.

Maella remembered searching the woods for Claritsa on that day, hearing Claritsa's hoarse screams, finding the shed and the rusty crow bar and breaking the lock—and discovering her brother was gone forever. Back then she had really believed he must have died after going through a door.

She looked at Barth with new eyes. Claritsa hadn't been sure what she saw, locked inside the shed. He had been there when it happened.

Claritsa hadn't seen Esson go through a door, but Barth had.

"Your family symbol is plainly written," Keeper Shaul said.

Maella pushed her thoughts about Barth aside while she focused on what Keeper Shaul was really saying. She pressed forward and tried to read the page again. Numbers, letters, her family symbol. Even after the Door on Shed or Fridge or whatever, there were at least a dozen entries.

"What does that mean?" Maella pointed at two entries, not daring to actually touch the page for fear of incurring Keeper Shaul's wrath. The entries were marked with her family symbol and had almost identical numbers and letters.

"These doors were opened in two different places at almost the same day and time," Keeper Shaul said.

"When?" Maella said.

"Approximately one year ago. Door in Field. But the other one is missing the location. As I said, the pattern is breaking."

Maella ignored the rest of what he said. The day her father went through the door, someone else in her family had also opened a door. But the only person it could be was Esson, right?

Her brain told her not to hope. For all she knew, this other Botron doormaker could be a long-lost cousin. It didn't matter what her brain warned though, her heart galloped away at the thought Esson was still alive.

"Foster said he killed Esson—" Claritsa started.

"Foster." Keeper Shaul sniffed. He read off several more entries before returning to Earth and the Door in Field, to the day—yesterday—she had opened her first door.

Hope bubbled inside her chest. Her father might still be alive. Maybe her brother too. She was still alive, wasn't she? "Tell me which door to open next. Tell me how to get home and how to find my father and my brother. Tell me—"

"Just tell us where this One-stupid-Door is," Barth said.

She didn't care about the One Door or The One doormaker. But she would do whatever it took to bring her father and brother back to her mother.

"There are two pattern-keepers for each of the three worlds," Keeper Should said.

"*Three* worlds?" Daniel said. "We're on a completely different *world*, not just time period, but world?"

Keeper Shaul inclined his head. "Time travel is impossible. In spite of our searchings, in spite of our schools and our scholars, no one of us knows where the One Door resides.

Each day, the worlds fall apart a little more. Each day, the
pattern breaks a little more. If the One Door is not found
soon, it will be lost forever."

"Then we'll find it," Daniel said, his eyes lit up with a sense
of purpose Maella could recognize. She felt that way about
understanding what had happened to her family, and now,
finding her father and brother.

"Even if we knew where the One Door *was*, it is not meant
for *her*." Keeper Shaul spoke the words with bitterness.

"She's done nothing wrong," Claritsa spoke up. "Why do
you keep talking like she's going to destroy everything?"

Maella cringed at those words. Hadn't she, though? She
had opened up the door and woken the Klylup and the
monster had killed all those men. They had tried to tell her,
but how many times had tears welled up in her mother's
eyes? How many times had her father's voice gone hoarse?
How many times had her grandmother rebuked her for
bringing up terrible memories best forgotten?

But what would her mother feel if Maella could bring back
her father and brother?

Everything.

It would mean everything, because even through the lies
and the terror and the silence—they loved each other. They
were all that was left in all the world who she knew loved her.

"She might," Keeper Shaul said. "The pattern is unclear,
but what is clear is the history of her family—"

"Maella?" Claritsa's voice rang out in the silence.

Except it wasn't silent.

It hadn't been silent for a long time. While they'd been
fighting over the book, while purpose had grabbed hold of

Maella, while she'd imagined the light coming back into her mother's eyes because Maella would be brave and smart and save her entire family and bring them home—the voices and steps and metal had grown louder.

Keeper Shaul swiveled dark, piercing eyes onto Maella. "You closed the door behind you—the door that brought you to this world and to me." He said this like it was fact, like it was the most basic of rules, like of course you put on socks before you put on shoes, like of course you can't have the peanut butter jar because it will open a lid to hell.

"No, she didn't," Claritsa said, standing at the cave door, looking back the way they had come.

Shame filled Maella. They were all there to see it, how like a baby she was, how absolutely, completely messed up and useless and dangerous her ignorance made her.

Keeper Shaul hobbled faster than she thought possible. "Fool."

The room filled with clanks, cranks, the whirring sound of fans, the drip of liquid. Light flared, glinting off metal, then flared brighter, before settling into a strong flame, which revealed a machine against one wall.

A mess of wheels and cogs and belts towered over their heads, taking up one length of the room. Keeper Shaul adjusted a lever, tightened a screw next to a belt spinning into a blur, then dug through a box of parts on the ground.

Daniel and Barth argued in whispered, urgent tones.

Maella searched the book for answers to a problem she didn't know existed two seconds ago. She hadn't closed the door. She was supposed to have closed the door.

Foster.

Something small and light hit her in the chest. She grabbed it before it could fall to the ground. A cup of some kind, made out of glass like the ones in the kitchen.

"Bring back a cup of the *licatherin*."

"The what?"

Keeper Shaul's gnarled fingers didn't pause from tending the knobs and belts and cogs. He uttered words in another language, but even though she didn't understand them, she did know they were meant as curse words. "The liquid from the pool we walked by. Do not let it touch your skin."

"But—"

He threw a look over his shoulder like someone would throw a dagger. "Would your family fail us again?"

Maella ran past Claritsa and the boys. They shouted after her, but their voices were drowned out by louder noises from above.

She raced to the pool and knelt. The dark shape of the Klylup slid smoothly under the water, drawn away by the noises—she hoped. Her reflection in the water was purple, dirt-streaked, clothes stiff from salt. The water acted as a perfect purple mirror, changing the color of her skin and allowing her to see the tears that she furiously tried to blink back.

Careful of Keeper Shaul's warning, she used a metal dipper attached to the edge of the pool by a chain and filled the cup. Her hands shook as her mind imagined a dark shadow rising from the water to drag her into its depths.

Drops of the liquid splashed onto her hand. She held her breath, waiting for some sort of pain. Instead, her skin tingled. She shook off the drops and wiped her hand dry on her shorts. Hot breath tickled her neck and she flinched.

"What are you doing?" Claritsa said. "We have to get away from here. There's a Klylup in there."

"Keeper Shaul said this was the only way." Maella did not let a single drop spill as she hurried back to the machine.

"I don't trust him." Claritsa jogged to keep pace.

"It doesn't matter," Maella said.

"Of course it matters!"

As if in response, the shouts that had blended together became clear. They were chanting in English—

*"Death to doormakers!"*

A great darkness emerged from the far end of the purple lagoon, creating a wave of water that swamped the walkway.

When she returned to Keeper Shaul and the machine, he took the cup and dumped its contents unceremoniously into a bronze funnel. He grabbed her hand, and before she knew what had happened, he sliced her finger, forcing her blood to drip into the funnel. She cried out, but he had already released her.

The liquids slipped into a transparent tubing that gurgled as it emptied into a beaker that sat over a candle flame. Keeper Shaul began turning a wheel. The whole machine came to life with a series of clicks and hisses. When the liquid evaporated into a purple mist, he hurried to a flat plate covered with a piece of paper that matched those in the book. Directly above the paper was a giant needle.

Maella looked around the room. The boys were gone. Claritsa was at the doorway, keeping watch.

"The door won't lock. Daniel and Barth ran," Claritsa said. "We should too."

"I can't," Maella said.

"I know," Claritsa said.

"You should go."

Claritsa sighed. "Don't be an idiot."

Keeper Shaul hissed as the needle dipped into the paper, then back out, again and again, each time leaving behind inky purple marks.

The needle was a pen.

But it might as well have been writing gibberish for all she understood what it spit out. Keeper Shaul caught her stare and used his body to block her view. Even still, she noticed his eyes grow wide, reading whatever the stupid needle spit out.

"Where's the door, Keeper Shaul?" Maella used her best adult voice, the one she used when she wanted her mother and grandmother to take her seriously. The one she used when she tried to bring them back from the memories that suffocated them all in the darkness.

The needle-pen stopped inking. He snatched the paper off the mount and looked ready to ball it up into trash.

"Tell me what door I need to open," Maella said. "We don't have enough time. Tell me my pattern."

He didn't look at her while he spoke. His words were so quiet, Claritsa could not hear them. "You have seven more doors left to open." His voice stalled. "The seventh door will kill you."

Adrenaline surged inside Maella. What was he saying? She couldn't have heard him right. It didn't make—

"But the *next* door you open," Keeper Shaul continued. "That one will take you...closer to your father...closer to home."

His hands crumpled the paper like the death sentence he had just announced was so much trash now. Pounding footsteps and shouting voices told Maella they were out of time. She wouldn't live to open even one more door if they didn't get out now.

"Which door?" She shouted, her mind spinning.

"The lighthouse hatch," Keeper Shaul said, his voice loud. Now sure of himself. "That one *must* be your next door. It must be. There is no choice."

"But that's past whatever army is coming down those stairs right now!" Claritsa said, turning at his words, her face full of panic. "He's crazy."

Keeper Shaul brushed at his eyes as if removing cobwebs. He shuffled behind the contraption. His voice was faint but clear. "Follow me. I will take you to the door you need."

# Chapter 9

BEHIND THE PATTERN-READING MACHINE was a narrow opening in the wall. Keeper Shaul vanished through that opening.

Maella dashed in after him, letting the darkness fold over her like a blanket—not thinking.

"Maella." Claritsa's voice sounded faint, almost strangled.

Maella stopped, the slap of her shoes echoing. Her toes felt icy in this new cold with this new fear. The sound of Keeper Shaul's steps became faint and then went silent. She ran back to the machine. Even in the warm torch light Claritsa's skin looked washed out. Her breath hitched into the beginning of hiccups.

Claritsa could not do small, dark places. Not after the shed.

People burst into the room. Maella's heart skipped a beat. They pounded the floor with their steps and now shouted at each other in a language Maella did not understand.

Keeper Shaul's pattern-machine hid them for the moment. But not for much longer.

Claritsa knelt, hiccups wracking her body.

Maella decided she would let herself get captured and that would be it. Claritsa did not have this awful thing inside of her like Maella. They would leave Claritsa alone because she was not a doormaker.

Tears shined in Claritsa's eyes. "Maella, you have to go." She whispered this. It wasn't even a whisper. She mouthed the words, but they knew each other so well that even in the dim light Maella knew exactly what Claritsa said—and refused with everything inside of her to hear it.

People shouted, stomped around, and began tearing apart the machine, sending gears and handles flying.

Maella thought of an idea. Not much of an idea, but a better one than waiting on their knees in the dark for people who chanted death to doormakers.

"Close your eyes." She hoped there was enough time for this.

Claritsa didn't protest. Tears slipped from beneath her lids.

Maella grabbed her hands. "Stand up."

Claritsa did, even though her legs wobbled.

Maella began a story that started in a green meadow and with a red tricycle, a story about streams and valleys, and can't you just picture the green grass, the blue endless sky, the way the sun warms your skin? Just take a step forward into the grass. It's squishy because of the mud underneath, but Cheyanne is waiting with her tricycle. Cheyanne said Claritsa could ride it first and it will just be the three of them, just the girls, so we can talk about cute boys and be as thrilled to ride a silly tricycle as we want, no one has to know, take another step, yeah, that's good, and we'll go to the flats and race around the parking lot strips, and take another step, and set up obstacles, and I'll win all the races, just you see, don't laugh, just cause I never owned a bike doesn't mean anything, this is a tricycle, try to cycle, you know, try real hard and stuff.

And Claritsa giggled because Maella was no longer making sense and they were both more than a little hysterical.

They were in the tunnel and the walls were cold. Maella's story was warm enough and they took enough steps that the noises faded.

No one entered the tunnel after them, and then they were at the end.

But at the end was a door and this door was closed.

# Chapter 10

IT WASN'T THE RIGHT DOOR. The sinking feeling in Maella's stomach told her that.

The door was wooden, splintered, old. It was arched at the top, and even though the torchlight shined faintly behind them, she could see the door's black iron handle. Well oiled. It would probably open at the slightest touch of her hand and suck them into a vortex.

She wanted to trust Keeper Shaul. Why would he close the wrong door on her? This *must* be the one he meant.

And then she heard it.

And Claritsa whimpered because she heard it too.

And Maella could see it, because something lit up the minerals in the walls like glitter.

The soldiers had entered the tunnel.

"You have to open the door," Maella said, not sure at all that she was right. "I can't do it. It's not the right door. It's not the one he said."

Maella waited for Claritsa to freeze, to fall apart, to protest.

Instead, Claritsa kept her eyes closed and reached out a hand. "Show me."

Maella guided her to the latch. As soon as Claritsa's fingers brushed the metal, Maella snatched away her own hands.

Claritsa barely touched the door and it swung open.

Keeper Shaul stood on the other side and looked shocked to see them.

If Maella hadn't walked slowly through the tunnel for Claritsa's sake, she would have run into the door and opened it by accident.

He shook his head and narrowed his eyes. "They're following you."

All around them was stone again. And another set of stairs.

Keeper Shaul pushed the door closed behind them and set the lock.

"It was closed," Maella said, accusing him with those three words of pretty much everything terrible in the world.

"It was not," Keeper Shaul said, sounding more like a child than an old man. He brought his robes together in one hand and held his cane in the other. "I am neither stupid nor the careless one here."

Maybe before the doors Maella would have fought back— she could hear the insult in his words just fine, but he was also speaking the truth. She had been very stupid and very careless.

Claritsa looked around like she had just woken up and didn't know quite where she was yet.

Keeper Shaul led them up the stairs. The light increased as they climbed, revealing fine cracks in the stone blocks. The steps were smoother in the middle, as if worn away by thousands of feet over hundreds of years.

Maella's hands grew slippery from the cold moisture of the wall she touched to steady herself. Her shoes were still wet, but the air warmed as they climbed. Sunlight filtered through a series of punched out stones she guessed were somebody's idea of windows.

The stairs led to a small landing. A large window opened to the sky on each of the four sides of the room. A smaller iron staircase with open railing grew from the center of the room and disappeared into the ceiling, twisting three times on its way up.

Maella's head spun. They were already so high it felt like they'd climbed a mile, but there was still more to go.

And then she saw the door.

An overhead door made of wooden planks. It closed off the spiral stairs to the top room—to the lighthouse.

Maella didn't get a good feeling about this door. Not at all, but she knew without needing to ask that this was the one Keeper Shaul meant for her to open. "Will the door let us off into the sky? Will we fall like before?"

"The pattern is incomplete." Keeper Shaul leaned against his cane like it was the only thing keeping him standing. He'd just climbed a mile of stairs too and even though he wasn't out of breath, his robes shook like his legs underneath had turned to jelly. "As sure as I can be since the pattern began to break down… this door will take you to where you need to go."

"Closer to my father. Closer to home," Maella said, even though those two things didn't make sense together, but there was no time—

"The worlds are falling apart," Keeper Shaul said. "The pattern is breaking."

Claritsa leaned against the wall for support, next to one of the window openings, and stared at the view of sky and water and beach. "That doesn't answer her question."

"Go through the door or not," Keeper Shaul said. "I have more than done my duty by a doormaker who does not know what duty means."

Maella jumped up, ready to argue.

Claritsa turned and held out a hand as if to say, don't waste your time with crazy. Except this crazy was sending them through a door to who-knew-where.

Noise on the stairs below interrupted them. Keeper Shaul hissed. "Go now or not at all."

But Claritsa was right, and so was Keeper Shaul. Either they waited to be captured or she opened the door.

The narrow stairs allowed for them to climb one at a time. Even though the railing was only simple wrought iron, at least there was something to hold on to. Keeper Shaul climbed behind them, making three strikes against the metal stairs—foot, cane, foot. Running sounds grew. Maella hurried to the top, Claritsa close on her heels, Keeper Shaul a few paces behind.

People burst onto the landing.

Maella looked down.

Curly mops of hair, ripped jeans, chests covered in plaid.

Barth scanned the room as if searching for weapons. Daniel looked up, shock opening his face when he saw the girls and Keeper Shaul.

"They're behind us," Daniel said, breathless.

"You led them here," Claritsa said, accusing.

"Stupid," Keeper Shaul said.

The shouting increased.

Barth looked from Maella to Daniel to Keeper Shaul. Something ugly appeared in his eyes. "You were going to open the door and just leave us."

"You had already left," Maella said, the flippant tone of her words barely hiding her shaking fear. She climbed even as she felt Barth's burning stare. There was only one way out. Her hands shook as she thought about what she was going to do next.

*Never open a door, Maella.* She heard the warning in her grandmother's voice for the millionth time.

Barth bounded up the stairs. He reached Keeper Shaul and pushed roughly past him. Daniel was close behind, but hesitated.

"Go." Keeper Shaul pressed himself against the metal railing to make room. "Go now."

Maella reached the hatch and rested the palm of her hand against the wood. It was rough and splintered.

She didn't want to do this.

Men filled the landing. Maella looked down again. Her muscles seized when she found Foster staring back at her. He wore a sort of leather-armored shirt, soaking wet—from the fall from the door into the water, she guessed. His hands held a lethal long knife.

"You," Foster said.

Maella's breath caught in her throat. The door was above her. There was no getting out of its way if something terrible barreled through.

Before she could think, she thrust open the hatch.

She felt a vibration, like a tickle, on her hand.

Foster shouted at his men to climb the stairs. Claritsa screamed in her ear to go. Keeper Shaul stayed where he was, holding onto the railing a few steps below.

White light shot out the door. For a horrifying moment, Maella feared it was flames, like the desk.

But the light did not burn, it only blinded. The outline of Claritsa's body stumbled past Maella, through the open door. Barth was close behind. As Maella's eyes adjusted, she saw Barth held out his hands, like he had pushed Claritsa through the door to meet whatever horror waited on the other side. There was a horrible grimace on his face.

Barth grabbed Daniel by his shirt and practically threw him into the open door. Daniel shouted and fought. He kicked Maella accidentally in the shin and she almost fell over the railing. He was bigger than her, but no match for Barth.

Daniel disappeared through the door.

Barth stepped forward. Maella couldn't help herself. She put out her foot because she hated him. She hated everything about him. She just wanted to wipe that look off his face, just wanted him to know he couldn't control them, or make Esson do what he wanted, no matter what kind of business Barth had with her grandmother.

His leg hooked onto her foot and he was too tall and the railing was too low to stop him like it had stopped her. He flew over the railing and into the waiting arms of Foster's people, who caught him and dragged him away.

Maella gaped at what she'd done. She hadn't meant—

Keeper Shaul moved. He stood right next to her. He wrapped one arm around the railing and held out his cane.

Maella saw Foster's angry face and the way it turned his skin reddish-purple as he bounded up. Through the blinding light of the opened door, the other side looked like the moon, except it had blue sky. But there was nothing alive as far as she could see. No trees, no buildings, no people, no plants, no animals. It was empty and gray and endless.

Foster had almost caught up. He held out the long knife like a spear.

"You are not The One." Keeper Shaul's face looked both grave and determined. "I am sorry."

He punched Maella in the stomach with his cane.

She tripped backward, up into the door, and landed hard on some rocks. The sun beat heat onto her skin. Wind whipped her hair and slammed the hatch door into her body, onto her foot still over the threshold, then the wind whipped the door open again.

The door was like a window. On either side was gray nothingness and higher piles of nothingness into the horizon. In the middle of her view was a rectangle. Inside that rectangle was a spiral staircase surrounded by stone and Keeper Shaul's surprised face at something long and terrible and metal that stuck out from his chest.

Blood trickled down one side of Keeper Shaul's mouth. A suction noise tore through Maella's frozen brain. The long knife disappeared. Keeper Shaul's face twisted in pain. He fell onto the last step, inches from the hatch. His eyes were open and he stared at her.

He couldn't see her anymore, but she got the message.

*Close the damn door.*

She moved her foot.

The door slammed onto Foster's hand holding the long knife—it didn't close.

Maella shouted.

Suddenly, it was the three of them. Maella, Claritsa, and Daniel bracing the door. There was a cry of pain as the door jammed against Foster's wrist. The long knife dropped on their side and the hand retreated.

The door closed.

A vibration hit Maella again. Through the same hand the drops of purple lagoon water had splashed. Her body felt off. The world seemed out of tune. The lines that marked the door's outline faded and disappeared into the stone.

Vibrations stopped.

There was no door, or anything even close to a door.

There was no going back.

Maella's mind filled with the image of Keeper Shaul and how the blood trickled out of his mouth and down his chin.

She didn't understand his last words.

He had said he was sorry, but he had not looked sorry. Not really.

She gulped for huge breaths of air to try to clear her light-headedness. Her hands shook as she checked her own chest for a knife sticking out of it like it had stuck out of Keeper Shaul.

Keeper Shaul had been killed while trying to help them, but the feeling in the pit of her stomach told her this thought was not quite right.

He had tried to get them through this door. Because of something important to him.

But Maella didn't think this something was meant to help them.

She didn't think that at all.

# Chapter 11

THE SUN BEAT AN EXHAUSTING kind of heat into Maella's skin. The breeze tore that heat from her, leaving her chapped and cold on the stones. The door had closed and the three of them had collapsed like deflated balloons. She wanted sleep to black out everything. The temptation to rest pulled at her muscles, unstoppable.

"Where's Barth?" Daniel asked, raising his voice. "What did you do to Barth?"

Maella could barely lift her head from her arms. The long knife lay on the ground next to her. Red liquid stained the blade. Oh.

She scooted away. The rock scraped her hands. This movement sent her head pounding. No matter how deeply she
breathed, she didn't feel like she got enough oxygen. For
some strange reason, the stones smelled like licorice.

Claritsa scanned the mountains of rock that surrounded
them. They were in a gravel bowl except the pieces of gravel
were the size of their heads. "How can it be both cold and hot
at the same time?"

"Barth didn't make it through," Maella said.

Daniel's face turned pale, then flushed. He walked away. A
sort of half-scream tore from his throat. A rock clattered
down the hillside.

"Be quiet," Claritsa said. "We don't know what could be
around."

Daniel turned red-rimmed eyes onto Claritsa. His whole
body shook. His hands formed fists. He opened his mouth,
and he let out a shout that went on and on. The sound
slapped against the rocky walls of their bowl and bounced
back. Stones danced, then slammed into nearby stones,
sending off sharp, bomb-like noises.

Claritsa stood up and slapped Daniel across the face.

Snot flew into the air. His dark, red-rimmed eyes lost
focus, then cleared. He turned a hateful gaze onto Maella.

She shrunk into the stone under that look. Daniel had
helped them in the field, but he wished he hadn't. It was
plain on his face.

The stones tumbled into each other for several more minutes, sounding a lot like rolling waves of thunder. Then
stillness returned and that was somehow worse.

JAMIE THORNTON 131

"Is this the moon?" Maella asked. She knew it was not, but this was what she would have imagined it to be like. All stone, no life. No sign of anything except rock. A hellish landscape for someone like her. Potential doors everywhere she turned. The thought exhausted her and she laid her cheek back down on the rock. If she just stayed in this spot forever, she wouldn't be able to make anymore mistakes.

"We can breathe, can't we?" Claritsa said.

"Barely," Maella said. The words took work to push out. "It feels like there isn't any air here. Can't you feel it?"

Claritsa shook her head and her dark braids whipped across her shoulder. "I don't know where we are. I don't know what's happening. I just know, I just—"

"Want to go home," Maella finished Claritsa's sentence. "I'm sorry."

Claritsa wiped furiously at her eyes. "It doesn't matter. It's fine."

"No, it's not." Daniel scrambled up the rocks, setting off more mini-avalanches.

Maella and Claritsa watched him climb. By unspoken agreement, neither of them followed. Maella didn't think she had the strength for it. Claritsa looked too mad to care what trouble he was about to cause.

Daniel crested the rocky bowl. His outline against the sky made him look like a stranger. He covered his eyes from the sun and pointed across the landscape.

Maella's head pounded. Claritsa said something felt wrong with her stomach. Maybe this world had poison for air. Maybe that's what the licorice smell meant. Maella didn't know how it all worked. Keeper Shaul would know, but he was dead. Killed while helping her, or throwing her away. She wanted to believe the former, but feared the latter was more likely the truth.

"I see something," Daniel shouted, causing more little shock waves of thunder.

Maella wanted him to stop moving, just stop. Just leave the stones alone. But even after he scrambled down, his neck flushed, sweat dripping down his face, the thunder continued. His skin looked reddened, like he had already begun to sunburn. Claritsa's dark skin protected her well enough. Even though Maella was covered in freckles inherited from her mother, she had gotten dark enough skin from her father to not be worried about the sun yet.

She would count herself the luckiest girl in the world right now if all she had to worry about was a sunburn.

"It looks like there's something not too far from here," Daniel said.

"Something?" Claritsa said without the usual sarcastic bite.

Maella still heard the thunder—a low rumble that felt both further away and somehow all around her. She scanned the rocks, searching for movement.

"It doesn't look natural," Daniel said. "It's something people had to have done. There *have* to be people here."

"That's what we want," Claritsa said. "More people like Foster."

"There's only one way to find out," Daniel said. "We can't stay here."

"They wanted to kill us before," Claritsa said.

"They wanted to kill her," Daniel said.

"Same difference."

"Not really."

Claritsa stared coldly at Daniel. "We don't need you."

Daniel shook his head.

Maella tried to stand up, but the dizziness sent her flat onto the stone.

"We're too high up," Daniel said. "You're feeling sick because of the altitude."

"What are you talking about?" Maella said with her eyes closed. She tried to keep her breathing steady.

"There isn't really anything alive. You can see it from up there." Daniel waved at the hill of rocks. "It's like we're at the top of the world. A world. Some world. Whatever."

His words brought her some hope. If they really were just high up somewhere, maybe they weren't dying from air poisoning after all. Maybe Keeper Shaul had helped them get home.

"I could flip over a rock to open another door."

"No." Daniel and Claritsa said in unison.

Of course Maella didn't really want to, but still, it hurt her the way they said it, like she was a freak. Even though she knew she was.

Even though she knew—if Keeper Shaul could be trusted —that she only had six doors left to open before she died.

This thought woke Maella up like someone had splashed her with icy water.

Thunder rolled again, and this time, on top of the rumble, some sort of horn and then a trumpet sounded.

The trumpet sound—it was familiar in a terrifying sort of way.

She needed to tell Claritsa about Keeper Shaul's prediction. Claritsa would be able to convince Maella that Keeper Shaul was lying.

She forced her eyes open, expecting to see blue sky.

Claritsa and Daniel returned to their arguing.

"You guys," Maella croaked. All thoughts about Keeper Shaul and her seven doors vanished. Her brain locked up stiff like her body.

They ignored her.

"Look up!" Maella shouted as lightning exploded the sky.

# Chapter 12

ELECTRICITY CHARGED THE AIR. FAT drops of rain fell in a staccato pattern.

They scrambled out of the rocky bowl as lightning turned the world blank with silver light, like the never-ending flash of a camera. The edge of the storm cut across the sky like a wound. The clouds were black and green and swirled like soup in a blender. Clear blue on one side and a mass of darkness and wet electricity and wind on the other that pushed down on them, pinning them to the rocks as they slipped and jammed and scrambled.

By the time they cleared the rocky bowl, sweat and rain drenched Maella. The view opened to a flat field of boulders.

"Can't stop," Daniel shouted.

A crack of lightning tore into a pile of stones a hundred yards away. The storm moved faster than they possibly could. She had never been in a place that felt both so big and so empty. Sky went on for an eternity and she wished for a bird, or anything other than the storm, to give it shape.

Thick, cold sheets of rain dumped on them, then stopped every few seconds, like someone turning on and off a faucet. Her mind tripped on the lavender tinted mist the rain formed off the rocks. Keeper Shaul had told her she had seven doors left to open before she died and she'd already opened one. But could she trust what he said?

Water pooled between the rocks, becoming dozens of mirrors that reflected a purplish light back into the sky. Lightning struck a nearby stone and the stone erupted like it had been struck by a bomb.

Claritsa and Maella raced after Daniel. He led them to where he swore he saw something human made. There was nowhere else to go.

Then he stopped abruptly. "Get back!" He held out his arms.

Maella was so focused on her steps and her hands to keep from tripping and accidentally opening a door, she stumbled into his arm. Her concentration shattered and her shoe slipped. She jammed her big toe into the wet stone and pain erupted. But the stone was heavy and didn't move. No door. Lightning cracked the sky. She bit back a yelp. She swore a trumpet sounded again, and she could almost name it, but the thunder swallowed it.

Wind picked up, driving rain into her face. Somehow, the sun still shined. Clouds surrounded it and the warm light stood out like a beacon in the sky. But even the sun didn't look right. A shape had taken a bite out of it.

No, that wasn't it.

There was something in *front* of the sun. A small, dark shape that sent shivers down Maella's spine. But she told herself it was just the clouds taking over. The storm would cover everything soon and if the lightning didn't kill them then the stones would.

"I think this is a mine," Daniel shouted over the wind.

They had stopped just in time to keep from going over the edge of a cliff. Maella looked down into a rocky bowl a lot like the one they left, but here the sides were steeper and dropped away to a sickly purplish pool of water. Carts, tools, pulleys, even some cloth, stuck out of the water in different spots. Maella searched for movement, for any sign of life. But there was nothing.

"Maybe we should go back," Maella shouted.

"I can see a way down," Daniel said.

Something moved. It was large and on the same level as them—to the side.

The storm paused, just for a moment.

And she heard it—a trumpet sound—and she recognized it.

"Klylup." Maella's voice hiccuped over the word. "Klylup. It's a Klylup!"

Lightning struck the pool of water at the bottom of the mine. Electricity raised the hair on Maella's arms. That licorice smell grew stronger.

The Klylup came out of the storm from the direction where they had entered this world. It slithered across the stones, using its belly to move. The tail lashed out behind it, as if steering it. She thought for a terrible moment it was the *same* Klylup, the one they had woken in the cave. Her brain registered that it wasn't—this one was ten times her size, but ten times smaller than the first one, or even the one in the lagoon. And it looked different, lopsided, like it was—

"It's missing a wing," Claritsa said.

"That's not going to stop it," Daniel said.

Maella's thoughts went on autopilot. She had opened the door, the Klylup had woken. Here was another Klylup. Because she had opened another door.

Its black body sucked up the light. Water ran off its sides in a dozen little purple streams. Its eyes were a glowing green and its ears were long and triangular. One leathery wing was gone—thin, grayish white bones stuck out like a cluttered handful of flutes.

Maella felt a hard yank on her shoulder.

"We have to run!" Claritsa screamed into Maella's ear.

The Klylup locked onto them. It trumpeted and lashed its tail, turning direction. Its massive body slid across the stones like a monstrous creek snake.

Adrenaline made blood roar across her ears. They ran. They tried to run. They fell. At each fall, Maella tried to watch her hands, and waited for a door to open and a stone door to take her. They shouted at each other to get up. Wind ripped at their clothes. Ragged breaths tore from her chest. The Klylup trumpeted its murderous intent. Thunder shook her insides. Water formed puddles that turned into ponds and made it impossible to see where it was safe to step. Maella ran as fast as she could, picking a zig-zag path that dropped her behind both Claritsa and Daniel. She had to land on the right stones. She had to throw herself onto the heaviest stones, those least likely to flip under her hands if she fell again.

Daniel reached these house-sized boulders stretched out in a line that formed a sort of wall. If they tried to go around, the Klylup would catch them. So Daniel scrambled up the side, but slipped back down, clawing at the stone with all four limbs like a dog.

Then she was at the boulders, the thunder masking the Klylup's trumpet call. She didn't dare look over her shoulder to see how close the monster was.

Daniel slid off the rock again as she threw herself at its surface. Her foot caught a sort of lip, just enough to bring her hands around and scramble up the boulder, even as Daniel slid down again.

She vaulted herself up—and saw two impossibly huge green eyes staring back at her.

Screaming, she fell backward.

A hand lunged out and grabbed at her jacket. She kicked and scratched. There was shouting, human shouting, and something that sounded like a growl. Maella fought harder. The sounds switched now to a higher, softer pitch. She could almost understand these sounds, like they were supposed to make sense to her.

"Are you from Earth?"

She stopped fighting.

The woman's skin was coated with gray dust, the rain leaving streaks of purple through it. The grunts and growls had been the woman trying out different languages. Everything smelled like rock but with a faint burnt overtone. Like when her family had been altogether—before Esson had gone through the door—and sometimes spent a hot afternoon at the creek. The sun would bake the wet stones and it smelled like this.

Green eyes switched languages again when Maella did not speak.

Now Maella could tell it was a woman's voice.

"I'm from Earth," Maella said.

"You must come," the woman said, switching back to English. "The Klylup always comes when they open the door, but the storm has made this day unlucky."

"My friends," Maella said.

The woman's eyes widened. "What does—" She looked behind Maella. "You must come now!"

"No!" Maella wrenched herself out of the woman's grip, almost flying off the boulder. She flipped onto her stomach and reached down for Claritsa's uplifted hands. Daniel had his arms wrapped around Claritsa's legs and braced himself, one foot in a growing pool of water, another on a stone above the waterline.

The Klylup barreled over—its mouth open, its long ears cocked parallel with the ground to keep out the rain. Purple-stained teeth lined its mouth against a pink gum.

Claritsa's dark bangs were plastered to her forehead. The rain ran off her in rivulets.

Maella grabbed for her.

Too slick, too slippery.

"Hold on!" Claritsa yelled.

Maella gritted her teeth and dug her nails into Claritsa's arms. Claritsa yelped, but Maella held on and pulled. She felt someone push down on her legs, holding her to the boulder so she wouldn't slip over the side.

Claritsa scrambled up, stomping on Maella's head in her rush to get up the rock. Then Claritsa flipped down next to Maella and they both reached for Daniel. His shirt hung soaked against his skin, outlining his chest and shoulders. A vein along his neck pulsed from adrenaline, fear, anger. His arms bulged with muscle as he reached for them.

The Klylup was yards away.

Daniel jumped. Their slim hands reached for his shirt, his arms, his wrists, anything they could grab. His feet dangled in the air as the rain slipped between them and their grip. Then his weight began to drag all of them down the face of the boulder.

"Don't let go!" Daniel said.

The Klylup coiled around the last boulder that separated them. Its trumpet call pierced Maella's ears with pain. She gritted her teeth and held on, even as she began to slip out from the woman's hands, even as she felt Daniel's shirt slip out from her hands.

"Daniel!" Maella shouted as she lost her grip completely.

Daniel fell, splashing to the ground. Claritsa slipped down the boulder after him. Maella snatched at Claritsa's skirt and then hooked her hands around Claritsa's bare ankles to keep her from going over. She scooted backward, up, across the rock. Her brain frantically searched for a solution.

The woman. The woman had to help them. She had to
have a way—

The Klylup was there—its green eyes level with Maella on
top of the boulder, its triangular bat-like ears parallel with
the ground, acting almost like an umbrella over Daniel.

The monster opened its jaw wider, impossibly wide, like it
could unhinge it. The smell that came out of its mouth made
Maella want to puke—like rotten egg and dead meat and
melted licorice. Maella screamed in frustration. She would
jump up and throw herself at this thing. Better she die than
someone else be murdered because of her. Except she
couldn't fight it unless she let go of Claritsa.

Claritsa twisted and Maella almost lost her hold. Something silver flashed into Claritsa's hand. Something long and
sharp.

The knife.

The knife that had been covered in Keeper Shaul's blood.

Claritsa struck out at the Klylup with one hand braced
against the boulder. The knife opened a thin line along the
Klylup's lip. It roared and flung its head about. The knife flew
into the air, flipping end over end. Claritsa slipped away,
down the boulder face, disappearing. Maella screamed at the
universe. The knife clattered onto the boulder near her. She
scrambled across the rock's wet surface, her shoes slipping,
thunder rumbling, as lightning struck again and again and
again. The knife handle felt warm in her hand.

She turned, shaking, to face the Klylup.

Maella screamed at the beast again. Her scream mixed
with the thunder and the Klylup's rage and it all became her
rage. The world split into a dozen arcs of lightning. Rain

pounded the stone. She felt outside herself, like she was a bird looking down, her friends somewhere beneath her, a monster raging against the boulders, like she raged inside.

She had opened a door and something terrible had happened.

This time, someone she cared about would die.

She swooped back into her body and let the fury take over.

Not without a fight.

She would break this Klylup or it would break her.

The Klylup stopped its thrashing and stared at her with one green eye. She ran for that eye, knife held out straight from her body like she'd seen Foster do. The Klylup shifted, opening its mouth. She tried to change direction, to keep from falling into its mouth. Her shoes slipped on the wet rock. She went down on all fours.

"No!" Maella shouted, her rage slipping away like the knife out of her hand. The Klylup's stink overwhelmed her. She was feet away from its teeth and still sliding.

A man appeared on the rock, jumping in front of her. He stopped her horrifying slide and swiped at the Klylup's nose again and again, knife in hand. Two slits at the end of the monster's snout opened up and poured a river of blood. The Klylup roared and the knife tumbled into its mouth.

He jumped off the boulder through the river of blood that fell from the Klylup's nose. Maella felt the taste of iron licorice on her tongue. The Klylup thrashed, falling away from the boulders. Daniel's head and shoulders appeared as if he were being lifted. Maella grabbed for him and held on until he was secure, then both she and Daniel helped up Claritsa.

The man vaulted up the rock like it wasn't a big deal. Like they hadn't all almost died. Clouds boiled overhead, green-black in color. The rain increased, coming down in sheets so thick it felt like they were almost swimming in it. Lightning flashed. An ocean was forming around them.

"Is this an earth-storm?" He shouted, worry thick in his voice. "These storms are not as bad as we were taught, right?"

Thunder rumbled in the sky and it seemed to shake the whole world like an earthquake. Lightning cracked. A rock split just a few feet away. The air smelled like electricity. Maella's hair stood up on her arms.

He wasn't a man at all. He was a boy who looked Daniel's age. Dark hair, dark eyes. A gaunt hollowness to his cheeks, dark stubble on his chin.

The boulder shuddered under them as the Klylup rammed itself into the stone, leaving a bloody mark on the rock.

"Come with me!" The woman shouted.

# Chapter 13

THE KLYLUP AND THE STORM raged outside.

They weren't really inside, but it counted as shelter enough. The boulders were grouped together to form a sort of open air room. Slats of wood created a ceiling over one section. This was the section they sat under, out of the rain, while trying to calm down, even as the rain made pools of water at their feet.

Daniel asked if they were safe here, if the Klylup could get in, if the boulders would protect them.

The woman replied, her accent swallowing the ends of the words. "This is what they have done for us so far."

Which didn't do much to soothe any of them. Nothing was safe anymore. But the truth was, nothing had ever been safe.

The woman's name was Lirella. She shared food, though it wasn't much. The young man's name was Sethlo. Other people hid in the boulders with them. Maybe several dozen. Men, women, some who looked very old, others who looked middle-aged, a few younger, but not as young as Maella and Claritsa.

Maella felt bad for taking food, but she couldn't refuse, not with the way her stomach rumbled. The food was this smashed, almost pancake-shaped thing. Gray dust covered it and crunched between her teeth as she chewed.

She was thankful for the food, and the little bit of gray water Lirella said was safe to drink. It gurgled in her stomach but seemed to clear her head and made her feel full enough to refuse more food. It was easy to see they didn't have anything to spare.

"Where are we?" Claritsa said. "What is this place?"

"It's Earth, isn't it?" Maella said, almost afraid to say the word. Because it was too much to hope for. She pressed on anyway. "Sethlo called this an earth-storm, so it has to be."

"But the Klylup," Claritsa said. "That's not—"

"What crime did you commit that they did not tell you where they sent you?" The whites of Lirella's eyes showed stark against the gray dust that coated her skin. Her lids looked rimmed with purple. She called back to someone in a language Maella did not understand. More gray bodies came out of the shadows.

Maella didn't know how to answer.

"Giffen was on watch at the door when Sethlo came." Lirella flicked her gaze at an older, solid-looking man with a solemn expression, and a bald head paired with a dark beard. He had a narrow jaw and he could somehow look at you without any emotion at all appearing on his face. "When the storm arrived and when the Klylup call sounded, he says he did not see you come out. They send their prisoners to Earth. So this is Earth, but it does not explain how you came here."

Maella felt a smile spread across her face. "We're home." She had brought her friends back to their world.

Daniel's face lit up. Claritsa burst into a shout of joy.

Keeper Shaul had helped them. He had meant what he said.

They would find a way home and Maella would see her mother and grandmother and Josa again and she would tell them that father and Esson were alive.

The woman looked at them with a puzzled expression. A different woman spoke up. Lirella raised a hand and the voice fell silent. She spoke quietly to those around her, and they dispersed. Gaunt and gray, they looked like they worked themselves to the bone and never ate enough.

The smiles dropped from Claritsa and Daniel's faces.

"*Where* on Earth are we?" Maella said.

The woman shook her head. "We do not know. You are from Earth. You know this place? If we could figure this out —"

"Bu—" Daniel said.

"You don't know where we are?" Claritsa said.

The woman's quizzical expression deepened. It carved her face out like she was a skeleton someone had hung skin on.

"We call this place…" She spoke words in a different language.

"I don't understand," Maella said.

Lirella called out to a man in the shadows. He was a thin, fragile-looking older man with dark, almost coal gray skin. The hair on his face and head was dark and kinked and growing out like he had been living in this place for a long time.

"This is Harry," Lirella said. "He is also from Earth."

He smiled at each of them and nervously touched his nose like he was trying to push up glasses that weren't there.

"What do you call this place in English, Harry?"

"Yes, it is not a direct translation." He spoke with an accent Maella thought sounded British, but she had never been very good at recognizing that sort of thing. "But basically, they call this place Rock Heaven." A half-smile formed on Harry's purple-stained lips. "It's a joke they—I mean, we— tell each other sometimes to make it easier."

"We watch the door and the door watches us," Lirella said.

The smile dropped from Harry's face.

"We are not supposed to know where our prison is," Lirella said. "Harry is also from Earth, and he does not know where we are."

The storm picked up again, drowning all ability to talk. The Klylup still raged against the boulders. Lirella retreated to sit on a stone. Claritsa's two braids were so long that when she sat down the ends dipped into a gray pool of water. Daniel saw this and gently lifted them out. There was nowhere else for the braids to go, so he held them for her.

Sethlo was next to Maella, pressed against the rock. He had listened to the entire conversation but added nothing. He stood taller than her and hunched his back. His face pointed away from the storm and toward the rock, to her. She felt his closeness unexpectedly. There was something dangerous about Sethlo. His skin was dark like Claritsa's, but his face looked like no one she had ever seen before. Some sort of mix of things that stirred a familiarity in her she didn't understand.

She knew enough from school to know about genetics and DNA. What part of her DNA was so messed up to have given her this terrible ability to open doors? What made Sethlo look just a bit different from anyone she had met on Earth before?

Thunder shook the surrounding rocks in a series of mini-earthquakes. Lightning whited out the world. Maella's head buzzed from the assault. Sethlo's arm brushed against her own and in spite of the storm that would drown them, she stopped feeling the cold. She could only feel his arm against hers.

Sethlo's eyes looked wild, and he flinched at every sound of thunder. Fighting the Klylup had been no big deal to him, but the storm was something else.

"Is this what earth is like?" Sethlo shouted. He swallowed the English words almost like Lirella did.

Maella's thoughts broke at his voice. She was thinking about DNA and Sethlo's closeness, and she had almost died. Fighting the Klylup had scrambled her thoughts. She felt numb, unable to think straight, unable to ask the million questions that needed answering. It was enough to be alive at the moment. Enough to let herself rest and her thoughts scatter on nothing that mattered.

Another round of thunder and lightning cut off her chance to respond. The water reached their ankles now. People moved onto higher stones.

Sethlo broke into another language, like he was cursing, then returned to English. "How do any of you survive on this world? We were all taught about the worlds. They are falling apart, at least for now. But this…" Sethlo shut his eyes and shuddered at another roll of thunder. "This is not right. I will fix this. I swear it."

"The storm?" Maella said. "How?"

"The worlds," Sethlo said. "I will fix the worlds."

# Chapter 14

THE STORM ENDED LIKE IT began.

In an instant and completely.

The sky cleared to a brilliant blue that hurt Maella's eyes. The friendly clouds came back, fluffy and pinkish-purple from sunrise. Gray dust sank away, leaving behind pools of water that acted like shining mirrors. As the camp of people came out from their hiding places—from rocks arranged and stacked to provide shelter and protection—the world became beautiful.

Even though the camp looked—she couldn't think of a better word than—pathetic, it was also organized. Everyone seemed to have a job. Someone had organized this place like she'd seen her family do after a neighbor had called Child Protective Services on them. Mother had thrown clear plastic over everything and clucked to CPS about the neighbors gossiping over a painting project.

Maella, her brothers, and father would sleep in the backyard in a tent that was basically a mosquito net strung up on a pole because the thick canvas of a real tent's zippered opening was too dangerous. They wouldn't be allowed to step one foot inside the house while the sheet-doors hung, but to CPS it looked like a backyard camp-out with Dad during a remodeling project.

The neighbor had called CPS on them once more, but nothing came of it, and the neighbor finally moved—though she left all her stuff behind until the bank took the house.

Maella knew that even when you had practically nothing, that was practically still something. And in the right hands, that something could turn into a lot. She studied the camp and counted. She had been right, several dozen people. Most of their clothes were ragged. Maella couldn't claim she had slept well on the rocks, but she wasn't numb anymore. What happened with Keeper Shaul and the door and the storm and the Klylup was too massive an event to process in one night. But she knew they couldn't stay here, in Rock Heaven, or whatever they wanted to call this place. She had questions and needed answers.

Lirella approached and waved Maella, Claritsa, and Daniel to their feet. "You must come along and begin your work today."

With a shock, Maella realized Lirella's skin was a deep lavender. In fact, looking around again, every person's skin was tinted a different shade of purple. Maella had dismissed it as an effect of the sunrise.

Maella and Claritsa exchanged a silent look. *Purple skin?*

"It has been many days between new members. I have not seen colors like yours in a long time. It is easy to forget." A half-smile crept onto Lirella's face. "There is something in the gray dust that reacts to the oils on our skin. Your skin will soon change color too. This happens to everyone here."

"My skin is going to turn purple?" Daniel said.

"What is this place?" Claritsa said.

The woman held up her hands—even her palms were purple.

"This place is a prison. But you should know this already. It is your turn to tell your story. And yes, your skin will turn purple. It is a happy accident from the viewpoint of our warden. If ever any of us should escape before our time is up, we will be well marked for recapture."

"The color is permanent?" Daniel said.

"No one has escaped Rock Heaven," Lirella said. "We do not know what happens to the color."

"But who is our warden? Where is he?" Maella asked.

"Our warden is not important. Who he works for is who you should worry about—a doormaker." Lirella spoke the label with disgust and bitterness.

Maella's heart skipped a beat.

Daniel opened his mouth. "But—"

Claritsa elbowed Daniel in the chest.

"Surely Doormaker Tain sent you through?" Lirella said. "There is no other way into Rock Heaven except through the one door."

"The One Door?" Maella said, unable to stop herself. "You know where the One Door is that goes where a doormaker wants it to go?"

"That door is a myth. You are too old to believe in such things." Lirella beckoned them again to stand. "The door to this place that is always left open. Surely—" Her eyes narrowed. "Walk with me and tell me how you got to the boulders. The Klylup was on your trail. Sethlo had already come, and yet you are not with him."

Maella pictured his dark hair and darker eyes. The way he had taken the knife out of Claritsa's hand, slashed at the Klylup, and slipped off the rock like it was a dance move. "No," Maella said. "We are not with him."

They followed Lirella through camp. She introduced them to a few people by name. Weird-sounding names, foreign alternate universe kinds of names. Though she realized their own names must sound just as odd. Erentia, Miall, Radovan, Aretha, and the ones she already knew, Giffen, Harry, Sethlo, and others she forgot as soon as Lirella said them because it was too much to take in all at once.

And as Lirella had said, underneath the gray dust, skin was different shades of purple. Some dark, almost inky black, others with skin almost a royal purple, and still others with lavender shades. Lirella said the shade of purple had to do with how dark a person's skin was to begin with and how long their stay had been so far.

As Lirella walked, she seemed to skip over the rocks—they never moved under her feet. Claritsa and Daniel followed, though not as quickly, since they weren't used to the rocks any more than Maella was.

Maella moved much slower, like she had an injury. Any wrong step or any misplaced hand could open a door in the stones. She clasped her hands behind her back—the way she had been taught. Walk with your head first, never your hands. Better to fall and injure yourself than fall hands first and risk a door. There were so many stones here. Heavy, flat, small, large. She would have to be careful. She would have to use everything she had been taught to prevent an accident.

Lirella, Claritsa, and Daniel were soon far ahead of her.

Lirella looked back once. "You walk like a doormaker."

Claritsa froze on the stones.

Maella did not freeze. Well, her heart froze. Lirella had not said the word doormaker kindly, but her foot had slipped on the sharp edge of a stone and she needed to focus on finishing that step.

"She pulled a muscle running from the Klylup," Claritsa said, covering for her like she always did.

After a long pause, Lirella continued across the rocks.

Maella knew she had dodged a bullet. All the questions bubbling to her lips faded. After Foster's treatment, once he learned she was a doormaker, she figured she needed to do everything she could to keep Lirella or anyone else at Rock Heaven from finding out her secret.

Warnings from her parents, her grandmother, the servants who had cared for her, all reared up. *Keep the secret. Never reveal yourself.* Lines would deepen with worry on her mother's forehead at each repetition.

Maella needed to understand, but there was a reason her family had trained her to hide.

When they left the outskirts of the camp, Lirella pointed to the east, into the glare of the rising sun, to the rock bowl in the ground, to where they had seen the carts and equipment. "That is our mine." She swept her arm around to point in the opposite direction. "In that direction is the door the door-maker uses to punish us far beyond our crimes."

The clouds bubbled across the sky like cotton candy that had tumbled off their sticks. Gray rocks mirrored back that same pink, filtering the world in a rosy glow. Pools of water gleamed crystal clear, shining back pictures of the pink and orange clouds.

Lirella moved fast across the rocks again. Maella tried to see how and copy it. Find the top ridge of the rock, bounce lightly from foot to foot.

Lirella finally stopped and waited.

Maella forced her arms to her sides as she followed. *Do not reveal yourself.* Her hands itched to clasp themselves behind her back.

When Maella caught up, Lirella said, "We watch the door and the door watches us," like it was a ritual.

Maella tried to brush the gray dust off her clothes. It covered her hands and she couldn't tell if it was the colors of sunrise or if her skin was already changing, but did it look tinged with purple now? She swept her gaze across the landscape and tried to ignore how her skin vibrated with that thought.

Claritsa gasped.

Lirella, Claritsa, and Daniel were all looking up.

She followed their gaze.

"This is the door you came through, is it not?" Lirella said.

Low clouds revealed a rectangular shape that didn't belong in the sky. The door was wooden, rotting, hastily built out of old fence boards. There was a small, rough handle on this side. Not that it mattered. The door hung too high in the sky to use it. Maybe several stories high. Light shined along its outline because it was not fully closed, but opened just enough for a cat to crawl through.

*Close the damn door.* The words repeated inside Maella's head. Grandmother's words. Keeper Shaul's words.

Lirella waited for an answer.

Maella's hands tingled and then went numb. She didn't know what answer Lirella wanted, so she did not answer at all.

Underneath the door, at their feet, was only gray stone. Jagged, hard, deadly. Anyone falling from the door would break more than a leg.

"How does one survive the door?" Lirella said.

Maella thought this was Lirella reading her mind. How did any of Lirella's people come out of that door uninjured?

But Lirella waited, watching them.

Maella and Claritsa locked eyes and a secret message passed between them.

*She's testing us.*

Lirella could not find out she was a doormaker. Not with the way Lirella had spoken the word earlier. Not with the way her family had fled and hidden themselves for years. It was important for Lirella to believe they were just like her. They were from the door and they were prisoners, too.

But Maella didn't know how to answer. Claritsa and Daniel had the same helpless look on their faces.

How did one survive a drop from a door that high?

"I—" Maella began, her brain spinning and coming up blank.

Lirella zeroed in on Maella like a hawk that had caught the movements of a mouse in the grass.

"The ladder, of course," a voice said behind them.

Sethlo.

He wore robes that reminded her of Keeper Shaul's robes. On him they looked too small, like he'd grown taller and more muscular since he had first been given them.

"Yes," Maella said, jumping at the chance he was offering. "We survived because of the ladder."

Lirella stared up at the door that hung impossibly high in the sky. She cocked her head to the side as if listening for something. "I see."

Maella's palms sweat. She clasped them behind her back like her grandmother had taught her, but then remembered Lirella said this was a sign of a doormaker. She brought her hands to her stomach. Everything vibrated just a little bit. Nerves. Lirella made her nervous. The pink of the clouds turned a sickly hue. No more candy cane lightness. Now it was more like Pepto-Bismol pink.

"Giffen saw Sethlo but did not see you," Lirella said. "But you are not with Sethlo. You are all so young and clearly not from Thrae in those clothes. What terrible things did the three of you do to be sent to Rock Heaven?"

Thrae? Was Thrae a world? A place? What would make someone force three teenagers through a door into a wasteland like this? She saw their lies unraveling before them. Lirella wasn't stupid. Her questions had been careful.

"It's my fault," Maella said. "They're here because of what I have done."

"Maella," Claritsa said.

"And what have you done?" Lirella said.

"I…" Maella thought about the truth. I disobeyed the one rule my father taught me never to break. I abandoned my family. I broke my mother's and grandmother's heart. I woke up the Klylup and it killed people. I got Barth and Keeper Shaul killed. I exiled my best friend into a universe so terrifying I don't know how she can stand to look at me.

But she could not say any of this out loud unless she admitted to Lirella that she was also a doormaker.

"Umm. I think something's coming through." Daniel pointed to the door in the sky. It had opened wide.

"Get to the boulders," Lirella said sharply. "The Klylup awakens when something passes through the door."

A rope fell out of the opening, twisting and dancing in the sky like a snake.

"This is not the time," Lirella shouted up.

A low voice boomed out of the door.

Maella turned to Sethlo. "What did he say?"

Sethlo stared at the door and the rope, as if calculating how to make a jump for it. "Trade."

"What?" Maella said.

"That's what he said," Sethlo replied.

"Giffen!" Lirella called, turning to a pile of rocks nearby.

A dark shadow separated itself from the rocks and hurried over. He carried a pouch not much bigger than a bowling ball.

Someone on the other side of the door blew a horn. Low and loud, it filled the empty world around them.

Maella heard the Klylup's trumpet return the call.

Lirella and Giffen spoke in angry tones.

Sethlo translated. "They insist on the horn because they know it brings the Klylup. But Lirella doesn't know why the pattern changed. The door opens every eighth day, but this is too soon, like they have run out. That's what she's saying."

"Where did the Klylup come from? What did they run out of?" Maella said, frustrated.

Sethlo shook his head. "I have only been here a few more hours than you. I do not have that answer."

The rope touched the ground. Giffen expertly tied a knot around the pouch and tugged.

Brown hands with rings on every finger glinted from the door's outline. The hands began pulling up the rope and pouch. When both disappeared through the door, a stick with a hook on the end grabbed onto the door's outer edge and began pulling it closed.

Lirella shouted in a language Maella did not understand. The only word she could make out was *licatherin*. The same word Keeper Shaul had used to describe the water that had told her fortune.

The hook paused. The door stopped halfway open. A crate was pushed across its threshold and tumbled end over end, smashing onto the surrounding rocks.

The hook closed the door, only leaving a big enough gap for a cat. Lirella and Giffen raced around, gathering supplies and then pushed them into Maella's and the others arms.

"On pain of hunger, do not drop what you are given," Lirella said. "But if you value your life, and what little of it remains once Rock Heaven is done with you—you must run now."

Lirella and Giffen, arms full of supplies, dashed away from the door that hung in the sky.

# Chapter 15

"INTO THE BOULDERS," LIRELLA SAID as they entered the camp's perimeter. "We must wait until the Klylup tires and returns to its hibernation."

The entire camp sat inside the safety of the boulders, waiting for the Klylup to begin its assault. The Klylup did not disappoint.

"Where did this Klylup come from?" Maella asked as others relieved her of the supplies. This was the first question she had dared. She needed to be careful. Questions revealed just as much about her as the answers might give her.

They sat in stony silence and no one spoke. Somehow, she had asked the wrong question, anyway.

"We do not talk about it," Lirella said finally, as the Klylup thrashed against the rock. "It is too painful."

Lirella turned to someone else and spoke in that language Maella felt she was on the verge of understanding. Like it was a language she had forgotten how to speak.

"How do you know English?" Maella asked Sethlo, frustrated with how little she knew about anything that was going on. Her family had kept her alive all this time, but also in the dark.

"I was taught it the way all my friends were taught it. Through our schools." Sethlo glanced at Daniel, then Claritsa, and finally Maella. "I come from the high house. I know the major languages spoken on all the worlds. English and Chinese from earth, Dealthin and Mort from—"

"Why were you sent through the door?" Lirella said, while relieving Sethlo of his supplies.

Anger flashed in Sethlo's eyes. "I am innocent."

"What crime are you accused of?" Lirella asked. "I did not ask if you were innocent or not. Ask anyone here—we are all innocent." Her laugh was harsh like this was another kind of joke. "And what was your crime, Aretha?"

Aretha looked like one of the younger ones, maybe in her 20s. She had a petite nose and delicate ears that showed through hair almost as kinked as Harry's. "They say I helped execute a doormaker."

Maella flinched.

"Giffen?"

He stepped forward like he was reporting for duty. "I was your servant in that previous life. Your crime is my crime. "

"And what is that?"

"Thrae traitor."

"Erentia?"

"My lover was a skillful fighter and one of the generals in the Doormaker Wars." She said this from her seat on the stones. Her hair was coiled around her head. She kept her face neutral and her arms folded over her knees. "They punish me because they cannot find him."

Lirella arched an eyebrow at Sethlo. "Answer my question, newcomer. Why were you sent through the door?"

Maella's hands had been full with food brought back from the door in the sky, but it would not go very far in their bellies. And now the number of bellies had increased by four, and three of those bellies were not supposed to be there. Maybe it mattered what type of crime brought someone to Rock Heaven. If he were a murderer, would Lirella let him stay in the group?

"They claim I stole *licatherin*," Sethlo said finally.

Lirella looked at Sethlo with steel in her eyes. "That is not a Rock Heaven offense."

"It is when you try to use it to find the One Door," Sethlo said.

Maella gasped. "You know about the One Door?"

A pained expression crossed Lirella's face. "Children. You are children. They are sending children to us. Children that believe in fairy tales. Hear me now. The worlds are falling apart. The evil in the doors has tainted the worlds and there is no coming back from it. You must accept this. You must grow up now."

"It is not true," Sethlo said. "I know the One Door exists. Why else would the doormakers search for it?"

Maella shrunk into herself. How did he know what she was? But he wasn't looking at her. It took her a long second to realize he meant other doormakers. Did he mean her family?

Lirella and Giffen said something in unison, like it was a chant they spoke often to soothe themselves. It didn't sound friendly and it made Sethlo pale.

"I have no love for the doormaker clan," Sethlo said, "But they do not all deserve death."

"Blasphemy," Lirella said. "You will get along well with Harry."

"Harry?" Sethlo said. "What kind of English name is that? To name someone after a part of the body?"

"It is an Earth thing," Lirella said.

Harry spoke up. "My name is not spelled the same as the word you are thinking of."

Maella made a mental note to talk to Harry and Sethlo more. Anyone whose first reaction was to not kill a doormaker seemed like someone worth knowing now.

"How many doormakers are there?" Maella asked.

Sethlo looked confused.

Maybe he hadn't understood her English. She tried again.

"They have been hunted almost to extinction," Sethlo said. "Except on Thrae. But how do you not know this?"

"They are from Earth," Lirella said, as if that explained the stupidity of Maella's question. "Yet somehow went to Thrae and entered back to Earth through our door in the sky. It *is* time you explained this."

Maella suddenly saw a way to satisfy Lirella's questions while also getting some answers. "We were taken through our first door by accident. It had been left open like your door, but no one guarded this one." She gestured to the door that still hung like a mask in the sky. "We didn't know what the first door was and we entered a world with another Klylup and people fighting in a forest—"

"This is likely Rathe," Lirella acknowledged. "The doors are stronger between places on Rathe and Earth than anywhere else." Her voice was cool, assessing, but not disbelieving. "We have many prisoners here who are from Rathe. They do great battle against the doormakers still."

Maella swallowed. It seemed like everyone was here because they wanted to kill, or had tried to kill, or had already killed people like her. She needed to balance revealing enough of the truth to be believable without revealing too much.

Claritsa bounced from foot to foot, nervous for her. Even Daniel had stilled.

"We were captured."

"By who?" Lirella said.

"I don't know," Maella said slowly.

What if they knew Foster or Keeper Shaul? What if those names meant something to them? She couldn't risk it.

"This guy, Foster. He was a real jerk," Daniel said.

Lirella's eyes widened.

Erentia's casual pose on the stones iced over. There were several others who stilled. All the ones Lirella said had come from Rathe.

Erentia and a much older man, Miall, exchanged a look. Erentia stood. If she were wearing anything but rags, she would have swept to her feet. She held herself upright and stared at Maella as if considering whether to curse the ground she walked on.

Maella should have been afraid. Instead, anger bloomed inside of her. The ground she walked on was already cursed —that's what she wanted to throw back at Erentia's look. She was a doormaker and she was surrounded by millions of doors made out of stones. They were all cursed.

Out of reflex, Maella clasped her hands tight behind her back like her father and mother and grandmother had coached her. Both Lirella and Giffen noticed her do it. Realizing her mistake, Maella turned it into a stretch and brought her hands back around to her stomach.

Claritsa raised an eyebrow. Maella gave a little shake of the head. *Later.*

"Foster is a Rathe hero," Miall said in broken, stuttering English. "Great warrior and general. Saved all of us."

That's when Maella realized Miall had only one arm.

Maella glanced helplessly at Daniel. What had he done?

Daniel did not return her look, though all the color had washed out of his face and his breathing shallowed.

Questions were dangerous here. Information even more deadly.

Miall glanced at Erentia. "He is the reason for Erentia here."

Claritsa's eyes widened. Maella's anger vanished. This was not good. Foster was Erentia's—

"They took us all at once," Erentia said, in almost perfect English, though there was a mild accent to her words. "They took my father." She bent her head in Miall's direction. "They took those near me." She inclined her head at Aretha and a few others. "But they could not take him. They could not take what they could not find." She turned piercing eyes onto Maella. "They will not find him."

Maella shrunk under her gaze. She felt like Erentia could read her soul and see the stains on it.

"They have not found him?" Erentia's body became fragile instead of strong, like the act of asking had wounded her.

Maella didn't know what to say. Everyone stared at her, at Claritsa, at Daniel. Their eyes and lavender skin and gaunt cheeks accused her of, she didn't know—accused her. They must know she was a doormaker. They must be waiting for her to confess so they could rip her to pieces.

"They haven't found him," Claritsa said.

All eyes turned from Maella. Relief flooded her.

"Foster," Claritsa said. "They haven't found Foster."

Erentia flowed back into a sitting position, bowing her head.

Claritsa and Maella exchanged a look. *Thank you.*

Erentia's head whipped back up. "They said Foster captured them." She spoke to the other prisoners. "They must be working with the doormakers."

Rumbles, arguments, shouts.

"We are not!" Claritsa shouted.

Daniel pressed himself back into the shadows and looked ready to run. Sethlo watched, not saying anything at all in words or expression, though his gaze kept returning to Maella.

Erentia's words were like a punch in the gut. This was Foster all over again. They would find out and they would finish what Foster had started.

Lirella raised a hand and called for silence in three languages.

When everyone finally quieted, she said, translating into the three languages, "Our Rathe companions suffered deeply in the Doormaker Wars."

Rumbling agreement.

"But we listen. We reason. We are from Thrae and Rathe and Earth and yet we do not fight amongst one another. Those on the other side expect this from us. We hated each other once. We fought each other once. But we have proven them wrong." Some looked away, some stared openly at the newcomers, including Sethlo. "We will continue to prove them wrong."

Maella breathed out a sigh of relief.

Lirella turned to Maella. "Answer Erentia's question. What offense did you commit that the Rathe hero Foster would capture you? How did you escape Foster and come into the hands of Doormaker Tain's forces and then go through the door into Rock Heaven?"

Maella didn't know how to answer. She suspected she should know who Doormaker Tain was, but she couldn't remember him.

The silence deepened.

Daniel stepped away from the boulder as if about to say something, but Maella could not let him make more trouble. "Foster did not send us through a door. We came to Rathe by accident and it woke the Klylup and people died. But it was an accident."

"What happened on Thrae that sent you here?" Lirella said, her voice stern. "Did you fight Doormaker Tain? Did you steal *licatherin* like Sethlo?"

Maella didn't reply right away. Lirella's prompting questions contained a trap. If she said yes to either one, Lirella could follow up with more questions about details Maella would surely get wrong. She felt sick to her stomach. She exchanged a look with Claritsa. Daniel tapped his foot, waiting for Maella to come up with something, but there was nothing.

Then it came to her—

She stood, fisting her hands to her sides to keep them from shaking, and turned her own stare onto Lirella. She let the terror of watching the Klylup fly and swoop and scoop up the people in the valley wash over her. She echoed Lirella's own words about the Klylup. "We do not talk about it. What Doormaker Tain has done to us…You know the evil these doormakers are capable of. You cannot make us speak about such pain. Please do not make us."

A few of the prisoners protested. Many others nodded.

Lirella made a sound. Maella braced herself for more questions.

Before Lirella could press on, Erentia stood. "Who died?" Erentia asked. "Who did the Klylup kill?"

Claritsa shook her head. "We don't know. There was already a battle going on and then the Klylup came out, but we don't know—"

"The Klylup stopped them from fighting," Maella interrupted. "It might have…it might have saved a bunch of

people from dying. They had been fighting each other and…"
she fell into silence as other prisoners shouted questions.

Maella bit her lip. There were holes the size of Klylups in
her story, but everyone became focused on Foster, Rathe,
and who the Klylup might have killed, and remembering
names of family and friends, and grieving for what had been
lost. They talked in urgent whispers and even Lirella seemed
to have moved on.

Sethlo looked at her strangely, but for now, the questions
had stopped.

# Chapter 16

IT WAS LONG PAST SUNRISE before Lirella and Giffen decided it was safe to leave the boulders.

Instead of sending them to work, Lirella called for everyone to meet out in the light. People talked quietly, many coughed as if the dust and the wetness did not combine well in the lungs. Some laughed together, others set out boxes covered in canvas.

They gathered near a section of stones flatter than the others. People placed the boxes between their legs and set panning buckets upside down. A drum rhythm began.

Someone passed a stack of pale crackers into Maella's hands. She looked up at a man whose skin was a darker shade of purple than many of the others. His hair made her think that maybe in another time and place, he would have been considered African.

"I'm Harry," he said.

Harry. The one with strange ideas about doormakers that didn't involve killing them.

"We all share here and we all help where we can," he said. "They're not as bad as it sounded in there. You just reminded each of them of home. Of the people they worry about. It will pass and you will become one of us."

She nodded, wanting to believe him, but she didn't plan to stick around long enough for that to happen. She took a cracker and passed the stack to Claritsa, casting a worried glance at Daniel, who looked lost in thought.

"Won't the noise draw the Klylup?" Maella asked, motioning to the drummers.

"That's not how it works. The Klylup is called by the door. Once it has exhausted itself, it leaves and will not return until the door calls it again."

"But the pattern is breaking," Maella said.

Harry did not disagree. Instead he said, "You are Americans, I think." Harry smiled. "The accent."

"What are they doing?" Claritsa asked.

"We celebrate being alive when the time calls for it," Harry said. "The storms and the Klylup come regular enough it's now become tradition—though we may be imprisoned and forgotten, we do not need to forget ourselves."

"But—"

"Everything here is a risk," Harry said. "Everything here can kill us. We take the risk because it matters to us."

"Why don't you just leave?" Daniel said, looking away from the stones. He stuffed his hands into his jean pockets and avoided looking at Maella. "There aren't any guards."

Harry shook his head. "The people who have tried have not survived. We are somewhere far away from help."

"But satellites or airplanes or—"

"I've had all of these thoughts. I came here full of ideas for escape. I almost died trying. Others who attempted escape were forced to walk the rocks."

"What does that mean?" Maella said. It didn't sound pleasant.

"Some of us tried to climb the ladder once, to get back through the door into Thrae," Harry said. "It didn't work and they were sent away from camp."

"There aren't any guards here," Daniel said. "Who sent them?"

"You act like guards are the only way to force us to do what is required," Harry said.

"Isn't it? It's simple," Daniel said, his voice rising. "No one's pointing a gun to your head making you do anything."

"It's as simple as this: they stopped sending food. We almost starved," Harry said. "We did not get food until those who had tried to escape walked the stones—until they left camp and didn't return. That's how we know there isn't an escape out there, otherwise our warden would not have made it the punishment."

Daniel shook his head. "Maybe they were tricking you."

"So you forced them out?" Maella said, shivering. She tried to imagine what that would be like.

"They left. We were all going to die, or they were going to leave. So they left instead of making us force them to leave." Harry shook his head. "But I believe it would've come to that, if they hadn't left on their own." He shook his head again. "Come on. There will be plenty of time to think about the darkness of this place. The Klylup hasn't eaten you yet, the storm has passed—and we always ask newcomers to drum. There's no hiding of talent here."

"I can't drum," Maella said. The thought of being put back in the spotlight terrified her. She needed to process everything and come up with a new plan without anyone finding out she was a doormaker.

Daniel echoed Maella's protest.

"Me neither," Claritsa said.

"That's not true," Maella said before she could think about it.

Claritsa scowled at her.

In the secret girl band they had dreamed about forming— because why not?—Claritsa always picked drummer and Maella would sing and play the violin. Though her violin had been sold years ago for money to pay for their most recent doorless house.

Harry laughed. "You'll find they will trust you much faster if you don't fear making a fool of yourself. They won't trust you at all if you don't try."

He motioned Daniel over to one of the boxes.

Flustered, Daniel flushed red. Erentia slowed down the beat, leaving gaps for Daniel to fill.

Claritsa tapped her foot in time to it all and Maella knew her fingers itched just a little bit for the stick.

Daniel turned out to be a terrible player. But as Harry said, people liked that. They laughed and slapped him on the back. Daniel seemed less tense by the time he finally threw his hands up and Harry took the sticks and gave them to Maella.

She felt the rough grain—they were little more than box planks whittled into shape. She folded her legs underneath her. Daniel had left the spot warm. She touched the top of the drum. Cloth, stretched tight, wearing thin.

She would have to be careful. The bottom of the box drum made a makeshift seal with the ground. If she moved the box too much, it might open a door. It was strange. It was like she could feel the potential of it send a mild hum through her.

Erentia flashed white teeth through dark lavender lips. Shadows circled her eyes, but she lit up as if the drumming gave her energy. And maybe it did, because its beat seemed to wash away everything the last few days had brought, leaving only the space to be present in this moment.

Erentia spoke softly in a language that was different even than what Lirella spoke.

Harry leaned over. "You must touch the stick to the drum to make some noise—that is what she is trying to tell you."

He switched to a different language and they all laughed.

Maella, embarrassed, looked at the stick and touched it to the drum, like she was petting a cat, faking like she had no idea what he was talking about. She was not afraid to make a fool of herself. She was very good at doing that, in fact.

Harry startled, "Not like—"

Maella gave Erentia and Harry a half-smile.

Erentia looked confused for a moment and then got the joke. She busted into a smile and said something that included 'Foster' and it got them all roaring in laughter.

Maella smiled and hit the drum like normal. She even caught the beat once. Maybe she could undo some of the suspicion their arrival had caused.

Erentia shouted her approval, but then the box shifted. Maella's anxiety about opening a door destroyed any hint of rhythm. After that, she couldn't get it back. Finally, she gave up the stick. Claritsa sat down and jumped into the beat clumsily, but still a million times better than both Daniel and Maella.

A few of the people danced halfheartedly, but most sat, too tired to do much more than sway or tap along.

Maella approached Daniel. Compared to everyone else, he looked ridiculously healthy. His plaid shirt had begun to unravel at the hem, matching his jean shorts. Her own khaki shorts had already turned gray from the dust. She needed him to know how important it was to keep quiet about everything.

"They hate your kind so much," Daniel said. "I don't understand it."

"Be quiet," Maella hissed, looking around. All her words of comfort disappeared. Her heartbeat sped up. She looked around, but everyone was focused on the drumming. For now.

"Do you have a plan?"

Maella shook her head.

"Barth would have had a plan."

"I'm not Barth. Why do you need him, anyway?" Maella said, heat rising in her. "Think up your own plan."

Daniel shrugged. "He's not as bad as you think."

"I doubt that."

He stared down at her. His brown eyes examined her like she was an animal at the zoo.

She shrunk into herself at his look. "You've been helping us all along. You've saved me and Claritsa twice already."

"I have a bad habit of helping people when I shouldn't. The only person you should care about is yourself."

"You have your mom."

Daniel stilled. "Don't talk about my mother."

"I wasn't—"

"Just don't."

"I wasn't!"

He looked away, up into the sky, at the door no longer hidden by the clouds that seemed to shimmer in the sunlight.

"Barth was right about you and Esson. He said something was wrong with your entire family."

Maella's skin prickled. "Tell me, Daniel, did Barth do this on purpose?"

Daniel grimaced. "He didn't know about this." He waved his hands around, taking in all of Rock Heaven.

"Did he do something to Esson?"

"To Eddy?" Daniel rubbed at the patchy whiskers growing on his chin. "They were friends at first, but Eddy's the one who betrayed us."

"I don't believe you." Esson was many things, but untrustworthy wasn't one of them. He had watched out for her and Josa their entire lives.

Daniel's hand stilled on his chin. His face closed up, like he realized he had revealed way too much. "Barth said something was wrong with your family and he still helped you escape."

"You helped us."

Daniel shook his head. "He was right about you."

"So what?" Maella said, anger rising in her again.

Claritsa gave the stick over to someone else and approached them now with a worried look on her face.

Maella was tired of people accusing her family of awful things they didn't actually do. "Are you going to tell them about me? Are you going to hand me over to them and let them kill me? What are you going to do, Daniel, since I'm so wrong?"

A muscle twitched in Daniel's jaw.

"What's going on?" Claritsa said. "You both look angry."

"She doesn't have a plan," Daniel said. "The one person who could actually do something about all of this doesn't have even a clue of a plan. How stupid is that?"

"I offered to open a door before, and you both shut it down," Maella said, remembering their quick denial after they first arrived in Rock Heaven.

"That's before the Klylup attacked us, and a storm almost killed us, and we found out we're in prison!" Daniel said.

Claritsa frowned. "Daniel, you can't be serious."

"I am dead serious."

Maella paused for a long moment. She took a deep breath. "I need to tell you both something."

She poured it all out.

Keeper Shaul and the *licatherin* pool.

His pattern machine and her fortune.

The prediction of her death.

As soon as she finished, she felt a great weight lift off her chest.

Daniel's face paled. Claritsa shook her head, her dusty braid whipping gray bits into the air, her dark eyes wide. Maella swore there were lines on her face that hadn't been there just seconds ago. She knew that look. "Don't, Claritsa. Don't take this on yourself."

"How do you know he was telling the truth?" Claritsa said, the lines on her face only deepening. "He didn't want to help you."

"I don't know," Maella said. "But I feel like it's true. As soon as he said it, I thought—this is true. Doesn't it make sense? What I can do…it's wrong, I'm wrong. Everyone here thinks so."

Claritsa's mouth formed a grim line and she swept her bangs to the side. "How could he know that? He said the pattern is breaking."

"Enough of the pattern is still there," Daniel said. "He might be able to."

"But—"

Daniel interrupted Claritsa, his voice excited. "If he's right, then it means he's seen that the next six *won't* kill us."

"Won't kill me," Maella said. "That's all he said."

"So you can't open a door," Claritsa said.

"I have six left. I can if you think I should."

"You can't," Claritsa stated like it was a fact. "But we can't stay here."

"We should try another door," Daniel said, his eyes eager, the muscles along his neck and shoulders tense with excitement.

Maella looked between Daniel and Claritsa. A pit opened up in her stomach. She didn't like that it was suddenly her and Daniel in agreement against Claritsa. That's not how this was supposed to work.

Maella took a deep breath. "I think we should, too."

She didn't want to open another door. The thought made her sick to her stomach and choked her with fear. Enough damage had come from her breaking the rules, but how else could they escape a prison no one else claimed they had ever escaped from?

Claritsa shook her head. "No. It's been a day. We don't know if there's another way out of here. Just leave it alone for now. Are you going to leave it alone, Daniel?"

He could destroy Maella at any moment if he wanted to. Tell them she was a doormaker and it would be over.

"Daniel?" Claritsa asked.

He shook his head. "How long will we wait? This is a prison. We could die here."

"We could die while opening the next door, too," Claritsa said.

"I'll take my chances," Daniel said.

"Give it a few days." Claritsa looked between both Daniel and Maella. "Just a few days. Please."

Daniel nodded, like he didn't trust himself to actually agree out loud. Then he stalked off to the boulders.

"We'll think of something," Claritsa said. "He won't tell them about you. He's not like Barth."

Claritsa left to talk more sense into him, but Maella didn't know if that was possible. Maybe he would give them a few days, but she suspected he would take matters into his own hands.

She hoped Claritsa was right. Her stomach twisted at the thought of opening another door, risking her own death, and the deaths of innocent people. But if she was going to prevent that from happening, she needed to find another way off Rock Heaven. Lirella, Erentia, and everyone else at camp believed their made-up story, at least for now. She needed to use that while she still had the chance.

Maella found Harry again. Her heartbeat expanded in her chest until it matched the drums. She hoped Claritsa really was talking some sense into Daniel.

"That was well done," Harry said.

Maella stepped back. Had he overheard? "What?"

"The drums," Harry said, smiling.

Maella tried to relax. Of course, the drums. "You can't be serious."

"Well," Harry said. "Claritsa was decent."

"The worlds are falling apart," Maella said, not caring to make small talk anymore. She needed answers. She needed to understand. "That's what Lirella says. Do you believe it too?"

"Yes," Harry said.

"Next you'll say it's all the doormakers' fault." Maella said, not intending to sound sarcastic, but that's how it came out. The expansive feeling in Maella's chest disappeared. She shouldn't have opened her mouth at all.

Harry lifted an eyebrow. "This has all been very strange for me, too. It's a lot to take in. I was a researcher. I deal with cold, hard facts. Not alternate universes."

She needed answers, but she had been trained to never ask questions and to always hide herself. In order to ask questions, she would have to get noticed. She couldn't have it both ways.

"Is that what the doors are?" Maella asked, forcing out the question. She was ready to believe anything Harry said to make sense of it in her own head. "They take us to alternate universes like out of some sci-fi show?"

Harry shook his head. "I don't think so. I don't...I don't really know. But they sure seem like different worlds, planets, I think. I don't have any conceptual framework to understand all of this."

Harry tapped a foot in time to a particularly complicated beat. "Thrae doesn't really have a concept for planets like we do. Lirella says the doors take people to different places, but eventually those different places become the same places, that is, they repeat—"

"Like a pattern," Maella said.

Harry nodded. "Some people think the doors all go to the same world, but to different time periods."

"Time travel?" That idea did not sit right with her. Wouldn't doors and portals and time travel have made it into the history books already? Unless—

"How come nobody from earth, from our time or place or whatever, knows about the doors and the other worlds? Time travel only makes sense if—"

"Maybe earth is the oldest time the doors go back to," Harry said. "If our earth, our present, is the first time this planet has encountered the doors…"

But Maella had thought that very first world, with the Klylup and Foster—the place Lirella called Rathe—seemed much older. Except what did she know when it came down to it? Her family had hid everything from her for so long.

"I don't think it's time travel," Harry said. "I'm just telling you what some people say."

"What do you think? How do you know any of this? What is a doormaker?" She tried to sound naive. It wasn't hard.

She knew the family rule.

She knew her family had basically fled to earth to escape something terrible.

She knew what Keeper Shaul had told her.

She knew that the door in the sky was behind a cloud for now, but that it called to her in vibrations that were out of tune. The doors had never called to her before.

Keeper Shaul was right.

Doors were not meant to stay open.

"I think it's on a whole other scale," Harry said. "I think the doors are like wormholes to different planets and the doormakers have something in their DNA that acts like a key in a lock. You know how some people are just born with great singing voices, or super-sensitive taste buds? I think what they call doormakers are people who have that kind of ability. A mutation. These wormholes must be everywhere and it's *more* surprising that more people can't open them—"

"I see Harry is trying to convince you that everything still follows the rules of his scientific religion," Lirella said. There was a smile on her face as she approached, and Harry didn't seem offended by her interruption.

Giffen stood next to Lirella. He had a face that looked like it didn't know how to smile. "Some believe the doors are openings to the afterlife."

Lirella closed her eyes briefly and inclined her head. "Yes, some do. They're called the Sechnel."

"They believe that when a doormaker opens a door," Giffen said. "It opens to death, and anyone who walks through a door becomes like death."

"So we're all dead?" Maella said. "I don't feel dead."

"Spirits do not feel much of anything," Giffen said.

"Giffen likes toying with the Sechnel ideas," Harry said. "It's the subject of many late night discussions."

"You cannot explain something that is unknowable," Lirella said.

"If we are here as spirits," Giffen said, "that is knowable."

Harry raised an eyebrow. "With enough tests—"

"Thrae has entire universities dedicated to studying the doors," Lirella said.

"So why do you hate the doors so much?" Harry said.

"We have learned nothing—not enough. And I am no Sechnel believer." Lirella glanced at Giffen, but Giffen had gone back within himself, holding no counsel except his own. "It's time to do away with trying to understand something that is determined to destroy everything. It's time to fight back."

"And that is why you're here," Harry said simply. "And not on Thrae."

Lirella sighed. "Yes, on Thrae, it is blasphemy to speak badly about the doors and doormakers. It's different on Rathe."

"I know," Maella said.

Harry looked at her questioningly.

"It seemed like that's all they talked about. Hunting doormakers," she said quickly.

"There is another way to fight the doormakers," Giffen said.

"No," Lirella said, without pausing. "I will never take that way."

"What way?" Maella said.

"Finish what the door started," Giffen said.

"Death," Harry said. "He's saying we should kill ourselves in order to remove the door's hold on us."

"That does nothing to fight the doormakers," Lirella said.

"I am merely sharing what the Sechnel have—"

"Enough," Lirella said. "I will not allow you to leave me. You are needed, Giffen."

Giffen inclined his head and lapsed back into silence.

"But why doesn't anyone on Earth really know about it?" Maella asked.

"Well," Harry said. "If it's time travel and—"

Lirella interrupted. "Earth ran the doormaker magic—"

Harry opened his mouth in protest.

Lirella held up a hand. "Call it a mutation then, if you like. Earth ran the doormaker mutation into extinction."

"We are really good at that sort of thing," Harry said. "It's one of the ways our world is destroying itself."

"Don't worry," Lirella said. "The doors will help that along."

"Fair enough," Harry said.

"Doormakers still exist on Thrae," Lirella said. "They thrive there, but they are gone from Earth and almost hunted out on Rathe. It won't be long."

"And then what?" Harry said without much heat, like they'd had this argument a million times over. "How does that solve anything to destroy what you fear? Earth has tried that a few times already, and it didn't end well—"

"The doors—"

"Will not keep the worlds from falling apart," Harry finished.

"It might slow down the destruction," Lirella replied.

"You have no clue if it will work."

"We must do something."

Aretha stood up. She was thin and bony, and her rags hung from her dark purple skin like a dress. Harry and Lirella stopped playacting at an argument. Erentia tapped out a complicated beat.

Aretha danced, throwing out her arms, stomping, twirling. Her dance was mesmerizing, strong, like a beautiful battle.

Claritsa appeared at Maella's side. She looked at Maella with a question on her face. *Are you okay?* Maella shook her head. She had asked the questions, in spite of everything inside her telling her to stop because questions were dangerous. Questions got you noticed. But then they had answered, and now…now she didn't know how to live with some of those answers.

Lirella knew it.

Giffen believed it.

Harry wanted to explain it away.

The one point they all seemed to agree on was this.

Doormakers made the doors, and the doors were tearing apart the worlds.

So what kind of person did that make her?

# Chapter 17

THE NEXT DAY, MAELLA WOKE up hungry, cold, and dirty. Sleep had wiped away pain from Claritsa's and Daniel's faces.

Aretha broke into a coughing fit that didn't want to end. By the time she had finished, Miall was rubbing her back as blood sprinkled onto the rocks.

Maella shifted and caught Sethlo awake. He wasn't looking at her, but at the rocky landscape that stretched to infinity around them. She felt the pull of that emptiness deep inside of her.

There must be a way to escape this place.

No matter what Harry said, no matter how many people had tried and failed—there must be a way to find her family —and make all of this right again.

Sethlo shifted, interrupting her thoughts. Light caught the dark shadow of stubble on his face. He stretched and his back muscles rippled. He caught her looking and smiled slightly. "You're thinking about it, too."

It wasn't a question.

"Thinking about what?" Maella said, blushing.

"Escape," Sethlo said simply, but with a fervor that made her skin tingle. He said the word like he would be capable of doing anything to get it.

A recklessness rose up in her, scaring her. Yes, she was thinking about escape, but more than that, she wanted the truth. And she thought she might be capable of doing any- thing to get it, too.

Even if that meant using up one of her six remaining doors, even knowing her family's rule, knowing what had already happened each time she'd opened a door, knowing it might kill them all. She would open a door like Daniel want- ed her to do, no matter how scared that thought made her, and no matter how dangerous it would turn out. She wouldn't let them die here. She had to find her family and find the truth. One way or the other, Maella would make sure they escaped Rock Heaven.

Breakfast was more of the fried pancake. Even though clear pools of fresh water from the storm had not yet evapo- rated, Maella and the rest were given cloudy gray water to drink. Lirella called everyone to work, including the new- comers.

"You have taken food and water and shelter from us that we cannot afford to have taken. You must go to the mines today."

Maella didn't argue. What was the point? They were at the camp's mercy. Yesterday's revelations about some of their crimes made Maella determined to keep as low a profile as possible. It was something she, Claritsa, and Daniel had agreed on in the night, before falling asleep from exhaustion.

But what would they make her do? Could she get away with refusing the work if it might open a door?

Do what they say. Keep Maella's secret. Wait for their chance. That's what they had agreed on during the night.

But what chance? None of them knew.

The camp walked to the pit. It was an awful kind of commute.

Clock in, clock out.

Try not to open a door and kill everyone in between.

She stayed near the back of the group, Claritsa at her side, hoping people did not notice whether she accidentally walked like a doormaker. Claritsa took the same careful, slow steps next to her—like they were just two clumsy girls on the rocks.

"Is it hard to not..." Claritsa said.

Maella bit her lip and nodded. "It's almost like I can feel the potential doors in the stones. I never felt it like that at home—how doors could hum." She stepped around a flat rock that hummed especially strong.

"That's good, then," Claritsa said. "It's like a warning bell. It'll keep you from making any mistakes."

When they reached the pit, the other prisoners were hiking down a narrow trail, scattering rocks along the way.

"It's safe enough." Lirella said, waiting for them at the top. "Being late will not shorten your work day."

Claritsa opened her mouth to protest.

Lirella held up a hand. "I was your age once. I remember."

"It's not—" but Maella stopped. Better to have Lirella think she was lazy.

"We're not used to the rocks yet," Claritsa said.

Lirella inclined her head, neither agreeing nor disagreeing, then began to explain how the mine worked. The *licatherin* hid in the special type of gray rock that surrounded them. Harry had one name for it, Lirella had another, Maella promptly forgot both of them. It was a mineral that somehow fueled the doors or stabilized them or—no one really knew how it worked.

The prisoners at Rock Heaven were there to take the *licatherin* out of the rock. It was traded for food and supplies.

The whole system was as simple and as easy and as horrible as that.

"There are many stations here," Lirella said, beginning the walk down the trail into the pit. "Some are more dangerous and more difficult than others. We take turns at each station to share the burden and the risk."

Claritsa followed. Maella hesitated.

Lirella looked back up. "Get a move on, girl. This is how we earn our food."

Maella's hands became slippery with sweat. She needed to choose the least dangerous path. Picking her way down, she forced her arms to lock to her sides. Claritsa waited at the bottom, a worried expression on her face. Lirella looked impatient.

Sethlo and Daniel already worked at the first station with sledgehammers. They broke big rocks into smaller rocks. Sweat dripped from them and their muscles bulged through their shirts. Sethlo went about the work methodically, as if he were performing a training exercise. Daniel attacked his stones, as if fighting off someone. He kicked up a gray cloud with his fury that caused hacking coughs to tear from his chest. They were the most attractive looking guys in camp and the only ones not yet sporting purple-tinted skin.

"Come," Lirella said. "There is no electricity or fire or any sort of machinery. They give us enough food, enough people, enough tools, to do the work, but not enough to fight back. Wearing us down like this seems to please them. This is your first day and you are both small. We will start you at the easiest tasks."

Maella made it to the bottom of the pit and sighed in relief. She followed Lirella and Claritsa to a sort of grinding rock—a large flat boulder with smaller rounded divots. Small pebbles were piled next to each spot. People were already working, backs hunched, twisting and pounding the *li-catherin* to dust.

"Once enough is ground, we transfer it to the panning pool," Lirella said, and motioned to a wheelbarrow leaned against the boulder to collect and dump the material into the pool. "We must all take our turn in the panning pool—you as well. It is the least favored job, but it must be done."

"What's so bad about it?" Claritsa asked.

"You must stand in cold water that will rot your flesh after too long, among other things. Until it is your turn, think of this as a gift we give to newcomers. Your first day is as easy as we can make it to be." Lirella beckoned them forward. "Come."

The first station sledgehammered the rocks into smaller pieces. What if she broke apart a rock in such a way that it opened a door? Using a tool to open a door didn't stop the danger. Her grandmother had told her stories about door-makers trying gloves and sticks and other artificial extensions—and failing. But then again, she didn't open a door every time her shoe lifted up from the ground, or every time she changed clothes.

No, it was too risky. She couldn't just test it to see what would happen.

Lirella and Claritsa stood on the grinding rock. People had stopped working and were staring at her.

"If you do not work, you will not eat," Lirella said.

The hardest station, the job no one wanted, the job that would maybe rot your flesh—Maella could see a way to be safe there.

"Don't go easy on me."

"What?"

"I want to do the pool," Maella said. "The panning."

"No one offers to do that job," Lirella said.

Maella bit her lip. "I do."

Realization dawned on Claritsa's face.

"You've fed us and given us shelter," Maella said. "My mother taught me to give back and help where I can."

Lirella shook her head like she couldn't understand the thought process of stupid young women who didn't know what was best for them—but it wasn't her job to fix that.

Maella followed Lirella to the soupy gray water.

People dumped buckets of dust into the pool. Others held panning buckets, scooped up the gray water, and swished it into other buckets. Those new buckets were taken to a sifting cloth. The *licatherin* was lighter than the stone, so what remained after the panning was *licatherin*-infused water, which the canvas filtered until little piles of dust remained. Once the *licatherin* had been filtered and dried, it was collected in a pouch.

Maella took the panning bucket from Lirella and thought about her next moves. She couldn't just jump in like the others. Every step had to be examined at every angle for potential doors. One slip, one badly placed hand, and it was all over.

The canvas cloth let off a slight hum because it created a seal with the ground, like the door in the field had done. But it should be safe as long as her hands did not lift its edge. The panning bucket should also be safe, as long as she did not drop it and pick it back up again.

She took a large step over the edge of the canvas cloth into the pool of panning water. The cold water quickly soaked her shoes. Miall was there, water already to his knees, but he ignored her awkward movements, and showed her the swish-swish-twirl for getting the *licatherin* to separate from the stone.

A rusted pipe stuck out from the hillside. When needed, Miall opened it up and murky water gushed out, refilling the pool. After the water turned the sand into sludge, they jumped back in with the panning buckets. She worked next to Miall and let him correct her technique. Finally, when he decided Maella had gotten the hang of it, he turned back to his own work.

She was alone in the panning pool with Erentia, Miall, and another Rathe prisoner whose name she overheard was Radovan. He looked Asian, mixed with a million other kinds of things, for all she knew. He didn't talk to her. It was Erentia who had supplied his name and said he had been one of Foster's warriors.

Most of the day passed before she made a mistake. The cold gray water had quickly numbed her feet and legs. Her back ached after bending over and sifting for hours. She could not take a break like the others when their buckets filled and they lifted them to the filtering station—not without risking a door—so she stayed in the water each time and gave someone else her break. This won her a grudging respect, even from Erentia, but it also made her skin feel like it was going to peel away from her body at any moment. She didn't know if the tainted water could work that fast or if she was only imagining it after the warnings.

It didn't matter.

Let her skin rot.

Staying in the pool kept everyone safe—and kept her secret safe, too.

Claritsa worked at the grinding station. Sethlo and Daniel were moved to a different station after their muscles had given out under the sledgehammer work. The two of them took regular trips with a wheelbarrow to dump the grinding stone product into what she began to think of as *her* pool of water.

It was when Erentia took away the next load of *licatherin* that it happened.

The panning bucket slipped out of Maella's hands and landed upside down in the water.

Maella looked at it in horror.

She was tired and her eyesight blurred from staring at her pan for so long. Her feet had gone numb and her lower back burned like someone poked a hot knife into her spine. She kept thinking about Lirella's words and the water rotting her flesh and the answers she needed and whether Daniel would keep quiet and how to escape and get home and find her father and brother and she had forgotten to be careful.

Such a simple thing for anyone else was an impossible task for her.

She didn't dare pick up the panning bucket. It might open a black hole, or spew out fire, or release a swarm of bees.

She stood there, tears of exhaustion leaking from her eyes, and willed it to move, to turn itself over, or to have Claritsa pick it up for her before anyone noticed.

But Claritsa was at the grinding stone.

Erentia returned to the pool, but stopped her work, looking at Maella with an unreadable expression on her face.

Maella bent over to pick up the bucket, but its hum increased. She snatched her hands away from it as if burned. Looking up, she locked eyes with Sethlo. He carried another wheelbarrow load but hadn't dumped it into the pool yet.

Her stomach seemed to lodge in her throat. She dropped to her knees in the water and placed her hands on top of the upside-down bucket. Her shorts became soaked and the water crept up, wetting the hem of her jacket. Her fingers were wrinkled, swollen, and stained dark lavender. She couldn't let them know she was afraid to lift the bucket.

"Take a break, Maella," Sethlo said, sloshing over, the water coming to his knees. He pulled her away, back onto her feet, out of the water, and guided her to sit on a stone.

"We all work," Erentia said.

"Just take a breath. You haven't taken any breaks," Sethlo said this louder than he needed to—loudly enough for everyone watching to hear him.

"We all work or we don't eat," Erentia said again.

Sethlo loped back into the water and grabbed the bucket. "Just give her a moment!" He returned to Maella and handed it to her.

"Thank you," she said, not daring to look at him, afraid she would discover the truth in his eyes. Did Sethlo somehow know she was a doormaker? He couldn't just be acting nice.

"I...I need to go to the bathroom," Maella said. "I'll be able to keep working after that."

Erentia grunted and returned to panning. She spoke in a different language, but it wasn't hard to tell the words were meant to be unkind.

Miall responded sharply.

Radovan laughed.

Maella walked away, leaving Sethlo to his wheelbarrow, forcing her hands to her sides—trying to remember not to walk like a doormaker.

She could have killed them all with a bucket.

# Chapter 18

AT THE END OF THE day, Maella left the pool of water numb and shaking from the cold, her skin spongy feeling. She was exhausted, feeling sick, yet almost high, her brain flying from thought to thought, her muscles twitching, like she'd had a gallon of coffee. As she set down the pan, she wondered how to get someone to pick it up for her tomorrow, but then that thought dropped out of her head.

On a piece of canvas sat a small pile of finely ground dust. Gray, but with a hint of purple that sparkled when the sun hit it just right.

There it was, their day's work.

She pinched out a thimbleful of the *licatherin*. It felt like salt against her skin. The sun was setting. She had spent all day at the worst job in the mine, she still had no answers, no plan to escape this place, no chance yet of seeing her family again, and this was what she had to show for aching muscles, numb feet, a cough in her chest, and skin that was turning purple.

Fury boiled up inside of her. All of this torture for a powder. All of this for something that symbolized everything wrong with everything. Her hand opened and the pinch of *licatherin* flew into the air, like it was the glass from when she broke all the windows.

The *licatherin* dust drifted to the ground, sparkling purple in the fading light, disappearing into the stone.

Maella's stomach twisted and threatened to empty.

She hadn't meant to do it. Her anger had taken over, and before she realized it—

"That was your dinner," Erentia said.

Maella jumped.

Erentia walked on, ignoring her.

The camp enforced Erentia's pronouncement. They gave her gray water, because there was plenty of it, and they said the *licatherin* in the water increased a person's energy, but Maella did not get dinner that night. The camp did not fool around when it came to their survival. That was the lecture she got later, when the meager meal was passed around and she sat there, embarrassed, ashamed, hands empty in her lap.

They wouldn't hold it against Maella—it became too much for everyone at some point.

"But it must not happen again if you want to be fed."

Lirella said this last bit with a severity that re-lit Maella's fury.

She wasn't going to spend the rest of her life working this gray stone until it killed her.

Claritsa broke her small share of dinner in half and offered it to Maella. Even Sethlo offered part of his food, though he'd worked the longest at the sledgehammer.

She refused them. "I'm not hungry."

Everyone knew that was a lie. Their kindness made her ashamed of what her anger had done.

After Lirella's lecture, Maella left camp.

She feared someone would follow and force her back, but then realized no one would. Whoever controlled this place killed people in Rock Heaven by forcing them to walk the rocks.

There was nowhere to go.

But that wasn't exactly true.

She made her way to the wooden door. It hung in the sky, steadfast and strange. Its outline glowed golden from something on the other side. She told herself she wanted to watch the sky change colors and hide from her embarrassment, but it was the door that drew her.

What had Lirella called the place on the other side?

Thrae.

She wondered about the ladder both Sethlo and Harry had mentioned. If she climbed up, would she find the same sun lighting the same kind of sky on fire with oranges, reds, and pinks? Had her family come from Thrae?

She waited for a moment beneath the door, almost believing that if she wished it hard enough, the ladder would appear.

Stumbling steps from behind spun her around.

Claritsa. Daniel. Sethlo.

Daniel held his right arm against his chest like it pained him. It probably did after his work that day. Dark purple circles shadowed Claritsa's eyes. Both of them stared at her, expecting something from her.

Sethlo looked like he wasn't sure why he was there, except he'd somehow managed to become part of their group. They were all newcomers and the youngest prisoners at the camp. Their skin had not yet turned purple.

"What are you going to do?" Daniel said, hope filling his voice.

"What can you do?" Sethlo said. "Do you know a way to escape?"

The sun was low enough now that she could stare at the door without the light hurting her eyes.

"Maella," Claritsa said, a warning note in her voice.

Admitting she was a doormaker to anyone was dangerous, and not just for her. Hadn't Foster tried to execute Claritsa for being Maella's friend?

"Maella," Claritsa said. "Come back to camp."

"You should do it," Daniel said. He rubbed hard at his face, trying to push angry tears back into his body. "We can't stay here like this."

"What can you do?" Sethlo asked. "I do not understand. *What can you do?*"

Maella stepped to stand directly beneath the door. From this angle, it was a dark line in the sky, like a trail of soot. Its vibrations seemed stronger than yesterday.

Had she only been here two days?

It felt like an eternity.

The door had called her from camp and she had answered. Yet like before, its hum didn't feel—right. This door had been kept open for a very long time, years, based on how long Lirella said Rock Heaven had held prisoners. It shouldn't be treated like that.

She reached up, but it was too high, many stories high. Cloud level high.

Whatever the door was—magic, machine, wormhole—it was telling her it didn't like being open.

# Chapter 19

THREE WEEKS PASSED.

Three weeks, three *licatherin* trades, three Klylup raids, two storms, four arguments where Claritsa talked both Maella and Daniel out of opening another door.

Claritsa hurried after Daniel now as the three of them headed for the door in the sky. Maella went more slowly, carefully picking her way, but also, she had been the one to set Daniel off at dinner. Since last week, he had stopped talking to her, looking at her, acknowledging her, but that evening she had caught his eye over another mouthful of *licatherin*-covered pancake.

His face looked so pale even under the purple. She had asked, "Are you okay?"

A strangled noise had left his throat and then he had left camp.

"What are you going to do?" Claritsa called across the rocks. "Daniel?"

"We have to try something!" Daniel yelled back.

By their tenth cold night in Rock Heaven, Daniel and Sethlo gave up sleeping alone. Maella would have cared before—sleeping next to two boys who could make her stomach flutter—but the mining work took care of that. They made a nest out of blankets among the boulders. Their skin had all turned different shades of purple, but mostly the gray dust covered everything.

Maella marked each day by carving into a special rock. All the prisoners had them. She did not ask about what happened to the people who had added marks before her.

The crates arrived every eight days in exchange for the *licatherin*. The horn sounded, the Klylup responded. They raced to collect the broken supplies, the mining tools their only protection whenever the Klylup won the race. The crates were always smashed. Harry said those on Thrae did this so the wood could not be used for drums.

But Harry ran *licatherin* experiments in the mine and found a glue recipe that stuck for a few hours—strong, unbreakable—but then fell apart after that at the slightest touch. The glue held long enough for Claritsa and Erentia to drum, which meant Aretha would dance and make them forget. Claritsa became a favorite of the camp.

Maella, Claritsa, Sethlo, Daniel—they searched every day for answers, escape routes, anything. The other prisoners were polite about helping. Eventually, the newcomers would figure out what everyone else already understood—there was no escape attempt that the camp had not yet tried.

Nothing.

Except—opening another door.

But Maella couldn't tell them that.

Daniel stood under the door now. The vibrations from it made Maella's teeth rattle. She had asked Claritsa once if she felt the vibrations very strongly. Claritsa had looked at her strangely and said she didn't feel any vibrations at all.

The way Daniel looked at Maella now—

"We should tell them about her." He stood with his two feet planted on two different stones. Sweat gleamed on his purple-stained forehead. The surrounding sky was lit in reds, oranges, and hints of purple. They should have been exhausted, and they were, deep in their bones, but the *licatherin* gave them an energy that burned out fat and muscle.

"That would kill her. That could kill all of us," Claritsa said.

"Then she should use her power. Keeper Shaul said it would be okay." The stain of Daniel's skin flushed a deeper lavender.

"That's not what he said," Maella replied.

"You know we can't!" Claritsa said.

"Maybe you can't," Daniel said.

Maella's panic grew like a stone in her chest. The door vibrated its wrongness in the sky above her. Lirella's words were on repeat in her mind. *We watch the door and the door watches us.*

"We can't talk about this here," Maella said.

"They won't just give you a pass," Claritsa said. "You'll be guilty too, helping her hide this whole time. They'll punish you too."

"We're already being punished. How could it be any worse than this?" He lifted up his shirt, showing off a purple-stained chest, rippling with muscle, yet also starved looking. There was never enough food. There was always more stone to break.

"Did you ever stop to think maybe there's something really wrong with her? Everyone believes it. Maybe it's really true!"

"Don't talk to me like I'm not even here," Maella said. "I've been trying to find a way out. I haven't been sulking like you. I've been asking questions and searching with Sethlo for a way to escape! What have you been doing?"

Daniel's expression turned ugly. He opened his mouth, but Claritsa held up a hand.

"Stop," Claritsa said, glancing up. "Maella's right. We can't talk about this here. What if they're watching?"

Daniel opened his arms wide and stared up at the door. "Is anybody listening? We're not supposed to be here! You hear that? I'm not supposed to be here!"

"Shut up!" Maella shouted, her voice frantic. "You'll kill all of us!"

Daniel froze. The fight left him and he hunched his shoulders. The door swung in the breeze. Light glowed from its outline.

Claritsa stalked up and pushed Daniel, making him stumble. "Am I the only one who hasn't gone crazy? You're asking her to go nuclear on us? Who knows what could happen."

Maella cringed. This wasn't the first time the three of them had argued about whether she should open a door, but it was tough to hear herself described like that. Even if it was true.

"Maella, go back to the boulders. Just let me—" Claritsa looked past Maella, back toward camp, and stilled.

"What's happening?" Sethlo said, approaching.

After helping her with the bucket, Sethlo had begun to watch out for her. Each night, they walked the stones together before darkness fell, searching for something no one else had yet found—an escape. But there was only stone. They talked about everything except their families. Of course, Maella couldn't tell him she was a doormaker. The light in his eyes when he looked at her would vanish. She couldn't bear that, even though he probably thought of her as little more than a sister.

"It's fine," Claritsa said.

"No, it's not," Daniel said.

Sethlo looked to Maella for answers.

Maella's head began to hurt. The door was pulling her apart little by little. Daniel had saved her and Claritsa twice. Maella had condemned him to Rock Heaven. "It's my fault he's in Rock Heaven. Because of what I did."

It wasn't exactly a lie.

"What did you do?" Sethlo said. "You know my crime, but you have never shared yours."

Daniel and Claritsa waited. Claritsa's silent expression told her to shut up and Daniel's encouraged her to confess.

"I don't want to talk about it," Maella said.

Claritsa sighed. Daniel gritted his teeth.

Once, during the second week, Miall had tried to convince her to switch jobs. Even Erentia told her no one should work the pool like Maella did. But Maella decided to collect the *licatherin* as a way to punish herself. The work burned away all guilt, all shame, all feeling. She did not waste another thimbleful. Her skin stayed soaked all day, cracking and bleeding once dry. The water never let her feel warm.

Claritsa had cornered her once and examined the bruises and cuts on her hands, legs, arms. "You can't keep doing this."

Maella had responded, "I can't do anything else."

Because if the other prisoners found out she was a door-maker?

They would kill her.

"She's not who you think she is," Daniel said, bringing Maella back to the door. To Claritsa and Daniel facing off. To Sethlo at her side. To the breathtaking emptiness of the stones and the vibrations that shook her all the time.

"Just go, Maella," Claritsa said, pushing Daniel ahead of her.

Daniel balked, but then let himself be guided away.

Claritsa locked eyes with Sethlo. "Take her away from here. Let him cool down."

Sethlo ran a hand through his hair. "I do not understand —"

"Then make her explain it to you," Claritsa said.

Maella stepped back. Claritsa couldn't mean—

"Maella, figure it out." Claritsa turned away. "Come on Daniel, let's take a walk."

Sethlo grabbed Maella's hand and tugged her from the door. "Come on, we should search while there's still light." His voice was calm and steady. His hand was calloused and warm.

She let him draw her toward the setting sun, away from Daniel and Claritsa. The clouds now fluffy and tinged pink.

Sethlo didn't say anything at first. He wouldn't ask about what Daniel said. Maella hadn't known him for that long, but she already knew he wasn't the kind of person to force answers from anybody, even when the questions really needed answering.

Finally, Sethlo said, "Daniel does not know who he is yet. You already know who you are. He is not like you."

"Like me?" Maella laughed. She had no idea who she was.

"You do not see it yet." Sethlo gently squeezed her hand. "That is all."

# Chapter 20

THE DARKNESS OF THE NIGHT made it difficult for Maella to see the outline of her own hands. All around her, people slept. Some snored, some cried out from terrible dreams, others lay as if dead.

"Daniel."

Maella whispered into his ear so softly she wasn't sure he could hear her. She couldn't risk anyone else waking up, especially Sethlo or Claritsa.

Sethlo's words echoed inside her mind.

*You already know who you are.*

A recklessness had filled her at Sethlo's words—a rebellion. She didn't know who she was, no matter what

Sethlo thought. No one had ever trusted her enough to tell her anything to help with the kinds of dangers she now faced. They had wanted to protect her. Instead, they had left her defenseless.

Claritsa wanted to protect her, too. For three weeks, Maella had let Claritsa talk her out of doing the one thing that might actually make a difference. She allowed that reckless feeling to rise up and take over now. It battled against the hum of the door in the sky until she couldn't tell them apart.

She needed to get them out of Rock Heaven before Daniel got her killed. She needed to find her family and find out the truth. All things that Rock Heaven didn't have.

Daniel groaned as he shifted onto his shoulder. During the daylight, he often held that shoulder close to his body. He said it never stopped hurting. Maella brushed her hand across his cheek. Rough facial hair scratched her fingers. Everyone looked rough now. She could only imagine how matted and crazy her hair looked. Better not to imagine.

He smelled like *licatherin* dust with a layer of boy underneath—licorice, musk, stone. He needed to wake up.

She squeezed his hand. "Daniel." She risked whispering it a little louder.

His breathing changed. His hand tensed and his entire body went still.

"It's Maella. Come on."

She let go of his hand and stepped away from the shadow of the boulder and their nest of blankets. Cold wrapped her in an icy hug. The moon glowed brightly enough for the boulders that formed camp to cast long shadows.

No one would notice how she walked in the dark, even if they were awake. She stepped lightly across the stones, clasping her hands behind her back. Her footing was more sure than ever. She knew how to walk across the stones with confidence. They'd been in Rock Heaven for three weeks, after all. If she hadn't accidentally opened a door by now, she wasn't going to.

But that needed to change.

Claritsa wanted them to wait. They hadn't seen the ladder come through the door yet. Maybe it never would. But after Daniel's breakdown earlier that evening and the way Sethlo's words had cut deep into her, she had to try something—the one something Rock Heaven prisoners, in all their failed escape attempts, had never tried.

Opening a door.

But if the door was going to be big enough for people to escape through, she needed help.

That's where Daniel came in.

Part of her felt guilty for putting him in danger like this, but she pushed those feelings down, down, down, until she could pretend they had disappeared. He wanted her to open a door. She needed help opening a door. So here she was, sneaking around at night with a boy.

Her mother would be scandalized. Her grandmother would smile and a little devilish light would shine in her eyes.

But it wasn't like that.

Her sneaking around might get this boy killed.

Not exactly romantic.

Daniel had saved her and Claritsa from Barth. He'd helped save them from Foster. He had fought off the Klylup with them. But she suspected deep down that he regretted each of those acts. He was heroic in spite of himself. He couldn't stand Maella and she couldn't stand him.

Except.

Claritsa didn't want Maella to open a door and Sethlo didn't know she was a doormaker. Daniel was the only one who could help her with what she needed to do tonight.

She took the path to the mine and then walked beyond it. Daniel breathed low and steady behind her, following. There were no birds, no insects, no frogs. Rock Heaven really was all rock. But it didn't mean the world was silent. The doors hummed around her and under her feet and the door in the sky hummed loudest of all. Sometimes the hum put her to sleep at night, but most of the time it robbed her of sleep.

Daniel didn't ask any questions about what they were doing. It was like he knew what she intended. She had woken that morning and spent another long day in the mine and her skin had cracked, bleeding around her fingers, when she ate dinner. Erentia made some sort of joke in Rathe about doormakers. She didn't understand most of the words, but she understood their cruel laughter. Daniel's shouting at the door, arms opened wide, played on repeat in her mind. Sethlo's words were on repeat too—*you already know who you are.*

That wasn't true, not really, not the way he meant it, but she knew she could open doors and her walks with Sethlo had produced no chance of escape so far—

—Well, that wasn't exactly true.

They had found a stone, thin like a plank, tilted on its side. The flat top of a boulder sat nearby.

Daniel and Maella came upon it now, in the dark, the only light cast by the moon and stars.

Maella stopped when she was a few feet away. "We need to lift it onto the boulder."

The world shone silver and looked like the moonscape she had first thought of upon entering Rock Heaven. The milky white brush of stars across the sky was so beautiful it made her heart hurt. Everything was quiet except for their breathing and the soft sounds of their shoes—and the humming. She was glad Claritsa wasn't with them. If something terrible happened, at least Claritsa would be okay.

"I need you to help me open a door."

Daniel had been scratching his head, but stilled at Maella's words. "Just like that?" His voice was rough from sleep.

"Why not?"

"I'm not complaining."

"You haven't stopped complaining."

Daniel grimaced.

"Forget it," Maella said. "I got you into this. I promised I would get you out. I'm going to keep my promise."

"I don't think Barth would agree."

Anger bubbled into Maella's throat. She flexed her hands at her sides. "I don't want to fight." Except that's exactly what part of her wanted to do.

"Maybe I do want to fight," Daniel said.

His words made Maella step back. "What?"

Daniel sighed and rubbed a hand across his face. "It's either fight or give up. I choose fight."

"We're on the same side," Maella said.

Daniel shook his head.

Suddenly a question burned on Maella's tongue. "What happened with Esson?"

Daniel froze for a second, then moved his hurt shoulder around, stretching it. He grabbed the plank-like rock along its edges and lifted.

Maella gasped. She thought it would take both of them struggling with it, but he had done the job alone. Then she remembered—while she might have taken the most dangerous, yuckiest job in the mine, he and Sethlo had been hammering rocks every day. Still, his muscles strained as he stumbled across the stones, gently tipping the plank-rock onto the boulder.

The humming increased.

"What does it feel like?" Daniel said.

"What?"

"Opening a door?"

"Like the world's going to shake itself apart and take me with it." Her hands opened and closed. She wanted to reach for the rock and get this over with, but—

"You didn't answer my question," Maella said, prompting. "Esson?"

She waited, hoping he would have an answer to something she still couldn't understand—why had both her brother and father left them? She was tired of not understanding. Daniel must know more than he was telling her. She needed him to know more.

"I don't know, Maella," he said finally. "I wasn't there and Barth never really told me."

"You're lying," Maella said, but she knew he wasn't.

Daniel was many things, but being a good liar wasn't one of them. It was why he had such a hard time keeping her doormaker secret from the other prisoners.

Maella, on the other hand, had lied her entire life about her entire life. Her lies had protected her family and herself from danger, but had also brought her to Rock Heaven.

"Are you going to open this door or not?"

Maella placed her hands on top of the rock. The surface felt rough and cold. Her feet went numb—was she really going to do this?

"I need your help lifting it," Maella said. "But then you should probably jump out of the way or something."

"It went fine with the door in the field, and with Foster, and even with Keeper Shaul. Nothing jumped out. Maybe they don't know what they're talking about. Maybe it's all just been a bunch of bedtime stories to scare you into following the rules."

Maella shook her head. Her hair felt both brittle and greasy against her cheek. "Remember the flames from the desk?" But he hadn't been there to see that. "We've gotten lucky each time, but plenty of terrible things have happened to other people after I've opened a door. Remember the Klylup?"

"Fine," Daniel said, an edge coming into his voice. "It's dangerous. That's why I'm here instead of Claritsa, right? Or Sethlo, right? You don't like me, so it doesn't matter if I get hurt or even killed."

"I..." But Maella's protest died on her lips because he wasn't exactly wrong. The realization made her ashamed. She hadn't meant it to be like that. Sethlo didn't even know she was a doormaker. It wasn't like she was going to hide this from Claritsa, but she didn't want Claritsa here in case something really bad happened.

"That's okay," Daniel said, a strangled note entering his voice. "I'm used to being used. It doesn't bother me. Hell, I'm using you."

"What?"

"To get me home," Daniel said. "You're still my best chance, no matter how crazy you and your family are."

"We're not—" Instead of throwing more words back at him, Maella blew out a long breath. What was the point? Enough.

"Let's just do this," Maella said.

"Finally."

Maella rested her hands on the stone again, its vibrations blocking out all other sensory details. Daniel stood next to her, ready to help lift the weight of the door. The humming increased and the moonlight seemed to pulse brighter around her.

The recklessness that broke windows and fought Klylups and scattered hard-earned *licatherin*—fled.

She didn't want to do this. What was she thinking? If she opened this door, it would likely call the Klylup, and she would only have five more doors left before she died—if whatever came out of this door didn't kill her first. The pattern was breaking—Claritsa was right—how could she trust anything Keeper Shaul said?

"You're not as bad as you think you are," Maella said suddenly, stalling, hearing all the warnings her family had drilled into her over the years. Their voices rose in volume inside her mind, screaming at her to stop and—

"Stop," Daniel said.

"You don't want to believe you're a good person." Her hands began to tremble on the rock. "You don't want other people to expect you to be like that, but you are anyway, in spite of yourself."

"You don't know me."

"I know you saved us from Barth and from Foster."

"All of which I regret."

"You don't mean that. And I know you haven't told anyone else my secret."

"Yet."

"You keep trying to—"

Daniel grunted and suddenly the plank-rock lifted up. Her hands slipped off as the rock tipped over backwards. A huge boom sounded, like an explosion. A column of tar-like liquid shot into the air. It was dark and thick and it blacked out the stars until it rained down on them.

Maella and Daniel scrambled away, but the liquid kept falling, coating her skin with slime. It smelled like rotten eggs and fresh asphalt. A drop landed on her tongue and tasted sour. She gagged.

Daniel raced back to the boulder, into the liquid blowing into the sky, and struggled with the plank-rock.

"Stop!" Maella shouted and scrambled after him.

Now that the door was open, she couldn't let him close it.

He grabbed the rock on either side and held it up like a weight-lifter, cried out as if from pain, then slammed it down, cutting off the liquid. It pushed back at him, but he forced it down and, with a click, stone met stone and the geyser stopped.

He collapsed, clutching his shoulder.

"What have you done?" Maella cried out.

"It wasn't going to stop," Daniel said, chest heaving.

"You don't know that. You should have waited!"

"It was oil, Maella."

Maella wiped the goo from her face. Some had gotten into her eyes, making them itch. "We'll try again. I can open it again and it will go to someplace different and this time it will get us out of here."

"We can't—"

Maella opened her mouth to protest.

Daniel held up a hand to cut her off. He was soaked from head to toe in the same oil as her. Everything was slippery and smelled like a garbage can that had been left out in the sun for too long. She missed the licorice smell of the *li-catherin,* though she hated everything else about it.

"That boom probably woke people up. Or what if the Klylup heard it? We have to get cleaned up and back to camp before anyone notices this was us. Unless you want to tell them you're a doormaker now?"

The trumpet sound of the Klylup cut through the night air and closed any further protest. In the back of her mind, she knew opening a door might bring the Klylup out—but why? The door in the sky was always open, yet the Klylup only came to it when those on the Thrae side of the door blew a horn and traded supplies for licatherin.

There was no cleaning up the oil spill, but it was far enough away from the camp and where they mined for the *licatherin that Maella doubted anyone would find it.*

"We can't go into camp like this," Maella said. "They'll know something happened."

Daniel looked both of them over. "The mine."

"We don't have time," Maella said. "The Klylup is coming."

Daniel turned and took in the surrounding landscape. Stone, door, camp, moonlight, stars. "No, it's headed for the oil. Maybe afterward it will come to the mine, but we have time if we're quick."

Daniel raced for the mine and Maella followed. They each stripped and, with their backs turned to each other, scrubbed their clothes clean from the *licatherin* water in the pool Maella worked in every day.

Maella dunked herself in the water while Daniel wrung out both of their clothes. She scrubbed and scrubbed until she couldn't feel her arms or legs anymore from the cold. Listening for the Klylup's call, she ran in place to dry off and warm up as Daniel took his turn in the pool. She tried not to notice how the moonlight carved out the muscles in his arms and chest, or how broad his shoulders had gotten, even as he cradled the injured one.

They put their damp clothes back on. Her teeth chattered and she wrapped her hands around her chest. She had her shorts, a shirt, a thin jacket, and her shoes—all well on their way to disintegrating from her work in the mine.

"They'll know we've been gone," Maella said through chattering teeth.

Daniel hurried out of the mine, not waiting to see if she would follow. "Then we'll say we heard the noise and went to go check it out."

They entered camp and kept to the shadows. If anyone was awake, Maella couldn't see them. She hoped that meant they couldn't see her and Daniel.

The two of them crept back into their nest of blankets next to Claritsa and Sethlo. All of her shook—from the cold, from the vibrations, from actually having tried to escape this place. It thrilled her and she thought maybe Sethlo was right after all.

She knew who she was—she was someone who wanted answers and would stop at nothing to get them.

The warmth of Sethlo's and Claritsa's body heat was a relief. She turned to shift a blanket better over her feet. That's when she caught Sethlo staring at her.

Moonlight made his eyes shine. A blanket was wrapped tight around his neck and shoulders. He lay on his side on the ground and watched her without blinking. She opened her mouth to say something, anything, but before she could, he shifted, turning his back to her.

Maella's stomach flipped. What was he thinking? What had he seen?

# Chapter 21

CLARITSA WALKED BY, SMILING A good morning to Maella. Her bangs had grown too long to be called bangs anymore. She pushed them back behind her ears and they curled onto her cheeks.

Maella couldn't tell Claritsa about last night yet. Claritsa would stop them and Maella wasn't ready for that.

Maella needed to talk to Sethlo and Daniel, separately.

Now that she had opened another door, she needed to do it again. She would use up all her doors if it meant getting them out of Rock Heaven.

But she also needed to ask Sethlo about last night. What had he seen? Why had he turned away from her? What could she say to explain herself that wouldn't give anything away?

If she could open a door that would allow escape, everyone would find out about her, but by then it wouldn't matter. Maybe they would even be grateful.

Until then, she couldn't risk anyone else finding out.

Sethlo avoided her, but Daniel gave her a knowing look. They shared a secret now and he looked more calm than she had seen him in weeks. She did not doubt that he would help her open another door tonight.

She marked the day with a scratch on her boulder. Her muscles had both grown and shrunk. Hunger pains never left her while awake or sleeping. If she filled up on the gray water, it gave her energy and made her sick and increased the vibrations.

She recognized the divisions in camp now. Who sat near each other, who said good morning to one another. There was Lirella and Giffen and their almost religious fanaticism about doormakers, so like Keeper Shaul—and yet Lirella was often fair and sometimes kind. Giffen spoke often about the Sechnel. Harry was skeptical about everything. Erentia and the other Rathe prisoners were both on Lirella's side and somehow not. People sided one way or the other, mostly based on which world they had come from, but that wasn't set in stone.

Ha. Stone.

She hated the gray stone. But so did everyone.

There was sunrise gray, sunset gray, afternoon gray, wet gray, dry gray, dust gray, *licatherin* gray.

The world around her had become more complex, yet more simple. Wake up damp and chilled. Licorice smells engulfed everything. Grind through the dust-covered pancake for breakfast. Gulp down the *licatherin*-infused water. Work in the *licatherin* pool until her skin cracked. Dream the door.

She had opened a door. No one had died. No one seemed like they had noticed anything out of the ordinary.

Well, no one except for Sethlo.

Breakfast ended and she fell in line for the walk to the mine. Sethlo looked starved, but confident. Purple stained his skin, but Sethlo owned it, like it didn't bother him.

"Sethlo?"

He kept walking.

"Sethlo!"

He paused, shook his head. "Maella—"

A shout from the direction of the door interrupted them.

All of Rock Heaven stopped and looked back.

"Newcomer," Sethlo said, his eyes widening. "Giffen says a newcomer is arriving."

Thoughts raced through Maella's head. A newcomer meant they would finally see the ladder. In the *licatherin* exchanges she'd witnessed so far, none of them had included the ladder—there had been no newcomer.

Claritsa hurried up to Maella. "This could be it."

Daniel and Maella exchanged a look.

Those on the Thrae side of the door sounded the horn. Far off in the distance the Klylup answered the call.

Maella was an experienced stone-walker now, but it still took her the longest of all to reach the perimeter of the door's blast radius—the safe distance needed to avoid injury by the supply crates dropped from the sky.

The ladder snaked out from the rectangle of light. It was made out of tree trunks and branches lashed together by rope. Sections of it lowered in lurches, connected and dropped to make room for the next. The ladder's feet eventually lodged into the boulders, twisting under the weight of the newcomer who immediately began climbing down.

Sethlo watched it all with an obsession she understood.

What if someone tried to climb up and into the door?

What would be on the other side to stop them?

The person climbed down the ladder slowly, painfully, keeping an arm pinned to the side as if from injury.

Giffen was at the base of the ladder, holding it still. The Klylup trumpeted, making the prisoners flinch, but the trumpet was far away. There was still time.

"Has anyone ever tried going up the ladder?" Maella asked, but then remembered. They had tried and been banished to walk the rocks.

Harry squinted down at her. "They always have guards waiting on the other side."

A bald, brown head appeared through the door. Hands, thick with rings that glinted in the sunlight, held the ladder. The face was difficult to make out. He looked down on them like a god surveying his subjects.

Maella's heartbeat quickened. Was this the doormaker?

"Lirella." The voice boomed.

Lirella stepped forward and bowed her head before upturning it again. She whispered something. By this time,

Maella had heard her say it enough times in all the different languages to understand.

*We watch the door and the door watches us.*

The man on the other side of the door spoke in Thrae.

Maella could almost understand him. The words reached for memories long buried. A language she might have spoken as a child. But it hadn't clicked yet and not understanding only left her frustrated. She turned nervously to search for the Klylup. This was taking too long.

Sethlo's face went white. "Maella."

"What's taking so long? The Klylup will be here soon."

"Maella."

She caught him staring at her. Eyes wide. A knot of worry formed in her stomach. She looked around. Erentia stared at her too and spoke to Miall in hurried whispers.

Actually, dozens of prisoners, all of them, stared at her.

"What is it? What is he saying?"

"There are three among you who should not be," Sethlo said. The words seemed to get stuck in his throat. "He says Lirella must make the three walk the rocks within eight earth days."

Daniel had shouted at the door.

They must have been on the other side, watching.

But immediately, another thought came to her. Maybe it hadn't been Daniel that gave them away.

Maybe this was her fault.

She had opened a door and it had alerted those on the other side.

Keeper Shaul had kept the pattern. His pattern-machine recorded the doors opened by doormakers. Keeper Shaul said every world had two pattern-keepers. What if these people in Thrae had their own pattern-keepers and pattern-machine?

Claritsa had been right. She should have never opened the door.

Daniel looked stunned. His eyes widened when she caught his gaze.

The two of them both knew—

This was because of the door they had opened last night.

"We won't—" Harry started.

Sethlo interrupted. "He says there will be no more food until the three who should not be are gone."

Maella looked around.

Everyone stared not just at Maella now, but at Daniel and Claritsa, too.

No.

"He says—"

The newcomer set both feet on the stones. The ladder snaked back up. Those deeply bronzed hands decorated with rings dragged in the last rung.

The newcomer turned around.

Sethlo turned an odd shade of sickly green gray. "Daj Dedion?"

Sethlo ran for the newcomer.

This Daj Dedion guy recognized Sethlo, too. Except that recognition was wiped away by something more awful.

Maella's mind spun on what Sethlo said and what that meant for them, but the look on this guy's face—she stepped forward. "Sethlo!"

Sethlo went to hug the man.

The newcomer threw Sethlo to the ground. His voice rose and spit flew from his lips. He advanced on Sethlo as he shouted in Thrae. Then he began punching Sethlo. Again and again.

Why didn't Sethlo fight back? Why was everyone frozen?

# Chapter 22

THE SUN SHONE HARSH IN the sky. Those on the other side of the door had gone. The Klylup called—closer now.

Maella ran for Sethlo. Giffen forced Dedion off and pushed him toward camp.

Radovan held Daniel back. Miall used his one arm to keep Claritsa from running to help.

The rest of the prisoners collected the broken supplies and hurried to the safety of the boulders. The cloudless blue sky filled Maella with emptiness. She waited for someone to snatch her away from Sethlo's hunched form. The stillness, now that the ladder had disappeared, and the door had

returned to its almost-closed state, did nothing to hide Sethlo's moans or the Klylup's trumpeting.

Or the words Sethlo had translated that were on repeat in
Maella's head.

*Walk the rocks. We watch the door and the door watches
us. Walk the rocks.*

Lirella told Miall and Radovan to take away Claritsa and
Daniel. And they did.

Claritsa kicked out, but Miall was strong, even with only
one arm. Daniel broke away, but Radovan caught him again.
She couldn't believe Lirella or Harry or anyone at camp
would make them go out there, out into nothing. Those on
the other side of the door knew about Maella and Claritsa
and Daniel. Did they know she was also a doormaker?

"Harry." Lirella's voice. Stern.

Maella winced. It was her turn.

Harry looked dumbfounded. He pushed at his nose at
glasses that weren't there. Aretha stood next to him. Maella
was pretty sure they were a couple.

"Daj means uncle," Harry said nervously.

"What?" Maella said, her thoughts pulling away from the
door's ultimatum. "He called him uncle? But—"

Harry rubbed at his forehead. "Dedion accused Sethlo of
killing his sister and niece—Sethlo's mother and sister."

The blood rushed to Maella's ears. "Sethlo wouldn't murder anyone."

Sethlo was ambitious, and he was obsessed with the door,
but mostly he was kind.

"Dedion said Sethlo's mother and sister came after Sethlo
was taken," Harry continued. "Dedion hid them for weeks,

but they were discovered. He fought off the Thrae soldiers, and they captured him and brought him here, but not before they forced him to watch the house burn down with Sethlo's mother and sister inside."

Maella felt sick to her stomach.

"Bring Maella back to the boulders," Lirella said.

"I won't go without Sethlo!"

"Harry," Lirella said. "You heard what they said."

Harry shook his head. "We can't make a bunch of kids walk the rocks!"

Lirella looked over her shoulder. "Be quiet."

Maella followed her gaze. The Klylup was in sight now.

Lirella back-stepped, almost dancing on top of the rocks, a small hammer, her mining tool, as her meager weapon. "Then leave her to die! It will be the same to those on the other side of the door."

Lirella's dance turned into a sprint.

"I..." Harry began. He looked at her, mournfully once, then Aretha tugged on his sleeve and the two of them darted away.

She couldn't believe it. He had left.

But maybe she could believe it.

Her brother and her father had left.

Keeper Shaul had thrown them away.

The door hummed above her. A dark wound in the sky.

But then she noticed Harry did not take a direct path to camp. He veered toward the Klylup, shouting and waving his arms until the Klylup gave chase.

Maella held her breath as she watched the race to the rocks. Even with its broken wing, the Klylup slithered so fast

across the rocks, faster than humans. But Harry and Aretha
had a good head start. Still, they darted to safety with only a
few seconds to spare.

She quickly knelt next to Sethlo. He pressed his face to the
stone. His arms were wrapped around his stomach, as if to
prevent himself from falling to pieces. She smelled the sweat
and dust on him, she felt the pain and anger that wracked his
body.

"Sethlo?"

He did not answer.

She placed a hand slowly on his shoulder.

He shuddered. She pressed herself against his back and
wrapped her arms around him. She thought about Claritsa
and Daniel and the Klylup, but she knew Sethlo would not
move. When he shuddered from angry sobs, it was like an
earthquake moved through her too, but she held on. She held
on because she knew the darkness that consumed him. She
knew those feelings, the guilt and the grief and the anger and
the shame.

The need to make something right that could never be
right again.

Sethlo clenched fists into his stomach, as if punching
himself, and mumbled words over and over again, broken
only by the hitch in his throat. He used words she'd never
heard before, but she understood well enough what they
were supposed to mean. Tears dropped onto Maella's hands.
They scalded her skin, wrinkled and icy from the day's work.
She held on.

She didn't know how long they stayed like that, only that
eventually he quieted.

The Klylup still worried at the camp. Soon it would give up and head for the door. Even if it didn't and it slunk away to wherever it hid itself, Lirella would be back with Giffen.

Harry might not obey what Lirella wanted done, but Giffen would.

She released Sethlo. They were surrounded by the field of gray stones, the impossibly clear sky, the stillness of a place that didn't want them.

"You shouldn't be here."

Sethlo sat up now. His tears had washed away the gray dust on his face, leaving behind purple tracks that looked like bruised gashes. His dark hair was plastered to his skin. He wouldn't look at her.

"Yes, that's what they said."

Sethlo struggled to his feet. "No, you shouldn't be here with me. I'm a murderer."

She didn't tell him that she was pretty much a murderer, too. She was a doormaker, wasn't she? But she wasn't ready for that confession. It was all too much right then, worrying about getting Sethlo on his feet before the Klylup came. Worrying about Claritsa and Daniel and what Lirella would do to them in exchange for the camp's food.

He pushed himself up and stumbled along the rocks, picking up speed until he was almost at a run.

Maella looked between him and camp. Between the Klylup and Claritsa and Daniel to Sethlo and the never-ending rock landscape ahead of them. The Klylup was snuffling at the boulders now, tired of its game.

If she let the Klylup eat her, she could not help Claritsa and Daniel. She could not bear to leave Sethlo alone out on the stones, even if he didn't want her with him. What she owed Sethlo—

Sethlo ran and Maella followed him.

She told herself Sethlo wouldn't make it far, not bruised and battered like this. He was grieving, but soon that grief would exhaust him and then he would stop. She would help him get back to camp safely.

Sethlo headed out across the stones, away from the door and from camp. When she looked back, there was only a dim rectangular glow in the sky. She thought someone called her name, but it was lost in the wind.

They walked, but she didn't know for how long, only that the sun had moved its position in the sky, or had they moved in relation to the sun? Sethlo would stumble, catch himself, then veer in a different direction. So lost in grief and anger, she suspected he didn't know where he was going or even that Maella followed.

In the pit, there was plenty of gray water to drink. Here there was nothing—no puddles, no pipes. Just gray rocks the size of bowling balls or bigger, and between these, smaller rocks. She became thirsty and hungry and exhausted from watching her steps. He had gotten far ahead of her. He didn't care if a rock slid out from beneath him. He was practically delirious, talking in his home language, calling out the names of those she assumed were his family.

It was important to keep him in sight. She could no longer see the familiar boulders of their camp or the outline of the door in the sky. Those landmarks had disappeared hours ago.

They were lost in a sea of rock.

She called out to Sethlo again.

He ignored her, like he had the last three times. Maybe he hadn't even heard her. Had she heard her mother or grandmother yelling at her to stop as she methodically broke each window in the house?

No. She hadn't.

But this wasn't like the windows. Sethlo would die out here if she could not get him to stop and think. Her lips cracked in the dry air. Her fingers grew numb and swollen. The sun sat low on the horizon but was obscured at times by the passing clouds that remained white and puffy for now but could change at any time.

"They would not want you to kill yourself!" She shouted finally, exhausted, scared of how low the sun had sunk in the sky, and how the wind wanted to steal away her breath. "But you will kill me and Claritsa and Daniel if you don't stop soon."

"I will not rest until I escape this place." He spoke in broken English, like he'd almost forgotten the language.

"They are going to send us to walk the rocks. We have to go back for Claritsa and Daniel. We have to—"

"If I die trying to leave, if I die trying to avenge them, then that is fair payment for what my actions have caused."

Maella understood. Even still, she said, "It's not your fault."

"It is," Sethlo said, choking on the words.

"Sethlo."

He continued halting steps across the stony landscape.

Her feet were two big blisters that blazed with pain. Her shoes had disintegrated in the panning pool the previous night. Most of them had no shoes, just calluses that the water soaked away if you stayed too long in the panning pit, and she was always in the panning pit.

Maella was trying to help Sethlo, but now part of her regretted it.

They were lost. They would die out here.

Lirella hadn't needed to force Maella to walk the rocks. She'd chosen this path for herself. She would never make it right for her mother and grandmother and little brother. Tears covered her vision. She blinked them furiously away and stepped onto the next stone. It rocked under her foot, slipping her balance out from under her.

Releasing a yelp, she fell on her side. Adrenaline shocked her with energy.

Had she?

She looked with her eyes and reached out with her inner senses for a hum.

Nothing.

The rock was only a rock.

She'd slipped, but it hadn't opened a door.

But now her bare foot was stuck between the stones.

"Sethlo, please stop. Don't let me die!"

He paused.

He looked back.

He looked away.

She thought for a second that he would keep walking.

She thought for another terrible second that if he did, she would turn over a stone with both hands.

She would turn over a million stones until she had destroyed all of Rock Heaven.

Sethlo came back.

The furious recklessness that made her break windows and throw pure *licatherin* into the air and open secret doors at night—faded. She placed her hands on the cold stone, her fingers damp from the shadowed corners of the rocks that still held a bit of water. Not enough to drink, just enough to stink.

He crouched over her, blocking the last of the sun's heat.

She shivered.

"How bad is it?"

Her feet were hot and swollen, but she could wiggle them. He lifted one stone away and she flinched.

No door. She was okay, except for how it felt like the Klylup had chewed on her toes, but at least she hadn't sprained anything.

But Maella wanted to give Sethlo a reason to stop, to wake up, to come back. "I can't keep going. Please help me."

Sethlo's eyes traveled up and down her body, evaluating the state of her injuries. She shivered under his gaze. It wasn't because of the cold. She hadn't only followed him because he needed someone's help. *She* had wanted to be that someone. Maella cared about him, and what he thought, more than she'd like to admit.

"I'll help you up," Sethlo said. "We have to keep going. There isn't any shelter here."

He held out his hand like he was offering her a peace agreement.

"Do you think that's going to change?" Maella said before she could stop it from coming out. She didn't mean for her tone to sound so cutting, but it was too late.

Sethlo flinched. Her words *had* pretty much rejected his peace offering.

She took his hand before he dropped it. His skin felt warm and rough from the mining work, but then again, so did hers. He brought her arm across his shoulders to help her walk. They tried stepping like this once, but Sethlo drew in a sharp breath, like someone had kicked him in the stomach.

"My daj," he said, which she took to mean the beating he'd endured at the hands of his uncle. "I'll be okay."

They took another step together. The rocks felt even more precarious as they struggled to find some sort of path.

"Do you know which way is camp?"

Maella shook her head. If this had been home—her creek, her field, her little bit of forest—she could use a dozen different ways to get them safely back, but everything here looked endlessly the same.

If this had been home, there would have been a soft bed and blankets, and if she asked, her grandmother would have snuggled into bed with her for as long as she wanted.

She would have asked.

They struggled across the stones, silent except for their labored breathing. And then, for no reason that Maella could figure, Sethlo began to talk about his family and about Thrae. Sometimes the wind whipped his words away. Sometimes she focused too hard on where to next put her foot that she missed a word. Sometimes he switched out of English altogether.

He spoke about a world filled with light and laughter. He spoke about a full table of food and fruit for dessert. He spoke about his sister's jokes and the way his mother would sing him to sleep. His father had died in war when he was so little there wasn't much space for pain about that, except he saw how it affected his mother sometimes. He spoke about getting old enough to make money to support the family. He'd gotten in with the wrong people on Thrae, with people who wanted to break the hold the doormakers had. He hadn't cared about any of that at first. He'd cared about putting food on the table and buying his sister a dress in her favorite color. But later he had begun to care about what the doormakers were doing, and even later still, he had gotten caught.

He had sworn to protect his sister, and now she was dead.

His mother had warned him to be careful, and now she was dead.

He lapsed into silence, and the wind howled around them. The clouds began to change color. She knew she should watch those colors to see if they turned dark and gray and heavy.

Finally, into the silence, he said, "Why do those behind the door say you do not belong here?"

She felt safe against him. His heat and his kindness protected her.

Before she even knew she had made the decision, her story began to pour out. She couldn't bear to let him think he was alone. He knew what it was like. He would understand.

She started with the door in the field and told him that all of her family were like refugees. Maybe from the same war that had killed his father.

She didn't look at him, afraid she would lose this spark of courage. "We are all doormakers." Her mouth twisted around the word. "My grandmother, my father, my brothers. *Me.* We ran from all of this. All of the doors and all of the worlds. My father made me swear never to open a door. He wouldn't talk about what happened. Neither would my mother. That's how I knew it was bad. We talked about everything except that, but it was there anyway. Haunting us. My family is haunted by whatever happened. My older brother opened a door, my father went next, and then there was me."

Maella took a deep breath. She didn't want there to be any confusion. She didn't want to keep this secret anymore.

"I'm a doormaker. Keeper Shaul, the pattern-keeper, said I only have seven more doors to open before I die. I've already opened two since then. So I have five. Five doors left before I die. We didn't come through the door you came through. We came to Rock Heaven through a door I opened."

Her last words somehow bottled up her remaining courage and threw it into the creek where Claritsa and she had fought with Barth. She regretted opening her mouth, but it was too late to take back her confession.

The wind filled the empty space with its howl. Clouds blew in—dark gray, heavy, treacherous.

Sethlo supported her arm and most of her weight. He hadn't interrupted her once. She wanted to take that as a good sign. Suddenly, she became unsure. What if she didn't know him as well as she thought? What if she had made a huge mistake?

People liked to chant death to doormakers around here.

"Sethlo?" Her heartbeat increased. What had she done?

"I *knew* it."

# Chapter 23

"COME ON!" SETHLO YELLED, INCHES from Maella's ear.

It sounded like a whisper over the noise of the storm.

They struggled over rocks that had turned into an apocalyptic meatball soup of sharp edges. Lightning struck, threatening to electrocute them. Thunder shook the world and rattled Maella's teeth. Everything smelled like licorice lit on fire.

She had told him she was a doormaker, and the storm had struck and made a response impossible. What had he known? What did he think of her? She had felt trapped before by the clear blue sky and the way the air made her breathless and cracked her skin. But this storm was different. This was a slow suffocation. A drowning.

Maella ignored the pain in her raw feet, gritted her teeth, and followed after Sethlo. He searched for the safest way across the rocks, trying to find anything large enough in the storm to shelter them. There was no time to talk, but that didn't keep her from thinking—

*I knew it.*

How did he know?

Lightning struck again, branching into the ground at five different spots, circling them. Thunder almost threw her off her feet. The hair on her arms stood up, zinging with electricity.

She opened her mouth to drink the water that fell in sheets because damn everything if she wasn't going to get some clean water to moisten her throat before she died of drowning, or electrocution, or smashing her head on a rock.

Sethlo shouted, but she couldn't make sense of the words. His face loomed in front of her. Water beaded along his eyebrows and his eyelashes held the drops like pearls. The chaotic, jagged pattern of the lightning that struck somewhere behind Maella shone clear and precise in the mirror of his eyes.

If Claritsa were here right now, she would have rolled her eyes and laughed. *Don't you know you're about to drown?* Her expression would have said. *This is not a good time to be crushing.*

"I think I found something," Sethlo said, not hearing the delirious, delicious conversation in Maella's mind.

He took her hand and heat bloomed in her stomach. Before she knew it, a black hole loomed in front of them. Stones ringed it, forming a haphazard arch.

A cave.

Sethlo pulled at her to enter the darkness. She couldn't see anything beyond the opening. That was enough to give her the chills.

She dug in her heels. "No, Sethlo. We can't. This could be where the Klylup lives. I saw a place like this before and—"

"We don't have a choice," Sethlo said.

"No." Maella shook her head. Wet hair flopped over her shoulders. Rain pounded her face. Wind tore the words from her mouth. "No."

Sethlo left her.

She stood there stupidly, balancing on a stone. He just— disappeared into the darkness of what was probably a Klylup cave. Every part of her was drenched but she could barely feel it. She was so tired, so cold. She shouted for Sethlo to come back—don't leave her alone. She wanted him to tell her, how did you know? But there had been no pause in the storm or their search for shelter. Now she stood with a sick feeling in her stomach, waiting for the Klylup to barrel out of the darkness with Sethlo in its jaws.

A shadow detached itself from the larger darkness. Maella held her breath. The shadow was too small to be the Klylup— but it wasn't until Sethlo stood inches away from her that she breathed again.

"The Klylup isn't in there," Sethlo said.

The next steps she took were practically in the dark. She couldn't see the outline of Sethlo or stone. Stepping between two stones brought water up to her thighs. Strong arms gripped her waist and lifted her off her feet. Suddenly she was in the cave, out of the worst of the wind and rain, soaked to the bone.

The landscape lit up silver under the flashes of lightning. It was like they were on the moon while it was being ripped apart. One flash revealed piles of sticks in the cave. White and brown. Another flash showed her the brown sticks were planks from the smashed supply boxes. It took a third flash for her to recognize the white sticks.

Bones.

From the people the Klylup had killed and eaten.

Because there was no food for the monster in this place except for them and their meager supplies.

She shivered and buried her face in Sethlo's shirt. He smelled like stone and water and boy. Sethlo wrapped his arms around her like she had wrapped her arms around him at the door.

Finally, after long minutes, she unburied her face because she hadn't survived this long by hiding.

*That's exactly how you have survived this long*—her grandmother's voice—*You must always hide who you are.*

Fine, she could hide herself from others, but she promised she would not do that to herself. So she looked around the cave. She smelled its musty, wet, dead smells. She watched the water rise in pools around them, eventually forming one large ocean that covered the stones. Rain pelted this ocean's surface, pitting the water with millions of white spots.

They stood there, shivering, water to their knees, holding each other. They faced the storm.

And then, like a light switch—the storm turned off.

The thick gray soup of clouds dissolved into thin streamers of pink, orange, purple—sunset.

The pooled water mirrored the clouds. It lit everything in otherworldly colors. Except this was supposed to be Earth. Her world. But not her world.

Sethlo stirred next to her. The *licatherin* hidden inside the stones still let off a faint licorice scent. The two of them could have been the only people alive in the whole world.

"How did you know?" Maella said.

"We would have smelled the Klylup if it had been inside."

"That's not what I meant."

A long pause. "I know."

Maella waited for it—the disgust, the hate. She had come to this world when she was six. That's what her family had told her. Earth was home, but even still, she could feel that six years of foreignness every time she faced a door, or sometimes in the way Daniel looked at her, or in the way she almost recognized Sethlo's home language. She did not regret telling him she was a doormaker, but now she had to live with the consequences.

"Your story about the Klylup and somehow going to Thrae and then here—it did not make sense," Sethlo said.

Maella nodded.

"And when you think no one is looking, you walk like a doormaker."

Maella's stomach flipped. "You were watching me?"

Sethlo grimaced. "I only meant that sometimes you would forget on our walks together in the evening. But I did not know, not really. They must not know either—those on the other side of the door—that you are a doormaker. They know you are here and should not be. Otherwise, if they knew you were a doormaker, I think they would not sentence you to walk the rocks."

"I think they know *something*—"

"What did you do last night with Daniel?" There was a weird note in his voice and he chose not to look at Maella.

She searched his face, trying to figure out what he was really asking, but didn't understand. Her whole life could be summed up like that.

I don't understand.

"I made him help me open a door," Maella said. She wanted to make sure Sethlo knew nothing romantic had happened. There wasn't anything like that between her and Daniel. "To try to escape."

Sethlo sucked in a breath. "You were going to leave us? Claritsa?"

"No. Of course not," Maella said, frowning. "Every time I've opened a door, something terrible has happened. I didn't want anyone else to get hurt. We were going to open it and— once it was safe—tell everyone else."

Tension disappeared from Sethlo's expression and he glanced at Maella, thoughtful. "But it was not safe."

Maella shook her head.

"And you think they know about you now?"

"They know something happened but—"

"The pattern is breaking."

"Would it be so bad if those on the other side knew about me? Isn't a doormaker in charge on that side?" Maella became excited. Why hadn't she thought of this before?

"Maybe if they know a doormaker is down here, they'll release us."

"You have a precious gift, but they will imprison you in a place worse than this for control over it," Sethlo said. His voice flat.

"But—"

"There was a war," Sethlo said. "It isn't over. Your kind is hunted down. Haven't you heard enough yet from the others?"

"But other doormakers—"

"Will kill you even faster. Why did your family flee if not to escape death?"

"I don't think..." but she stopped because deep down she felt the truth of his words and she also felt shame. She had opened that door with Daniel so recklessly. She had ignored everything her family had taught her. She had ignored Claritsa's worries and warnings. She had done what she wanted—no matter that someone like her doing what she wanted got people killed. Claritsa had seen it: Maella was a nuclear explosion waiting to happen.

She couldn't bear the thought that pretty much everyone on multiple worlds wanted to kill her and she just might deserve it, so she changed the subject. "You sounded so sure—how did you know I was a doormaker?"

"I didn't," Sethlo said, his voice also quiet. "Not for sure."

Clouds floated by, turning the scene into a moving picture of colors. The beauty of it hurt. They might freeze tonight, but it would be pretty while it happened.

"But I thought, maybe," Sethlo said. "I thought it could be true, but if it wasn't..."

"Do you… Do you hate doormakers too, like the others? You don't care? Do you?"

"I hate the ones who have done things like this."

The door wasn't anywhere to be seen, but she knew what he meant all the same.

Maella remembered the door after escaping from Foster's noose. She had opened the door and left it open and Keeper Shaul had been murdered and Barth had been left behind. That probably counted as something 'like this.'

She shivered and sunk deeper into Sethlo's warmth. His arms tightened around her. Clouds drifted by, changing now from pink and orange to a deeper purple. The sun continued on its track, able to travel far from here, unlike the two of them.

Sethlo shifted, making a small wave in the water that lapped at their knees.

"We can't stay here," Sethlo said. "We'll freeze."

"I know," Maella said.

"You could open a door—"

Maella flinched away from Sethlo. The cold cut like a knife between them.

"What?"

"Could you not lift a stone? You did so with Daniel. Why not with me? If we found one big enough, I could help you lift it and—"

"Lava could spew out, or a lion could attack, or it might empty us into space for all we knew."

"Space?"

Maella tilted her head. He was from Thrae. He knew about the doors, pattern-keepers and their machines, and doormakers, but he didn't know about space. She tried to describe it. The more she explained, the more confused he looked in the fading light. Finally, she gave up. "It's not like it matters. Just know if I opened a door to that place, we would die in an instant."

Sethlo raised an eyebrow, like he wasn't sure if he should believe her. "But still."

"Claritsa and Daniel are too far away. No."

"This could be the way out. For all of us. You could open a door to one of the other worlds, or even just away from this place. It could be a door back to camp—back to Claritsa and Daniel."

"It doesn't work like that."

"Only because you won't try."

"No!" The cave swallowed up her shout. She had been ready to try opening a door again with Daniel that very night. Here she was, telling Sethlo opening another door was impossible. But the way Sethlo looked at her right now—greediness shined in his eyes. He saw power and control and they were too far away from camp, but he couldn't see that—and that scared her most of all.

"Do not be a coward! We're going to die out here, but you are afraid to try the only—"

Maella stepped away from him, deeper into the water. She felt cold now even in the places the water did not touch. "I tell you I have five doors left in me until I die—"

"If Keeper Shaul told you the truth—"

"I tell you about all the people in my family who have died opening doors. About my father and brother—"

"Who both are likely still alive."

What was this? Who was she talking to? What had she done, telling Sethlo she was a doormaker? Maella stepped back again. Her foot rocked on a stick. She looked down.

No, not a stick. A bone.

She looked back at Sethlo. There was a gleam in his eye as he returned her stare. He looked at her like she was a tool he wanted to use. But then the gleam faded.

He shook his head as if shaking off water. "I'm sorry, Maella. I didn't mean it. You don't—you don't have to open any doors. We'll find another way. There has to be another way."

He stepped through the water to the cave's entrance— away from her. Pausing, he hunched his shoulders, and then he turned back and held out his hand. "We should go out on top."

She looked at his hand and then at him.

"It's dry up there. It will be cold, but at least it's dry," Sethlo said. "And if the Klylup comes back, it won't be able to trap us in the cave. We've been through colder nights than this."

She wondered if he was remembering last night, when she'd returned cold and wet after opening a door—the very thing she now refused to do.

His hand reached out to her, palm up. The expression on his face was—she didn't know—a sort of apology, almost embarrassment.

But he was right about the cold and the cave.

She took his hand. He guided her out.

# Chapter 24

MAELLA'S ARM FELT LIKE SOMEONE had rubbed ice on it. She shifted, trying to bring her arm closer into her body and hit something soft and warm. Her eyes flew open. The starlight filled her vision with silver spots. Her head pounded from a headache, echoing the first headache she had gotten after arriving at Rock Heaven.

The scratchy cloth of Sethlo's clothes brushed her cheek. She sat up. He lay there on the boulder on his back. One arm thrown across his face, the other arm out along the rock. She had been sleeping against him, nestled into his side and using his arm for a pillow.

She didn't know how she felt about that. It was no big deal when it was the four of them sleeping together for warmth in their pile of blankets. Here, it was just the two of them and it felt different. Important somehow.

And—she would only ever admit this to Claritsa—it felt really, really good.

And that felt most dangerous of all.

Maella stood up even though this let the cold spill over her. She shivered and lost Sethlo's musty warmth, and the way his skin smelled like earth, like the only earth around in a world of stone. But it wasn't only that.

Something had woken her up. Something more than the cold on her arm.

Her dreams had been filled with fire and doors and black holes that sucked people apart limb by limb. The dreams left an ache. Her mother used to rub orange oil on her feet after a bad dream. The citrus scent would remind her of orchards, lazy summer days, and grass stains on her clothes while imagining adventures with Claritsa in fake worlds. Thinking about that helped a little bit, but made her even more sad. It had been almost a month since she had seen her mother.

With a start, she realized that meant she was sixteen years old now. Not that her age changed anything in Rock Heaven.

Everything had gone so still, like the wind had never existed. The pooled water still acted like a mirror. It was hard to tell where the milky whiteness of the night sky ended and where the stones began. Sometimes the stars moved. She knew these weren't really stars. They traveled too quickly in their orbit across the sky.

Satellites.

Somehow, this place existed. Somehow, the rest of Earth hadn't found it yet.

She wondered what the doors were made of and why all the cameras and satellites and surveillance people hadn't noticed. This was Earth. People didn't get lost here, did they?

Except the camp hadn't been found. While she thought that Harry and Lirella and the others were capable of lying just like any other human being, she didn't think they were lying about this being Earth. She could see the satellites in the sky after all, and the moon and the stars felt like she remembered them feeling, even if mining for the *licatherin* felt so very wrong.

Sethlo stirred at her feet. She held her breath, fearing he was about to awaken. He said he didn't care that she was a doormaker. He didn't hate her. But then he had called her a coward because she wasn't willing to open a door.

Was she a coward?

The silvery light cast long shadows on the stones. She could almost smell the water in the air as it evaporated. By morning, most of it would be gone.

A small stone stuck out of the water below them, near the cave entrance. She let the cold air touch every part of her lungs. The world was calm and that calmness bled into her. It made her movements easy. She slid down the side of the stones that covered the cave, the rough grain of it scraping her bare skin raw. Her feet splashed into the water that was now only an inch or so deep.

The shock of the water's icy coldness made her want to climb back up and nestle into Sethlo's warmth. She forced herself to crouch next to the stone. It did not vibrate as strongly as the ones near the door in the sky.

She could just pick it up.

It would take some physical effort. She'd need to use her legs, not her back, as her grandmother would shout.

It wouldn't be like earlier, when she had felt such a flash of anger she'd wanted to turn over a million stones. Or like with Daniel, when that recklessness threw away all sense of control and reason.

It would be a simple experiment.

Her hand grazed the top of the stone. Smooth to the touch, vibrating against her. Maybe it had existed for hundreds or even thousands of years at this exact spot. Maybe storm after storm had pounded it smooth. She traced her family's symbol onto the surface of the rock with her finger. Invisible, yet it made her so homesick she could cry.

*A curved quarter moon, its points sharp like knives—that's us, the doormakers. Three links, separate yet attached, pierced by the moon.*

A rush of memories overcame Maella. Along with these memories, Grandmother and her mother and father whispered stern warnings in her ear. They reminded her of all the supposed deaths that had come before now—her great aunt and uncle, her cousin.

But her brother and father had opened a door, and according to Keeper Shaul's pattern-machine, might both still be alive.

She could use another one of her doors and have four left. Just to see.

Maybe Sethlo was right. Maybe the door would open to her house. To her mother and her creek and her younger brother.

Maybe the door would suck her into a starry void.

She looked around.

Wait, that had already happened.

She let a small smile creep onto her lips in the darkness.

Starry void.

Check.

She took her hand away from the rock. No, she wasn't going to open it.

Though she desperately wanted to return to her family, this rock would not take her there.

Still, something important changed inside of her.

If she needed to open another door to save herself, to save someone she cared about—she would, but she promised herself she would not do it recklessly, or foolishly, or for greed, or power. The doors and everything they stood for still scared her, but sometimes you had to do the thing that scared you most.

Only one door fit what she needed right now—both open and safe on the other side—if you didn't count the guards waiting to kill them. She and Sethlo had searched all of Rock Heaven and everything kept coming back to the door in the sky, but how—

Maella heard a snuffle. She looked around, afraid of what she would find. The darkness that sucked in all light. The green jeweled eyes. Thinking about opening a door couldn't have drawn out the Klylup, could it?

Far away, a large shape slithered across the stones.

Lirella had finally told the story one night during a storm, about how the Klylup had been pushed through the door to Rock Heaven while it was still a baby and small enough to fit. How it had not been old enough to fly. The crash to the stones had torn off one of its wings. Some prisoners argued for taking care of it because—well, even knowing what it would grow up to be they could not stand watching a baby in such pain. Before Lirella and the others could kill the Klylup, some of the prisoners stole it away, kept it hidden, and cared for it until there was no food and the Klylup became big enough and finally turned on them for food.

She waited for the Klylup to notice her. After all, she was near its cave with the sticks of wood and bone.

The silence ran deep. No birds, no insects, no breeze, not even Sethlo's breathing. Just her hand on the stone, waiting for the monster to turn on her.

The Klylup disappeared in the dark, headed away from the cave. She thought about following it. Where could it be going?

Wait.

There really was a sound now.

A beat. Like the drum circles they played to celebrate surviving the storms.

Maella stood up.

Maybe they had only dragged Claritsa away to protect her from the Klylup. Maybe she was drumming to help Maella and Sethlo find their way back to camp!

She scrambled up the boulder, ignoring the pain that flared in her feet, and shook Sethlo awake. He groaned and jerked his arm off his face. His eyes flew open, shining in the starlight.

"Do you hear that?"

Sethlo sat up. He looked around and then at her. "What is it?"

"You don't hear that?"

Sethlo stood up and turned in a circle, listening, looking. That's when Maella realized.

The drumming came from inside of her—it was her heartbeat.

"What's wrong?" Sethlo said. "I don't hear anything."

Embarrassment flooded Maella, drowning out the heartbeat she'd mistaken for the camp's rescue. "Forget it."

"No, what did you hear?"

She couldn't look him in the eye, fearing he would read the truth of her stupidity. "It's nothing. I thought I heard something, but it's nothing."

The Klylup had disappeared instead of returning to its cave. A part of her wondered, like the drum beat, if the Klylup had been there at all. She turned her face to the night sky. The stars were so bright, the Milky Way like a brush of white paint.

She thought it was just a trick of the eyes this time—like her ears had tricked her. Focusing on this trick, she tried to will it away because she didn't want to be a fool twice over.

Sethlo kept asking what she had heard, what she was hearing. Finally, he turned to see what she was looking at.

She feared her eyes were making another mistake until he stilled.

"Do you see it?" Maella finally risked the words.

Sometimes star patterns made shapes like dippers and unicorns and twins and fish and belts. But Maella had only ever seen *this* shape in one place—a dark rectangle outlined in light.

The door.

They had traveled all the way around to the front of it and by luck—really bad dreams—Maella had woken while it was dark enough to see how its wrongness spilled light out from another world and into this one.

If they followed the door, they would find the camp.

Maella slid down the boulder again, ignoring the rawness of her skin. Sethlo followed close behind. She passed over the stone that had held her attention so completely, her feet splashing in the water, and finally felt in control of herself.

Soon her feet went blissfully numb as she walked to that strange rectangle in the sky. Maella smelled the sterile, coarse rock, and that hint of licorice that spoke of hidden *licatherin*. Little clouds of moisture puffed from their mouths. The world felt spookier around them for what it lacked: the buzz of insects, the call of animals, the organic dampness of plants, the decomposing smell of soil, the sense of being part of all life on earth. Here they were separate, alone, abandoned.

Stars began to fade. She didn't notice it at first, and then it happened all of a sudden. The sky turned from deep purple to light purple, and then to gray. Opposite their skin color transformation. Sunlight threatened to spill over the horizon.

The door's outline disappeared in the light. It didn't matter, though. They had the direction now.

Her feet hurt, but Sethlo let her set the pace. She had spent enough weeks on the rocks that she wasn't as slow as she had been at first. And she had finally broken the habit of keeping her hands behind her back. They walked for a long time, but not yet as long as it had taken for them to get lost. Sethlo complained of a headache. They were hungry, thirsty, tired— no surprise that it affected their minds. But Maella noticed an odd shape breaking up the stones.

It was brown, not gray.

She veered toward it.

Sethlo jerked to a stop. "What…"

"Wait there," Maella said. "Hold our path. I need to see…I just need to see."

Sethlo sat down on a rock, following her request without protest. He cupped his hand into one of the nearby puddles and drank from the water and gazed across the stones, lost in thought.

Maella hurried forward, knowing she was wasting time to get back to Claritsa, and afraid they would lose the path back. But then she realized there was no way for her to lose the path now, not this close to the door. She could feel its vibrations, like how she imagined a water-seeker's stick might shake.

Except in her case, she was the stick.

She stopped.

That's what it was. That's what had seemed odd to her.

She had seen a stick.

"Maybe it's a magic stick, Maella." She said this out loud, mimicking Claritsa's voice because that's what Claritsa would have said seeing all this.

"What?" Sethlo called out.

Maella shook her head. Magic stick indeed. She rolled her eyes at herself. But it still wasn't right. Or rather, maybe this was the only right thing she'd seen in a long time. As she got closer, she saw gnarled branches connecting to a pitted trunk. All of it well on its way to crumbling into a bunch of bark chips.

A tree.

A tree had rooted itself in between the stones. Its roots had the strength to dig into the bedrock and take what it needed to grow into something that would have been taller than her if it were still upright.

It wasn't, though. It was dead now.

But she imagined it alive. She imagined it taller. She imagined the knots on its twisted trunk making the perfect holds for hands and feet. She imagined the rough feel of bark, a welcome texture compared to the endless stone that scraped her skin raw. She imagined climbing into the limbs, the green leaves shaking from a breeze and hiding her. She imagined tripping down from its branches and laughing because it was Claritsa's turn now to hide somewhere in their little fairytale world.

"Maella?"

Sethlo's voice brought Maella back to the dead tree in front of her. She didn't know if it was the kind of tree that even grew leaves. It was too small to carry anyone's weight. She brushed its bark with her hand just to remember what it felt like to touch something other than stone. Brown flakes fell away at her touch. She could see the black scar that ran down its center. The trunk had been split by a lightning strike.

She stood up. It was a tree. It was dead.

It would not get her home or even free Claritsa and Daniel.

It would not keep Lirella from making them walk the rocks.

It wouldn't make her the One Doormaker to find the One Door or whatever other crappy beliefs people had that would make them hurt her and her friends just because she was born a certain way.

She turned away from the tree. Sethlo was a little dot on a little rock. Had she really walked that far? How had she seen the tree?

Shaking her head, she told herself it didn't matter.

She looked back once, because it was nice to see something that wasn't a rock. She wanted to fix its shape, texture, and color in her mind to describe it to Claritsa and make her smile at the memory of the silly hide-and-seek games they had played in their forest.

Maybe it was a trick of the light again. Maybe the angle of the sun had shifted. Maybe Maella had taken just enough of a different path back to Sethlo. The tree's shape transformed into a sort of crude ladder lying broken and twisted across the stone.

She didn't know why her mind saw such a thing out of this poor dead tree's decomposing body. But she did.

Her imagination conjured up crates dropped from the sky to smash to bits on the ground. The collection of bone and wood in the Klylup's cave. A ladder smoothly gliding into and out of this world.

A whisper of an idea made her shiver in spite of the sun.

# Chapter 25

"WHAT DO YOU THINK THE doors are made of?" Maella asked.

It helped to take her mind off what might be happening to Claritsa and Daniel. They traveled across the stones as fast as they could, but there was nothing she could do until they got back to camp.

"I do not know," Sethlo said, but he didn't seem sure about not being sure.

He had asked about what she'd seen. She told him about the tree and her idea about the ladder. He quickly dismissed it. There wasn't enough wood at camp, tree included, to build a ladder tall enough to reach the door. But Maella could not let go of the idea so easily.

"Harry says they're wormholes," Maella said.

"What are wormholes?"

She tried to explain, but it went a lot like the space conversation. Finally, she gave up. "Some of them say it's all the same world, just different places." But Maella couldn't believe that either. She grew up in a world that claimed every part of it had been mapped and photographed and posted on social media. Places like Foster's town and the Klylup monster and Keeper Shaul's *licatherin*-eating machine didn't exist in a world like Earth.

Except Maella and the rest of them were here, weren't they? Here with an open door that no one else on Earth had yet found. Maella shook her head. No, not the same world. Not even the same world at different times. Time travel was for science fiction movies.

"What do you think?" Maella asked again.

"Some people think you're visiting the dead. Some people think going through a door opened by a doormaker makes you one of the dead. That it's an entrance to the afterlife. Or that you might as well be dead after going through a door because it makes you not quite human anymore and you'll carry the taint for the rest of your life. That's…that's what my uncle believes."

"He's a Sechnel believer?" She had heard enough of Giffen's late night debates to understand it was a religion focused on the righting of wrongs, death, and cleansing, and that the doormakers and doors were essentially their version of devils and hells.

"He's one of the leaders," Sethlo said. "Or he was."

"So he believes we each die after passing through a door and that this is the afterlife?"

Sethlo nodded.

"But you—"

"I don't know what I think." Sethlo rubbed his face with his hands. "I've been taught all these things and yet I always thought they were fairy tales until I saw a doormaker open a door. And then all I saw was power. I saw power and people using that power to hurt others. And I wanted it—to stop it. It doesn't matter who or how. It just matters."

Maella tried to wrap her mind around Sethlo's words. People thought going through a door made them dead or visit the dead? No wonder people were afraid of her. No wonder they hated people like her.

"I don't want to hurt anyone." She may not understand what was wrong with her, but she at least knew that.

The sun passed the halfway mark in the sky. Water from the storm the night before was gone—dried up—though they had plenty to drink before it evaporated. But food was a different story. The water had filled her up for a time, then had left her feeling even emptier and more exhausted. It was not the water they were used to anymore. It had been clean and refreshing, but all she really wanted was a drink of the camp's gray water and a stupid mashed pancake infused with *licatherin*.

They saw the familiar boulders of camp. The place looked quiet, though off in the mine's direction floated sounds of people working.

Maella and Sethlo exchanged a look. Neither of them knew what to do except to just see what they could see. But when they reached the door and the stones where Sethlo's uncle had beaten him, Lirella stood up from the guard's spot and met them.

"So you are still alive," Lirella said, stopping a few feet away. "It would have been better if you had not returned."

Neither Maella nor Sethlo said anything.

From this angle, from just at the front of it like they were, the dark wood slates of the door were the most obvious mark in the sky.

"You have made those on the other side of the door very angry with us."

"Where are Claritsa and Daniel?" Maella said.

Lirella held up a hand. "You lied to all of us." She held Maella's gaze, her expression hard and unreadable. "You must walk the rocks. The door commands it."

"You can't send her away!" Sethlo said. "You can't just kill her."

"Where are they?" Panic began to close Maella's throat. Lirella would not have already sent them out to walk the rocks, would she?

"She will kill us, just by staying," Lirella said simply. "Just by existing, because they will know." She cocked her head toward the door in the sky.

Maella's stomach growled. She wanted to shout at Lirella and the door and the world. She couldn't think straight. She was so hungry, so thirsty.

"Come away," Lirella said. "Come drink as much of the gray water as you need before you follow after your friends. It will help your headaches."

Claritsa and Daniel had been sent to walk the rocks. That's what Lirella was saying. Maella wanted to throw up.

"It is plain on your faces." Lirella inclined her head. "The *licatherin* acts as a...I do not know the English word. It creates the desire to do things. It helps you stay awake. It helps you work without feeling the work as much."

Barth's face appeared as if conjured by her words. His father had been involved in that sort of thing. She didn't know exactly what, only that Barth had mixed Esson into it before he had gone through the door.

Part of her wanted to follow after Claritsa immediately. Another part of her wanted to sit for just a moment. And a part that scared her more than a little was how she desperately wanted a long drink of the gray water.

Lirella stared up at the door. "Come away." She turned and left them to follow.

Maella hurried after Lirella as fury coiled into her chest. She could threaten them. All of them. She could make them listen. She could make them pay.

When they broke into the ring of boulders that protected them from the Klylup, Maella turned on Lirella. "There is something you should know about me."

She crouched low to the ground, next to a stone much like the one from the night before, and rested a hand on it. Smooth, rounded, heavy, but not too heavy. She had promised herself not to open a door in anger, but that promise held no power over her now.

"Maella," Sethlo said.

Lirella looked between both of them. "Your friends are safe. They are hiding in the mine."

Maella jerked her hand away from the rock like it burned. "But—"

"We watch the door and the door watches us."

Maella wanted to scream.

Sethlo looked confused. "That was—"

"A necessary disguise," Lirella said. "We can only hope it works. At least, at least you have eight days to prepare. You must understand, we will all die if they stop the food. But many of us think they won't stop the food. They need the *licatherin* too much now."

"But they could send in more prisoners for that. They don't need us, they only need someone to mine it," Sethlo said. "If we won't—"

"That is the gamble we are making," Lirella interrupted.

"I don't know what to say," Maella said.

"You are one of us," Lirella said simply. "No matter how you got here."

Maella felt ashamed at her fury, her suspicions, her selfishness.

Lirella brought out a hardened pancake and handed it over. It had never looked so delicious.

Maella broke the pancake in two, but it didn't break exactly equal. She sighed and looked at the two portions and how Sethlo towered over her.

She handed him the bigger piece of the two without looking.

He gobbled it down.

Eating her portion more slowly, she took great gulps of the gray water. It did not settle the grumbling of her stomach, but did flood energy back into her body.

She pretended that it was enough.

She pretended she hadn't just drugged herself.

Lirella closed the crate of food. The planks reminded Maella of the tree and how, just for an instant, it had looked like a ladder lying on its side.

The door in the sky called to her like a siren.

Sethlo's eyes were bloodshot, his eyelashes crusty from salt. He was still fully purple, like her. The gray dust hadn't overtaken them yet after the storm had washed it all away. The mine would fix that soon enough once they were back to work inside its pit. A dark greenish circle marked the underside of his chin, a bruise from one of his uncle's punches.

"Ready?" Sethlo said.

Maella nodded.

They passed along the cliff's lip at the edge of the mine. Just hearing the hammers and grinding and pulleys made her bones ache and her skin feel soggy. Maella silently apologized for taking even the little bit of food that they had eaten. She promised herself she would make up for it.

They just needed a ladder.

# Chapter 26

TWO FIGURES WORKED IN THE shadows of the mine, out of sight of the door in the sky.

"Claritsa?"

Claritsa stopped pounding the stone. Her braids were thick with gray dust that sent a cloud over Maella as they slammed together in a fierce hug.

Maella cried her welcome and Claritsa returned it.

"Where did you go?"

"Are you okay?"

"Did Lirella tell you?"

"We can't let them starve because of us."

They talked over each other, laughing—and trying not to cry. It had all been too much. It was all still too much.

"I told her about what happened," Daniel said, coming up. "About the oil door." He glanced at Sethlo.

"He knows," Maella said, and then turned to Claritsa. "I should have told you from the beginning."

Claritsa shook her head. "You should have."

"I'm sorry," Maella said. She had opened the door and the oil had spurted out and Maella was pretty sure it was her fault those on Thrae knew about them now.

"Sethlo."

Dedion approached. Emotions washed over the older man's face. They came and went too quickly for Maella to read them all. His words were low, steady, carefully chosen, spoken in Thrae.

The Thrae phrasing tugged at her memories. This time, Maella thought she caught the words for death and door.

Another silence, and then his uncle returned to the far side of the mine.

Sethlo looked after his uncle with a pained, almost horrified expression on his face.

Aretha walked up with Harry. "He believes we all died when we went through the door." She spoke in English with a guttural Rathe-English accent. Next to Dedion's lighter brown skin, her deep purple skin glowed. "He is a Sechnel believer. One who thinks of the doors as an afterlife where people get stuck. He believes that he is paying for things he did wrong by being here with the murderer of his sister and niece. He apologizes to the Sechnel for his violence and promises to do better as penance and as a way to earn himself a spot out of this hell."

Sethlo's face had gone pale lavender.

"That was all of it," Aretha said, kindness in her eyes. She did not look at Maella with that kind of kindness—ever—even in all the days Maella had worked with her in the panning pit.

"Not all of it," Sethlo said in a strangled voice. "You did not tell them about the last part."

"I did not..." Aretha started. "I did not think there was need."

Sethlo drew in a breath that made his body shudder. "He thinks I am dead, just like him, just like all of us. Because we all went through the door. Except he thinks that I'm an evil spirit who has been sent to torture him in his grief. We had never been close, but this—he says that I am not even human now."

Aretha hung her head. "We did not need to know—"

"But he went through the door too—" Maella said.

"We have to escape this place." Daniel looked knowingly at Maella. "Aretha's been translating—"

"Daniel—" Claritsa interrupted. There was a grim set to her jaw.

"I'm sorry, but your uncle is crazy, Sethlo. He thinks—"

"Daniel!"

"He thinks the only way is to close the door once and for all. He thinks the only way to make things right again means we all have to kill ourselves."

"But that doesn't make sense," Maella said.

Sethlo's face turned a sickly, washed-out lavender.

"If he believes we're already dead," Maella said, "how could we kill ourselves?"

Aretha shook her head. "That is not what you should worry about. You should worry because Dedion has convinced others that he is right and that it is their duty to act soon."

# Chapter 27

MAELLA AND HER GROUP WORKED the mine, out of sight of the door. She thought of them as her group now. Claritsa, Daniel, Sethlo, maybe even Harry and Aretha. She didn't know why others weren't included. Lirella had been kind. Giffen had been fair. Erentia tolerated her. Yet, they did not belong to her.

Maella, Claritsa, and Daniel were not allowed to return to the safety of the boulders that night. They stayed in the mine pit. Sethlo stayed with them.

She told Claritsa and Daniel her idea about building a ladder. Daniel agreed with Sethlo—there would not be enough wood. But Claritsa thought they should try, anyway.

With their own ladder and a big distraction and Harry's glue, it might work.

Harry stayed behind in the mine, too. He and another prisoner named Jessuf worked on Harry's glue experiments. Maella and the rest worked long past when the other prisoners returned to camp to get him more *licatherin* for his experiments. She would need that glue for the ladder. Plus, it was the least they could do while a death sentence hung over everyone in camp because of them.

Maella thought it was hilarious, in a hysterical sort of way, that she pretty much agreed with Dedion. The difference in their plans was in one very important timing detail.

Dedion wanted to close the door for good.

So did Maella.

She just wanted to wait until they were all on the other side.

"It's not fair," Maella said.

Claritsa frowned and paused after the next swish-swish-twirl of the panning bucket. They both stood knee deep in the water, sifting for *licatherin* for Harry.

"Don't lose it now."

Maella glanced up. Surprised. She shouldn't have been. This was Claritsa. You didn't rattle Claritsa. Well, you could, but she would die before showing it.

"You're the only person giving us a chance and keeping things together right now," Claritsa said. "Every day I feel like this place is going to suffocate me. I taste the rock, I chew on it, I sleep with it in my lungs. Someday I'm not going to wake up because it will have filled me up." Claritsa blinked tears away and scratched at her eyes, revealing purple streaks under the gray dust.

Jessuf walked up and took one of the full, sifted buckets. Instead of bringing it to the next station, he took it to Harry's experiments.

They spent the night together, all of them in a sort of dog pile for warmth. Thinking, dreaming, scheming. Maella and Claritsa argued for building the ladder. Sethlo and Daniel argued for Maella opening another door. They finally decided on both. They would build the ladder, but Maella would be the back-up plan.

When the prisoners returned to the mine in the early morning, Maella forced herself to walk over to the pipe of gray water. Turning the valve, a water flooded her cupped hands. She took large gulps of it to drug herself into waking up and working.

When Maella returned to Claritsa, she told her what Lirella had said about the water.

Claritsa shook her head. "Daniel figured that out a long time ago."

"What?"

"He was working with Barth's dad. He said the *licatherin* is sort of like…you're not going to like this."

"Just tell me."

"It's a stimulant. Sort of like cocaine. Especially with the way we breathe it, eat it, and absorb it."

Maella looked down at her skin. Gray dust, purple underneath. Gray grit in her lungs, gray water down her throat. "Why didn't you say—"

"What can we do? It's the way it is here. It's the only way to survive."

Maella looked around the pit with new eyes. Were they all drug addicts now?

Screams cut off her thoughts.

Someone on the path out of the mine was running and shouting.

A dark shape appeared at the rim, the sun behind it. The creature stepped onto the path, but the path wasn't large enough. Stone crumbled under its feet.

Maella dropped her panning bucket.

Klylup.

"We have to hide," Claritsa said.

"It's never come to the mine like this," Maella said. What had woken it? The door had not opened, otherwise they would have heard the horn. It seemed like she was cursed to bring the Klylup with her wherever she went.

The monster took delicate steps down the path while the human before it ran for shelter. Maella remembered the cave, its muddy coldness, the way the air smelled both rotten and damp. Adrenaline raced through her as she relived the camp attacks, huddled with Claritsa, Daniel, and Sethlo, hoping that they would all make it through the night.

The Klylup reached the bottom of the pit. Its body was the size of a small car and its weight had destroyed the path. Large eyes blinked, surveying the mind. The Klylup struck out a claw, and a cart disintegrated. Shrapnel sprayed Maella's cheek. Claritsa grabbed her hand. The Klylup lunged, lashing its tail around. Another shout, and then there was a low, terrible scream that cut off abruptly. Maella's stomach twisted as she remembered the valley. The Klylup would take out everyone in the mining pit like it had in the valley.

Maella's heart pounded. Her eyes searched for where to go. Erentia and Miall were at the grinding rock—closest to the Klylup. Aretha, Harry, and Lirella were nearby. No one knew where to go, no one knew what would hide them. Jessuf crossed their path, equipment jumbled up in his arms. The whites of his eyes showed. He looked at them but didn't see them.

Another scream tore across the pit. Maella wanted to slap her hands over her ears. Instead, she forced herself forward.

"Jessuf!"

He stared at her blankly.

"Jessuf, where do we go?"

His eyes cleared for a moment. He looked at Maella and really saw her, but then all of his equipment fell out of his hands and crashed against the stones underneath their feet. He looked beyond Maella, at something behind her.

She turned as if in slow motion.

The Klylup had locked on.

Its green eyes shined like jewels even though its face was in shadow. The sun was behind it again, but its massive body blocked the light. If it took just a few more steps forward, she would enter its cold shadow.

Claritsa shuddered next to her.

This caught the Klylup's attention, and it cocked its head and long ears. Its tail lashed against the mining equipment. The bones from its broken wing stuck out against its dark skin, reminding Maella of the Klylup's cave full of bones. Red blood rimmed its lips. Purple lined its eyes. Maella fought off nausea and stepped back. The Klylup froze. Alert. Focused. Maella looked for escape without moving any part of her. Then she saw it. The grinding boulder rested against another smaller boulder. In between there was a gap large enough to fit people, but maybe not large enough for a Klylup.

Maella squeezed Claritsa's hand and didn't let up until Claritsa saw what Maella saw. Understanding bloomed across Claritsa's face.

Maella mouthed the count. "One…two—"

"Run!" Claritsa shouted. She seized Maella's hand and dashed for the boulders.

The Klylup roared. Its hot breath seared the back of Maella's neck. Claritsa pumped her legs across the stones. Maella ran, stumbling, feet still raw. If Maella didn't know better, she would have thought they were back home, running from Barth through the grass instead of from the Klylup across the stones. Both creatures had wanted to catch her. Both wanted to hurt her in some way.

But Barth had been left behind to die.

No. *She* had left him behind.

The Klylup trumpeted. The sound echoed until it felt like there were dozens of Klylups in the pit.

She stumbled and fell. Hands grabbed her by the arms and lifted her. Dark purple arms, dark stubby hair, a face framed in sweat and gray dust. Giffen. He said something in Thrae. She didn't know what he said, but knew what he meant—get up or die.

Claritsa was now in the shadow of the boulders, in the safe space between. Maella and Giffen slid in next to her, the Klylup almost on top of them. Every part of Maella screamed in pain. Scraped skin, throbbing head, bloody knees. She scrabbled deeper into the rock, wedging herself between Claritsa and Giffen.

The Klylup hit the boulders like a truck slamming into a wall.

The boulders shifted but held. They came together at the other end as if forming the corner of two walls. Maybe a mouse or a bird could get through that gap, but no human.

There was only one way out and the Klylup blocked it.

The boulders shifted again, as if moved by an earthquake. A hot gust of swampy licorice wind blew over them, leaving Maella sticky.

Its snout was right there. Stained with both red and purple. Maella reached out a hand. Its trumpet sound blew through her ears, her brain, her body, her soul. When the sound stopped, the ringing began. Her ears felt hot and like liquid dripped out of them. All she could hear was the ringing. All she could see was how Giffen's hands shook as he braced himself on the ground and how Claritsa's grim set to her lips said she was ready to die.

The Klylup slammed against the boulders and lifted them, raining down dust.

She could reach out and touch the rock if she wanted to. The vibrations called out to her, telling her the rock had formed a door somehow. They could escape through that door. If it didn't kill them first. Or if the Klylup didn't drop the boulder and turn them into bloody human pancakes.

She reached out her hand again, this time moving it from the Klylup's snout, hot breath, white teeth, and to the boulder. Her hand wavered in the air, inches away. The rock lifted again, skidded a few inches backward, dropped. Stones beneath it pulverized into dust. Claritsa coughed. Giffen shouted something.

The Klylup pressed its green eye against the gap. Its pupil rolled around and locked onto each one of them. First Claritsa, then Giffen, and finally Maella. It looked at her like it knew her.

She had been in its cave. She had seen the bones. Maybe it did know her. Maybe it knew her better than she knew herself. There was no escape. It had to be the boulder. It had to be the door.

Maella's ears still rang. Her hand trembled as she brushed it against the stone. Nothing happened because the stone touched the ground. She pulled her hand back to her side like it had been burned. She had already left Barth behind. If she did this, she would leave behind Daniel, Sethlo, Harry, everyone here who had helped them. If she got the timing wrong, they'd be crushed trying to make it through the door when the boulder dropped on top of them. If she opened the door, something worse than the Klylup could come out.

Claritsa shook her shoulder. "Don't do it!" Not that Maella could hear her over the ringing. But she could see the words Claritsa's mouth formed.

She could list all the reasons why she shouldn't. They were good reasons, but those reasons wouldn't save them.

Claritsa pleaded with her eyes.

Maella forced her hand to touch the boulder. She held her breath, waiting for the Klylup to hurl itself against the stone one more time.

Giffen slammed into Maella, pushing her away from the boulder. He scrambled out. Toward the eye.

There was a hint of something gray in his hands.

A stone.

He raised the stone above his head and brought it down on the green eye.

The Klylup screamed. Light flooded in. Everything was dark gray—wet from the humidity of the Klylup's breath.

Before Maella had time to react, Giffen raised the rock again, even though there was nothing to strike. Everything around him was light, so bright. He was a dark shadow, holding that rock above his head. Something darker swooped down.

Giffen was lifted into the air. He hung there, like the door hung in the sky—as if from nothing. Except this nothing was dark and monstrous and had its white teeth around his hands around the stone. Maella screamed.

The Klylup tossed its head and Giffen flipped end over end in the air like a horrifying acrobatic performance.

Maella screamed. "No!"

The Klylup opened its mouth. Giffen disappeared head first, the Klylup gulping him down.

Her mind didn't want to believe what it had just seen. Fury and pain let her ignore everything except what was in front of her. She rushed forward.

Something grabbed her ankle and she went down. Hard.

Her face slammed into a stone. Her nose went numb, and then she felt hot liquid drip before her nose began to throb. She scrabbled forward, determined, but the Klylup had already rushed away to look for another target.

Maella screamed and pounded the ground. "Come back! Come back and fight me!"

Claritsa crouched next to her, hands flat on the stones. All scratched up and looking far too delicate for work like this— grinding stones, getting high, dying from starvation.

The ringing took over all sound, except Maella *knew* Claritsa could still read the words Maella's lips formed. "Why did you try to stop me? I could have saved him!"

# Chapter 28

NOW THAT MAELLA KNEW WHAT the *licatherin* did, she guzzled the gray water. She took only a few bites of the pancake they brought for breakfast before sharing the rest with someone else. She impatiently waited for the *licatherin* to flood her veins so that she could beat all thought out on the rocks.

Giffen had been killed. Lirella was inconsolable. Much of the mining equipment was destroyed.

Claritsa was not to blame for any of that. Except. Maella had hesitated and Giffen was dead. If she had been faster, maybe she could have saved him.

After the attack, after the Klylup had retreated, after they had held a moment of silence for Giffen even though there was no body to bury, Erentia directed the others to salvage the equipment and take inventory.

They could mine with what was left, but it would take twice as long to produce the same amount of *licatherin* as before.

They would not make the quota in time for the next exchange.

But the next morning, the door opened.

When the horn sounded, Maella, Claritsa, and Daniel hid in the mine. Though they had been given eight days, Erentia wanted those on the other side of the door to believe the camp had already sent the three to walk the rocks. No one knew why the door had opened before the normal time, but Sethlo was not condemned with them and so he went to find out.

The three of them huddled against the wall of the mine, in the warmth of the sun, out of sight of the door. For once, Maella was dry and even warm. Claritsa sat next to her on the stones, splaying her bare feet out in the sun. None of them had shoes anymore.

"Do you really think you could have saved Giffen?" Claritsa said. She had bitten her lip until it bled.

Maella touched her nose. Still sore, but not broken. Maella knew what it felt like to have guilt eat you up inside. She didn't want Claritsa to live like that. Not ever.

"No," Maella said. "I don't think so. You're right, it would have killed all of us."

But part of Maella knew that wasn't true. Terrible things happened when she opened doors, but it wasn't anything like what she had been taught. She had survived three doors now. That was proof enough.

But this she knew—Claritsa had only ever stood by her side and done what she thought was right.

"Giffen is not your fault," Maella said, putting every scrap of sureness she could into her voice.

Claritsa sighed as if relieved, but also not quite believing.

Maella squeezed her hand.

It seemed like they waited an eternity in the mine, straining their ears for a hint of what was happening. And, of course, on the lookout for the Klylup. When Sethlo returned, slipping down the trail of stones to the bottom of the pit, his face was grim and pale from gray dust. He had snuck away after the Klylup was sighted. Everyone else had made it back to camp in time. To the safety of the boulders. The Klylup worried at the camp now. They were safe in the mine for the moment.

Sethlo said Erentia told the Thrae guards about Giffen's death. Everyone thought he died trying to protect the two girls. But only Maella and Claritsa knew that Maella could have saved him.

Maybe.

The door could have killed him too, she told herself. But what if she had not hesitated? Would Giffen still be alive?

"The bald man, with the rings on his fingers," Sethlo said. "He called himself Ambassador Utheril. He appeared and called out Lirella by name. They had to go get her from camp. She explained about the equipment but he said the *licatherin* production must continue. And then they argued, shouting at each other, separated by all that sky. Erentia told him we had sent the three of you to walk the rocks but that we were out of food and down a worker and had broken equipment that needed to be replaced."

A strange look came into Sethlo's eyes.

"Tell us, Sethlo," Claritsa said.

"First, they...they sent down tools. Duplicates of everything, whether it was broken or not. It wasn't new equipment. Everyone could see the way the metal had been worn and pitted in spots, but it all works. Then they sent down a crate of food."

"So they believed everything," Daniel said, slamming his fist into the stone. "They've rewarded Lirella and everyone else for doing what they were told, for sending us out on the rocks!"

"But Daniel," Claritsa said helplessly. "They lied for us, they—"

"No," Sethlo said. "That's not the end of it. They know we've been hiding you. They know you haven't been sent to walk the rocks."

"But that can't be," Maella said. "Why would they give us equipment and food?"

"That's not the worst of it—or maybe the best of it—if you're Jessuf right now. The door was wide open but no one paid any attention to it. They were cracking open the food. They were going over the wood, because they had lowered the crate with rope. Nothing was smashed. There were actually real pieces of fruit and lettuce—"

All their mouths salivated.

"Sethlo—"

"They let Jessuf go home."

Maella rose to her feet. "I don't understand."

"They said he had served his time and it was up and they brought out the ladder and he climbed it and they...they let him through the door."

The four of them looked at each other in stunned silence. No one in Rock Heaven knew how long their sentence was supposed to last. No one had ever completed their term. It was assumed Rock Heaven was a life sentence.

"I checked," Sethlo said finally. "That's never happened before. No one remembers them ever taking someone back through the door. But they said—they said everyone's sentence would be extended and they would cut off the food if they continued to hide the three of you after the eight days. Or their sentences would be shortened if they got rid of you."

It was a twisted sort of hope. Prisoners didn't know how long they were condemned to Rock Heaven, yet Ambassador Utheril was offering to wipe it all away. It didn't matter if Lirella and the rest disobeyed. Maella knew without needing to say it out loud that both she and Claritsa agreed. They would walk the rocks before letting the rest of the camp be punished for hiding them.

The door had opened, bringing Dedion, four days ago. Giffen had died three days ago. They had grieved and regrouped yesterday. Today, the door had opened and it was already midday.

Including today—they had four days left.

It wasn't enough time.

It would have to be enough time.

They needed to build a ladder.

# Chapter 29

"It's not going to work, Maella." Sethlo shook his head. "There isn't enough wood, especially after what the Klylup destroyed."

"There's the new crate," Claritsa said.

"It will not be enough. We must open another door." Sethlo wouldn't look at Maella while he said it, like he knew what she must be thinking.

And she *was* thinking it—what did Sethlo want to use her for? Was it only to save them? She remembered the look of greed in his eyes, but then it had disappeared. She didn't want that look to come back.

"We watch the door and the door watches us," Daniel said. "I agree with Sethlo. You have to try another door. The ladder won't work. We'll die out on the rocks. Or Lirella or your uncle or someone else in camp will kill us. Because it's us or them. Barth knew that better than anyone."

"Who's Barth?" Sethlo said.

"A jerk and a criminal!" Claritsa said.

"He would find a way out of here," Daniel said, growing more agitated. "He would do whatever it took."

"We don't need him," Maella said. "We never did."

"You're wrong." Daniel said, backing away. He headed for the cliff trail that led out of the mine.

"What are you doing?" Maella shouted at him. "You can't go out there. They'll—"

Daniel turned around and held out his arms. "They'll what? Find out we haven't been sent to walk the rocks? A little late for that, don't you think? What a great phrase— walk the rocks. Don't you think that sounds nice? Let's go walk the rocks. Let's go murder some people—just doesn't have the same ring to it."

"Daniel," Maella said. "The Klylup might still be out." But by the ringing silence that always followed a Klylup attack after the horn was blown, they all knew the Klylup had given up on the camp a while ago.

Daniel vaulted up the trail and out of the pit.

Claritsa looked after him.

Maella put a hand on her shoulder. "Maybe you should—"

"Oh, let him go piss himself for all I care."

They ignored words unsaid and feelings unnamed because there wasn't time. Because there wasn't energy. Because none of them quite understood any of it.

"Sethlo's right," Maella said. "There isn't enough wood." But it was the Klylup attack that had made her see the solution. It had been there from the very beginning, when they had run out of the Klylup cave and into Foster's world, through the mud and muck—

—and bones.

"We can build the ladder out of wood *and bones*."

Sethlo sucked in a breath.

"Bones?" Claritsa said.

But Sethlo did not need to ask. He knew exactly what she was talking about. They had found the Klylup cave together, after all. They had stood on a stone in the cold water, holding each other in the storm, and he had confessed his family secrets and she had confessed her own secrets, and he had promised not to make her open a door, and they had been surrounded by bones.

As Maella explained, Claritsa's expression became more grim. She folded her hands together, her knuckles turning white.

"This could work," Claritsa said.

Maella let out a sigh of relief. Claritsa thought it was a good idea. This had to work.

She looked at Sethlo. He had to see it. "It's our best chance. You know it is. If I opened a door right now, if I turned over every *licatherin*-stinking rock in this mine, there's no guarantee where any of them will take us or what will come out. But this door—we know where it goes and you know what's on the other side."

"And if it doesn't work?" Sethlo said, a challenge in his voice. "What then?"

"Then I'll open whatever door you want me to open. I'll open a million doors until all of Rock Heaven is gone."

Their conversation was cut short as people returned to the mine. Now that new equipment had replaced the broken pieces, the camp needed to get back to work beating *licatherin* out of the stone. Maella, Claritsa, and Sethlo helped. Daniel stayed gone. This worried Maella at first, and then that worry became a spark of anger. Daniel saw her as just another tool to use. A small voice inside of her whispered that she had been rightly accused of the same thought about him. She pushed that voice aside and made herself not care where he was or what he was doing.

Maybe Daniel would be right about the doors. Maybe it would come to that in the end, her using up her four remaining doors—but he should see that it was a last resort, and they had a responsibility to try everything else first.

The light faded. They returned to camp with Sethlo and the others. There was no point hiding now. Maella and Claritsa waited in the little nest the four of them made each night together to keep warm. It felt different in there now. Like they should say goodbye. Maella brushed her hand along the marks she had made in the stone. It had been more than a month since she had last seen her mother, grandmother, and Josa. More than a month since she and Claritsa had run through the damp grass, eager to see Cheyanne's new red bike.

She had thought her life was pretty complicated back then —she knew better now. But she was more determined than ever to unravel the tangles, get her friends home safely, and find out the truth about her family.

Maella's curls had grown long, hanging just below her shoulders. Claritsa had twisted her hair back into two braids again, her gray-dusted bangs folded into the braids that framed Claritsa's face like a crown. Wisps of hair flew out in every direction. When this was all over, the first chance Maella got she would find a way to give Claritsa her fabulous movie star bangs again.

"If we don't make it out of here—"

"We will," Maella said.

"If we don't."

"*We will.*"

"I'm not sorry this happened," Claritsa said. "I mean, I would have rather gotten to ride Cheyanne's bike, but—"

Maella let out a laugh. Not because Claritsa said anything particularly funny, but more that the universe had proved again why Claritsa was her best friend. They had both just been thinking about Cheyanne and the time before the door.

"I'm with you, Maella. That won't ever change."

They clasped hands and made whispered plans that transported them back to their creek, to their field of grass that grew knee high, to the door in the field that had started all of this. They finished each other's sentences and fed off each other's energy.

"I can't find Daniel," Sethlo said, appearing. He held out a canvas pouch. "We should start the ladder tonight after it gets dark. I asked Harry for glue. He did not ask what it was for. The problem is we watch the door and—"

"The door watches us," Maella said.

"Yeah, we know that," Claritsa said.

"Even if we're able to build the ladder tall enough," Sethlo continued, "and even if the ladder is able to take our weight —as soon as we bring it out, don't you think they'll see it? They knew about the Klylup attack and the broken equipment before Lirella even said anything."

"No, I don't think that's exactly true." Maella had been thinking about this part. "How many times on our walks together did we see any sign of someone at the door?"

Sethlo frowned.

"Not once," Maella said for Claritsa's benefit. "I don't think they *have* been watching us."

"But Daniel shouted at the door," Claritsa said. "And the very next day they called out the three of us to walk the rocks."

"I think it was the door I opened with Daniel that night." Maella glanced at Sethlo out of the corner of her eye, trying to gauge his reaction. "What if they have a pattern-keeper or a pattern-machine or something that marked that door when I opened it?"

Sethlo shook his head. "All that means is even if they weren't watching before, they're watching us now. Otherwise, how did they know about broken equipment? They know you haven't left camp yet. They'll be watching."

"If we bring the ladder up from behind the door," Maella began.

"And set it up at the very last moment," Claritsa continued, catching on.

"And at night," Maella added. "If we set up the ladder and climb it at night, even if there are guards on the other side, they won't be expecting it. The last time Rock Heaven prisoners tried to climb the ladder—it was the one they let down from the Thrae side, right?"

Sethlo nodded slowly.

"Then they won't be expecting our *own* ladder."

"And if we climb the ladder and they do expect it?" Sethlo said.

"We'll have a distraction ready," Claritsa said.

"What distraction?" Sethlo said.

Claritsa and Maella looked at each other. "We don't know yet."

"Seems like a pretty big flaw in the plan," Sethlo said.

"That kind of flaw will get all of us killed."

The voice made the three of them freeze.

Erentia appeared inside their little nest. The fading light deepened the shadows under her eyes into trenches. Her hair was dusted gray and coiled around her head like a snake. She had not drummed and Aretha had not danced since Dedion came down the ladder.

"Your presence here puts in danger our freedom—our chance, finally, to leave this place and return to our loved ones."

To Foster, is what Erentia meant.

Maella's heartbeat increased. How long had Erentia been listening to them? Her imagination conjured up how when Lirella asked what crime she had committed to be sent to

Rock Heaven Erentia had sat regally on the stones and said, *My lover was one of the most skillful fighters in the Doormaker Wars.*

Maella couldn't forget that for all of Lirella's pronouncements about Maella, Claritsa, and Daniel being a part of the camp, it would mean nothing if they discovered Maella was a doormaker.

"Come," Erentia said. "Lirella has called for everyone."

Claritsa looked at Maella. There was no choice but to follow.

Erentia brought them to the gathering space inside the shelter of boulders. The whole camp, what was left of the camp, sat in a circle. She counted. Twenty. Lirella made twenty-one. Maella, Claritsa, and Sethlo made the total twenty-four. The others were dead now, eaten by the Klylup.

She startled. No. The total was twenty-five.

Daniel sat in the circle next to Dedion. They looked like they had been speaking about something, but Maella's entrance stopped their conversation. Dedion looked at Maella with a cold, calculating stare. Daniel did not look at her at all.

Where had Daniel been this whole time and what had he been doing? Why did the sinking feeling in her stomach tell her that whatever he had been doing, she wasn't going to like it?

Lirella took a seat on a stone next to Daniel.

Dedion and Lirella looked like Daniel's guards, or protectors.

Maella forced herself to relax. Daniel did what was right in spite of himself. Every time Barth had crossed a line, Daniel had stopped him. He and Claritsa had argued back and forth night after night about what was the right thing to do next. He had closed the door they opened together that night because he saw even before she did that it could not be allowed to stay open. He might try to deny it or dismiss it, but she meant what she had said that night—he was a good person in spite of himself. He would not betray her.

Still, the way he looked at her—and then away—it made Maella's stomach twist.

The clouds above them changed into sunset colors, unaware, uncaring, of the tension beneath. Lirella sat in such a way that she could watch the door at its low angle in the sky above their heads. Maella put her back to the door, because looking at it made the vibrations, the wrongness of it, worse. She sat cross-legged on a stone, focusing instead on the cold that seeped through her clothes instead of the way the door called to her.

"They have demanded we make the three of you walk the rocks," Lirella said in a halting, hoarse voice. Purple tracks streaked her cheeks through the gray dust. Giffen's death had hit her very hard. She spoke first in a language from Thrae, then Rathe, and finally in English.

Claritsa stood and launched into a loud rebuttal.

Lirella held up her hand.

"We are not here to answer the question yet about what to do with you. Our question," she exchanged glances with Erentia, "is this—why you three? What makes you different than us?"

"We don't know," Maella said, too quickly.

Dedion leaned across Daniel to whisper something in Lirella's ear.

"Stop lying," Lirella said. "We cannot help you if you keep lying to us."

Claritsa's gaze burned into Daniel, but he kept his head bowed and could not see it. Maella bet he could feel it, anyway.

"You must explain yourself." Dedion's voice. He spoke in heavily accented English. Similar to how Sethlo spoke it, but the accent was much deeper, with a roll to his R's and swallowing of the T's. He glanced once at Maella. She didn't understand what he saw when he looked at her. All she saw was anger and grief mixed together so thoroughly that they could not be teased apart.

"Explain what?" Claritsa said. "Explain how you're going to send the three of us to die out there now that you have a chance to go home?"

"Doormakers have ruined our worlds," Dedion said. "That open door is an abomination and must be closed. We will have no peace until it is so."

A few others grumbled in agreement. Maella remembered what Aretha said. Dedion was a Sechnel leader and there were others here who he had convinced to his side.

"Enough," Erentia said, translating into all three languages again. Erentia and Dedion exchanged a fiery stare. "I do not care what a Sechnel believes. If you want to die, so be it, but you will not take me with you."

"The worlds will not be fixed until all of this has been wiped clean," Dedion said.

Erentia sighed and refocused on Maella. "Daniel has told us that you want to build a ladder and attempt an escape. You know this is foolish. It cannot be done."

Others nodded in agreement.

Maella stood. "What did you do, Daniel? What did you tell them?"

"Only about the ladder, Maella. It's the only way." Daniel's face was scrunched up like he held in a great deal of pain. "You don't see it, but it's the only way."

And Maella saw what he was trying to do. If he took away any chance at building a ladder, it would force her to open another door. It would be the only chance they had left.

"You would risk our freedom. You would risk our chance of leaving this place like Jessuf," Aretha said. "I have children waiting for me."

"Your children do not want you back like this," Dedion said.

Aretha stood up and slapped him across the face. His head whipped to the side, but otherwise he was like stone with how little he reacted.

"They've never taken one of us back before," Harry said.

"We committed treason in their eyes," Erentia said. "There's no sentence for that except death."

People began speaking over each other, almost none of it in English. Sethlo translated quickly.

"They've changed their minds."

"They are more desperate now for *licatherin* than ever. We should use that."

"If we blow this chance we might never get it back. They've offered us a way out—you're going to throw it away?"

"They're tempting us to work ourselves to death for a chance."

"It's a small, almost impossible chance of getting out of here."

"Jessuf would say otherwise."

"We don't know what happened to Jessuf. He could be dead."

"We are already dead."

People protested that.

"You don't think—"

"He's safe. He made it through—"

"They wouldn't harm him—"

"Why would they have let him through—"

"Enough," Lirella said in a strong voice. It stopped all conversation.

"Even if it were true," Dedion said into the silent space Lirella made. "We cannot come back from what the door has made us into. We cannot come back alive. We cannot go back to our families like how we are now."

Others mumbled agreement.

Sethlo kept his thoughts to himself, but looked carefully at each person who had agreed with his uncle. He was planning something, but Maella couldn't figure out what it might be. She was too shaken up to think much beyond Daniel's attempt at manipulating her.

Aretha stood up. "We cannot do anything that might take away this chance. My children—"

Aretha had told Maella about herself once when they were together in the panning pit after a long day. Aretha had come to Rock Heaven pregnant. Sent as punishment here for something her husband did. But the *licatherin* water they were all addicted to also ended the pregnancy. Something about the water also stopped all their periods. Whatever it was, there were no periods and no babies in Rock Heaven.

"We will follow what we have always done," Lirella said, translating herself again. "It has kept us alive. We work for food. They want the *licatherin*. We will get them what they want in exchange for our lives. If that gives us a chance, even a small chance of winning our freedom—would any of us truly fail to take it? Any Sechnel who does not want that chance can find their cleansing by walking the stones."

"What about us?" Claritsa said. "You can't just send us away to die. We have to try something. They're trying to get you to believe everything's going to be okay. They took Jessuf because, because—"

"Because they want you to hope again," Maella said, realizing as she said the words how true they were. Her voice was low, careful, thoughtful. Sethlo looked at her in surprise and something like respect. She took courage from him and continued. "If you have any hope of getting out and surviving this place, if you have any hope of seeing your family again, you'll endure, and *do*, almost anything for that hope, won't you?"

Hope had driven Maella this far and gotten people killed along the way. It drove Claritsa too. Her parents had left her with her grandmother while taking her brothers with them, but Maella knew, even after all these years, that Claritsa hoped they would come back for her.

"So that's what they've given you," Maella said. "Hope. It's like a drug. Like the *licatherin*. You're high on hope and you don't even see it."

A few people grumbled. Others shouted she was wrong.

Lirella held up a hand. "You know what waits on the other side?"

Erentia picked up where she left off. "Guards, weapons, death. They need the *licatherin*. They are sending us a message, but they need us to survive. They will not leave us to starve. Not unless we give them reason to starve us. If we try to escape again, it will give them all the reason they need."

"The last time we tried to escape," Lirella said, "they starved us out until half of us were gone."

"Just let us try the ladder," Maella said.

"And when they capture you and tie you up and make it impossible for you to escape, what about then?" Daniel said.

Maella wanted to shout at him. What was he doing? "We don't need your help—"

But she stopped talking because she knew she would not convince him. Maella wanted to laugh. No, she wanted to cry, but she would die before she let that happen.

Daniel was going to do whatever it took to try to force her to open a door. If that included ruining any chance to find another way out of Rock Heaven with their makeshift ladder, so be it.

All this time, she had been worried about the greedy light in Sethlo's eyes. All this time, she should have worried about Daniel and how he did what he thought was right, in spite of everything else telling him to do the opposite. She saw his actions in a new light. He had done what he thought was right, and it didn't matter at all to him what she thought. She had used him, but he had also been using her.

The rocks underneath her hands vibrated from the potential doors in them. She shook to their beat. She shook with his betrayal. She shook with the realization that she had lost control—that she never had control.

"We cannot put in danger our chance at leaving this place," Miall said.

"We will not let you build the ladder," Lirella continued. "And any Sechnel believers who would risk our chance at leaving this place are also not welcome in camp anymore."

Claritsa stood, ready to continue arguing. "What does that even mean? Are you going to make us work in the mine? Send monsters to eat us? Oh wait, that's what counts for normal around here."

"We want to leave this place as much as you do," Harry said quietly. "More. This place has used up more of our lives than it has of yours."

Daniel would not look at her. Maella couldn't see anyone else. She stepped toward him. He froze and shame flushed his cheeks because he knew telling them about the ladder had destroyed all chance of building it. He had gone behind her back and told them, anyway. He was worse than Barth. Worse than Foster. She thought they had been friends.

"You've gotten used to it," Sethlo said to Erentia. "You don't remember how it was before the door. You don't remember and you don't see how wrong this is. You don't see that even death would be better than this—than them keeping us on the edge of death, ready to do what they want."

Sethlo's words made it through her tunnel vision and only confused her. They suddenly sounded a lot like something Dedion would say. She tore her gaze away from Daniel and examined Sethlo. What was he saying and why? Sethlo's expression was locked in a fierce neutrality, like he was made of granite. This disturbed Maella more. He was always expressive and passionate. Sethlo was pursuing some plan Maella couldn't even see the beginning of yet.

"They must be sent to walk the rocks," Erentia said.

"Yes."

"It's the only way."

"Send them."

A half-dozen people repeated the words.

Others shouted them down.

Others stayed silent.

Lirella bowed her head. "We make this decision with heavy hearts. We will not undo the guilt and blood on our hands from this, but it must be done."

Daniel's head shot up. He was getting what he wanted.

She would not let Daniel control her like this. Fury boiled underneath Maella's skin and something inside her broke. If she were a wild animal, it would have just escaped its cage. Even though she could see the rage filling her up and ready to spill over and break windows, she couldn't stop it. It was like she stood outside herself and this big circle of people, and knew what she was about to say, and that she shouldn't say it, and that she couldn't stop.

"If you make us walk the rocks," Maella said slowly, pouring her rage onto the stones like someone would pour out a pouch of gray water. "Then I will open a door and destroy all of you."

Sethlo stopped translating. The granite neutrality of his expression transformed into alarm. "Don't."

Daniel rose to his feet, panic on his face. "Maella!"

But it was too late.

It had become dark, but the moonlight was more than enough to see outlines and recognize faces. The door shone bright in the sky, like a disfigured, smaller second moon, high enough that the boulders did not block it.

Maella's anger could not be stopped now. She was done hiding. She was done playing this game. She would not let anyone control her like this, no matter what the cost.

"What did you say?" Erentia said. "What did she say?"

"If you try to kill us," Maella opened her arms like she was trying to embrace the whole world, "I will turn over a million stones until my doors have destroyed all of Rock Heaven."

# Chapter 30

"It's not possible."

"I knew something was wrong with her."

"Claritsa must be her *tenbl*. Disgusting."

"This is why they told us to get rid of her."

"She's been spying for them the entire time."

"We can't stay here with a doormaker."

"She'll kill us all."

The accusations, the fears, the threats, flew like frantic birds among the boulders.

Maella's fury kept her from sinking into the stones.

Her pride kept her from defending herself any further.

She had worked alongside all of them, but now they looked at her like she was an animal. No one shouted down those who wanted them to walk the rocks now.

Sethlo didn't say anything at all, but searched everyone's faces again, looking for answers to a question Maella couldn't fathom. She knew him well enough by now to know that he was furiously trying to figure out how to fix what her rage had just broken.

"She's not a doormaker," Claritsa said, desperate.

"*Tenbl*," Erentia said, the darkness unable to mask the disgust in her voice.

Maella had no idea what the word meant, only that it didn't mean anything good.

"She's lying," Claritsa said, panic rising in her voice. "She's not a doormaker. But she's scared to walk the rocks and her, her…" Claritsa looked around, reaching for a story Maella didn't think anyone could possibly believe.

She felt bad for forcing Claritsa to grasp at straws like this, but the feeling chipped away at her anger and made her feel weak, so she pushed it away.

"Her brother married a doormaker," Claritsa said, stumbling over her words. "He married a doormaker and that's why—"

"Then she's *melain* and tainted by family association," Erentia said. "Either way, she cannot be sent to walk the rocks. Her kind is hunted down in my world. We must make sure she dies."

All eyes turned to Erentia. Most seemed to consider her words final. They looked at Maella with the same violence in their eyes she had seen Dedion turn on Sethlo.

Her father, her mother, her grandmother. They had run from world to world to keep their children safe from this.

Maella's rage began to ebb like the tide. Horror filled its place. What had she done?

Claritsa grabbed her hand. They were at the creek again. The water soaked their socks and gurgled across the rocks. Trees lined the creek bed. The grass grew waist high this close to the water. Sand itched in their clothes. Barth waited on the other side, an arm's reach away from doing terrible things. Everyone had abandoned them. There was no one left to save them but each other.

"Run!"

# Chapter 31

INSTINCT MADE THEM RUN BUT did not give them direction.

Maella and Claritsa danced across the stones, light, silent, quick. They had learned how to walk the rocks, even if they didn't know where to go, even if they had given the camp exactly what they wanted by running away.

Like a magnet, the door pulled Maella to it.

They scrambled past the door, though Maella paused, unable to keep a shudder from shaking her body when they crossed underneath it. The door's light bounced off the tears streaming down Claritsa's cheeks.

When the door was a small rectangle in the sky at their backs, when they had run for what felt like hours and the moon had risen, Claritsa collapsed on the rocks.

Her breaths came in ragged gasps. "I can't—"

Maella's legs had turned into jelly. Jelly—her stomach cramped from hunger. They had run without any food, or the gray water they had become addicted to. Looking around and using the position of the door in the sky, Maella realized they must be near the Klylup's lair. They'd never find the cave in the dark, but she only hoped the same would be true of the Klylup and them.

"I'm sorry, Claritsa. I don't know what came over me. I couldn't bear... I'll turn over a stone. I'll turn over a stone until one kills us or we find one that takes us back home." Maella wiped at her face and her hands came away wet with her own tears. She had promised herself to never open a door foolishly like this, but she had been foolish for thinking she had that kind of control over herself.

"You'll die. Keeper Shaul said—"

"We're going to die anyway," Maella said, feeling that truth down to her very bones.

She had opened the door in the field and wakened the Klylup. She had opened the desk drawer and it had burned to ash. She had opened the trapdoor to an ocean and Keeper Shaul's death. She had opened a door to Rock Heaven and imprisoned them inside this hell. She had opened a door that would have drowned them in oil if Daniel had not closed it.

Daniel. Fury rose inside her at the thought of him.

"Do it," Claritsa whispered.

Maella looked around, wild with intention, but then thought of Sethlo and slowed down. Daniel had betrayed them, but Sethlo had not.

It didn't matter. She only needed to pick a rock, and just, just—

"Just do it, Maella. Do it before we can talk ourselves out of it."

"Stop." Sethlo's voice echoed across the landscape. "Maella, wait. Please."

As soon as Maella heard Sethlo's voice, she knew she would not open a door, not without him.

Claritsa turned a pale, moon-washed face to Maella. "What if he's not alone?" Her face twitched with panic. "Maella!"

She didn't know what to do. Claritsa was right. What if they had forced Sethlo to come after her? Or was she a fool to trust Sethlo like she had trusted Daniel? She searched the ground quickly for the right sized stone. Big enough to fit them at least one at a time, small enough for the two of them to lift together.

There.

Flat, sharp-edged, circular, like a sewer cover from back home.

"Get on this side with me," Maella said.

Claritsa let out the breath she had been holding. She scrambled over to Maella and held the edge of the stone with both hands. "Ready when you are."

But Maella did not touch the stone. Not yet. "We have to see if he's alone."

"I know," Claritsa said, accepting. "I hope he's alone. I hope—"

"Just be ready," Maella said.

Sethlo's feet slapped the rocks as he sprinted into view. His shoulders were broad, his feet were bare.

"Stop," Maella said. "Stop right now or I'll open a door."

Sethlo skidded to a stop. His chest heaved. Sweat shined in the moonlight and plastered hair to his face. He looked dangerous and beautiful.

Five others moved into view behind him, some distance away, but closing the gap fast.

"Come on, Maella." Claritsa said and strained to lift the rock. "He's not alone!"

"Wait," Sethlo said, his eyes almost bulging in the moonlight as he bent half over and gulped down air.

"You sided with your uncle," Maella said, but she didn't know that for sure. The others were too far away to recognize, but who else could they be? The hum of the rock's edge called to her. Claritsa was already lifting. Maella only needed to help.

"I have not, Maella." Sethlo pushed his hands against his knees and stood upright. His face shined silver, full of sincerity. "I have not—hear me out. I swear I have not betrayed you."

He held her gaze and she drowned in his eyes and wanted to believe him.

# Chapter 32

"MAELLA, YOU MUST DENY YOU are a doormaker." Sethlo spit out these words quickly and quietly, looking over his shoulder as if to gauge the hearing distance of those who followed. "I believe I have convinced him you are not one, but he will kill you at once if he believes you really are."

Maella wanted to believe Sethlo was still on their side. Needed to believe it. "Who? Why?"

"My uncle. I think I made him believe I could be converted into Sechnel, like him. I think… I think I can get him to help us."

"You think he really believes that?" Maella said, mind spinning on this new development. She wanted to believe

Sethlo so badly she ached. "After what he did to you after coming down the ladder?"

"Lirella and Erentia made all the Sechnel believers walk the rocks, fearing they would kill the camp in their sleep." Sethlo shook his head, still speaking quickly. "Even if he doesn't believe me, he's willing to help us build the ladder."

Realization hit Maella. "Because he wants to use it to close the door for good. With all of us on this side."

"Yes," Sethlo said, eyes shining. "But do you not see? We need his help. We cannot build it in time without him and the others he has convinced to his side."

Maella's doubts resolved. She believed Sethlo. And if she was wrong? At least for now, they were all headed toward the same goal—to build this ladder—even if it was for different reasons. Deep down, she sensed she could trust him and only hoped that she wasn't wrong about him the way she had been wrong about Daniel.

"Maella," Sethlo prompted. "They are almost here. What more do you need to know to be convinced I am on your side? I am trying to fix this so that we all leave this place alive."

Maella looked at Claritsa. "I... I believe him."

Claritsa closed her eyes briefly. "Yeah, I guess I do too. Not like we have a choice."

Maella turned back to Sethlo. Claritsa agreeing with Maella's own desire to believe Sethlo was telling the truth went a long way. She released her doubts and was glad to still trust the boy who made her heart thump whenever he looked her way. "So your plan is for us to all build this ladder together like one big happy family—and then fight each other over it?"

"Yes," Sethlo said. "It is the best one I could think up in the moment. I would like to avoid fighting, but—" He shrugged helplessly.

"One big happy family," Claritsa said sarcastically. "Sounds about right."

Dedion and the others arrived. Maella tensed. She believed Sethlo, but did Dedion also believe him? When no one attempted to immediately murder her, she told herself to relax. Sethlo seemed to have convinced Dedion that Maella wasn't really a doormaker. Maybe Sethlo had even convinced Dedion he was open to Sechnel ideas. Whatever the truth of it, Maella would stay on high alert until it was all finished.

Deep down, Maella knew she was lucky to have both Claritsa and Sethlo still on her side. After the mess her rage had made, after she had revealed her greatest secret to those who murdered her kind, it was amazing that Claritsa and Maella had escaped at all, and that Sethlo had managed to repair any of what she had broken.

They slept on the stones, away from each other, forming the three points of a triangle. Harry and Aretha at one point. Claritsa and Maella made a second point. Dedion and his followers, and Sethlo, created the third.

Maella told herself it didn't mean anything. Sethlo knew what he was doing, and it was important for Dedion to believe that Sethlo had been converted to the Sechnel side of things. Claritsa agreed with her, and yet the space between the two of them and Sethlo seemed impossible to cross.

The cold woke Maella long before the sun fully rose. It had also woken the others. She searched for the door in the sky, but it had disappeared in the sunrise.

They had three days until those on the other side of the door returned.

Three days to build the ladder.

All of them sat together on the stones. Maella, Claritsa, Sethlo. The five people who had followed Sethlo in the night. Harry, Aretha. Dedion. Two more prisoners who Maella had heard speak favorably before about the Sechnel.

It seemed like each person contemplated how it was possible to have ended up on the same side—for the moment.

"Are you what you claimed," Dedion began, his voice rough from sleep and spoken in a heavily accented English. There wasn't much heat in his voice. It sounded like he felt compelled to ask, even though he already knew the answer. "Do you deserve death? Are you a doormaker?"

"She is not," Sethlo said quickly. "It is as Claritsa said. She is *melain*."

"I want to hear it from her," Dedion said, not looking away from Maella.

"I… am not," Maella said and focused on keeping her expression neutral. All Dedion had to do was test her like Foster had tested her with the desk drawer, but he seemed satisfied by her answer. With a flash of insight, Maella realized Dedion was likely desperate to believe Sethlo, his nephew, had joined him in embracing Sechnel ideas. His grief, maybe mixed with some loneliness, blinded him, at least for now.

She wondered what her own mixture of grief and loneliness was blinding her from seeing.

"We are all now *melain* since passing through the doors," Dedion said. "The sooner we close this one, the better it will be."

"We won't let you murder us," Harry said. "We're going through first. But Sechnel or not, for now, we have the same goal. To build a ladder to the door."

"What comes after will come," Dedion agreed.

Aretha's tears had dried into streaks of gray. Her eyes steeled themselves as she looked at Maella like she was a worm. Like she was *melain*, ruined, tainted, by being willing to associate with doormakers.

"How will we build the ladder?" Dedion said.

"That won't be a problem," Harry said. He pulled around the sack resting on his back. "You can use my *licatherin* glue to put it all together."

Aretha leaned into him as if needing his support. Their intimacy touched Maella. It seemed like the time before this place was all a dream. Why had she ever resented living in a house with no doors? She had gotten angry and broken the windows in their house because she couldn't understand.

Well, she understood now, more than she ever wanted to, and she wished she could go back and tell her family she was sorry.

But there was no going back. She knew that now.

There was only going through the next door.

One door in particular. The door that hung open and wrong in the sky. The door that called to her bones and woke her up at night with bad dreams. The door that left her mouth dry and desperate for a drink of the *licatherin* water.

"But where will we get the wood?" Dedion said, having switched back into Thrae as Sethlo translated.

"Even with wood, they're still watching," Aretha said.

"They are not. Not like before," Dedion said. "The door on that side is metal. It opens into a courtyard that they've built a wall around."

"It had no wall when I went through," Sethlo said.

"Things have become worse in Thrae since you went through," Dedion said quietly.

"Is it guarded?" Maella asked.

"Not really. Not anymore," Dedion continued. "There were guards when they took me through. But only to guard me. The wall keeps others on that side away from the door. There aren't guards watching the door. They check maybe once a day, no more."

"That doesn't make sense," Sethlo said. "How did they know about the equipment if they weren't watching? The Klylup attack? That we hadn't walked the rocks yet?"

Dedion shook his head. "The pattern is breaking. The doors are a corruption. Thrae is in chaos. Almost all the doormakers are gone. Doormaker Tain leads, but he is not well. He searches for the One Door. He searches for the doormaker meant to find the One Door."

Claritsa glanced at Maella.

"The pattern-verses say this doormaker will come as a child and he will find the One Door—"

"And fix the worlds," Sethlo finished for his uncle.

Dedion shook his head. "Only if he destroys the One Door."

"That is not what it says," Sethlo said. "I studied them—"

"That is what the Sechnel pattern-verses say," Dedion said.

"But that will end the worlds," Sethlo said, emotion breaking through.

"It will end the connection to the afterlife," Dedion said, scrutinizing Sethlo. "And to the corruptions in this world that are brought to Thrae."

As if realizing he was giving himself away, Sethlo let his expression go blank like stone. "Yes, of course, uncle. I see what you mean."

Dedion said nothing for a long moment and then grunted once. "Good. You are learning."

It didn't matter how many times Claritsa side-eyed her. She wasn't the doormaker Dedion spoke about. She. As in— girl. As in Keeper Shaul's you-are-not-The-One. But that thought brought back how his face had blanked out, blood leaking from his mouth, blade sticking out of his chest. Maella became sick to her stomach.

"And what about Rathe?" Sethlo said.

"Rathe is also a corruption."

"So only Thrae is real," Maella interjected, upset by the images in her head and the guilt in her heart. "Only where *you* come from gets to be real?"

Claritsa pinched her arm.

Maella startled. Right, they were supposed to act on the same side. But how could Dedion believe people from Earth thought themselves so despicable they would willingly destroy themselves?

But then she remembered—she wasn't actually from here.

Dedion sighed, ignoring Maella's interruption. "Those on Thrae do not watch the door like they did before. That is the truth."

"Then how did they know the three hadn't been sent out to the rocks?" Sethlo said.

"Simple. They know Lirella," Dedion said. "Her first instinct was to hide you. If I had been one of those guards, I would assume you were being hidden somewhere."

"Brilliant," Harry said in English, excited. "They called our bluff, and we gave away our hand."

"Bluff like a cliff?" Sethlo said.

Harry shook his head. "Nevermind. It means something different in this case."

"And the equipment?" Maella said. "They had it all ready and waiting, didn't they?"

"You do not understand the importance of *licatherin* to Thrae and to the doormakers who control it," Dedion said through Sethlo's translating. "I would believe they had a dozen buildings full of the needed equipment for just such a happening."

Maella thought it over. "You said the machines were old and pitted. I thought because they didn't care enough to give us new ones—"

"Or because they had been sitting in wait," Claritsa finished. "Just like Dedion said."

It made sense in a convoluted let's-take-over-the-worlds sort of way. If it were all true, if they really didn't watch the door like before, then they had a real chance to make this work.

"But there are no materials to make this ladder," Dedion said.

Maella's mind conjured up an image of the tree, dead, lying on its side. For just an instant, it had looked like the most crooked, shakiest, flimsiest ladder. But the wood wouldn't be nearly enough.

Maella exchanged a look with Sethlo and Claritsa.

"There is a tree and the Klylup has a cave…"

# Chapter 33

THEY BEGAN BUILDING THAT SAME morning.

They found the tree and the Klylup cave. When they discovered the Klylup was not inside, they emptied the cave.

After the first day, they ran out of wood.

It didn't take much talk, but it did take a lot of courage to do what was necessary.

They used the bones to get the height they needed.

Arms and legs and ribs. The *licatherin* glue worked just as well on the human bones as it did on the wood. Better.

Harry had found the trick for making the glue last. It needed to be kept warm against the body until the very moment it was used. They all began sharing the weight of this. It reminded Maella of the egg-baby Claritsa had carried around back in middle school. Maella had been home-schooled because it was safer that way. But she often grilled Claritsa on all the things they did. When Maella told Claritsa about it, she agreed it was kind of like that, except, you know, failure at the egg-baby experiment didn't result in the parents' deaths by starvation or cold or Klylup.

Maella giggled at that and a brief smile had played across Claritsa's lips.

"That was a long time ago," Claritsa said.

"Just a couple of years," Maella said.

"An eternity."

Maella carried the glue like it was a weight around her soul. If she ever got a little careless, she remembered all the awful things that had happened because she'd broken the family rule and opened door after door to something worse than before. And if she still felt careless, she reminded herself of Keeper Shaul's seven door verdict.

They worked into darkness that first night, one of them always on watch for the Klylup and for people from camp. Clouds marched across the sky in pretty parades that acted like they would never dare change into a storm. They fueled themselves with a sack Aretha had thought to steal from camp—a sack full of the gray *licatherin* water. It kept them working and able to ignore the hunger pains, but was empty after a few hours.

They gave themselves two days to finish the ladder. Then they would use it to slip through the door the night before it was supposed to open again.

Maella touched each piece of ladder as it was finished. Wood, bone, glue. *Licatherin*. Everything had to happen soon. They were starving. The *licatherin* water had run out. Eventually a storm or the Klylup would find them.

She would use up the rest of her doors—if it came to that. But the door in the sky was a sure thing, a known place, with known dangers. What doors her hands might open could kill them all in an instant. And if it didn't, Dedion surely would.

Even this far away, the odd vibrations from the door in the sky drove their hum into her bones, though the rhythm had become oddly muted. She passed it off as *licatherin* withdrawals. They were all dealing with it: shaking, hunger cramps, a brain fog that sometimes tilted the world onto its side, the exhaustion that ate away at muscles and made people snap at each other.

With the glue and the bones, they could build more than enough ladder. They would finish in time. Somehow, they would not let Dedion close the door until everyone had escaped this place. They'd make it through and take everyone from camp with them. Even though the other prisoners didn't want anything to do with Maella anymore. That didn't matter.

What mattered was making things right.

What mattered was getting Claritsa and Daniel home.

What mattered was finding her father and brother.

They finished the ladder in the afternoon. Now it was time to wait for nightfall. In case the Klylup returned, they had made sure to set up away from its cave. Someone formed a simple arrangement of rocks to simulate the comfort of a campfire. There was no fire, of course.

That night they would carry the ladder to the door and somehow stop Dedion from trapping them forever on Rock Heaven.

Maella finished up at the spot they had designated for their camp's bathroom and then carefully picked her way back to the circle of stone. The *licatherin* had stopped her and Claritsa's periods. It was a relief not to have to deal with that on top of everything else, but she wondered what other damage the *licatherin* had done to her body. She was sixteen now, Claritsa too. That is, if time passed the same way on all the worlds. Their birthdays fell in the same month and had only been a few weeks away before they'd gone through the door in the field. Her mother and grandmother would have baked a cake for her and her mother would have sliced it for them to make sure no door opened while they enjoyed it. They would have reused the candles from the year before. They would have taken her and Josa down to the creek for the day.

She held all her intentions in her mind like they were written in the sky.

Use the ladder. Escape with everyone. Close the door.

And then.

And then find her father and brother. And—

A horn sounded.

She didn't think she could ever hear a horn again without it speeding up her heart, numbing her hands, and twisting her stomach in fear.

The door. They were opening the door.

It was too soon.

She began to run for their makeshift ladder. Thoughts tripped in her mind, but her feet were stable as they slapped the rocks. They would have to speed up the plan and take the ladder as it was—in the daylight.

It won't work. It won't work. Her mind screamed at her. They were supposed to have another day—

Something snuffled behind her.

The horn. Maella stopped running and balled her hands into fists at her sides. The creature let out a hot snort, as if to laugh at how long it had taken her to notice.

The Klylup.

It must have been nearby already. The horn had sounded and drawn the Klylup and she was in its way.

She turned and stared into the Klylup's green eyes. Scars marred the skin around one eye and it looked cloudy—the eye Giffen had battered. The bones of one wing stuck out, like it was waiting to become part of the collection of bones they had used to build their ladder.

The monster slithered across the stones on its belly. Its ears twisted this way and that, taking in the sounds of the surrounding landscape. Their makeshift camp was out of sight, too far away for help, even as the sounds of their ladder work carried to hers and the Klylup's ears.

Adrenaline surged, clearing her brain. The Klylup lowered its head, blew on her once, just to see, it seemed, if it could scare her into running. Its jaw opened and rows of lavender-stained teeth glinted in the sunlight. Licorice-laced rot blew over her.

Maella stepped backward. Panic welled up inside of her, but it was more than panic. Her heartbeat sounded loud in

her ears, drowning out the Klylup's breathing. All her muscles shook. She had been so close. The ladder was finished.
The door was right there.

Rage filled her like an empty cup and spilled over the
sides of her, blacking out the stones and the sky and the
door. The feeling was familiar, like seeing an old friend.

The Klylup would destroy her only chance to get her answers.

She was tired of others controlling her.

She would not let this Klylup destroy her chance.

She would not be controlled.

Crouching, she rested her hand on a stone, like she had
done at camp, when she had been ready to threaten Lirella
with an open door. It hummed with potential. She cupped
the rock in her hand and stood up with it. The smooth surface felt like the shell of an egg. She threw the rock like she
had smashed the windows, in fury, without thought except to
break something, her only goal to spend the anger inside
until it was used up.

The rock hit the Klylup on its bad eye. The monster reared
up. The stone fell to the ground a few feet from the small
door she had opened.

A screech sounded—like a bird dying.

*Never open a door.* Grandmother's voice.

*Four doors left.* Keeper Shaul's voice.

The fury that had made her see red disappeared, and left
her like it always did, feeling empty and sick.

The Klylup cocked its head and turned one green eye to
the open door on the ground. A beam of light shone out of
the ground, straight into the sky. A bird's cry tore through

the air again. The vibrations from the open door battered Maella's body, making her nauseous, but also clearing her head even more than the adrenaline. Energy surged into her veins and she scrambled to her feet.

She waited for the terrible creature she had unleashed from the opened door to come out.

Nothing came through.

The Klylup turned its attention back to her.

Wait.

Little bits of things fluttered up from the ground. They flew odd paths in the beam of light. Colorful, oddly shaped. They looked no bigger than—

Butterflies.

Dozens of butterflies.

She was hoping for fire, or a black hole maybe, even the oil from the last door would have been welcome, or at least some bees. She was hoping to die in style and all at once. But no, she got butterflies, and the stone she had unturned wasn't even big enough to fit her foot. There would be no escape for any of them through that door.

She waited for the Klylup to eat her.

It snuffled at the air and its one good eye rolled around, trying to keep the butterflies in its sight all at once. The butterflies flitted out of the beam of light and flew around the Klylup's head. It shuffled its feet on the stones, attempting to avoid the flying insects, and rolled stones around like pebbles.

Something else came out of the door. Something dark that moved like a wave of dots.

The first dot reached her bare feet.

There were so many they blocked the light of the door altogether, like someone had clicked off a flashlight.

Ants.

The one that crawled onto her skin bit down hard. The shock of the pain tore a scream from her throat. She slapped the insect off.

The Klylup turned from side to side, trying to keep all the flying creatures in sight and getting confused when it couldn't. Rocks went tumbling under its feet as it skittered away from the butterflies.

One rock flipped onto the door, sealing it, closing it. Like the light, the vibration turned off.

Maella slumped as if someone had turned off the electricity to her body. Another ant bit into her leg and she surged to her feet again. Other ants headed for Maella like they could sense she was the easier prey.

She ran away, looking over her shoulder once, twice. The butterflies distracted the Klylup even as the dark mass of ants disappeared into the rocks. But then the butterflies headed her way, and the Klylup followed, opening its jaw wide, almost unhinging it, as it bit at the butterflies.

She knew she had to warn the others and keep the Klylup from destroying the ladder.

Even as the adrenaline pumped all thought out of her brain. Even as her heartbeat rose in her ears, drowning out how close the Klylup was behind her.

She counted.

Four doors left until she died. And who would pay for this door? The butterflies and the ants weren't the end. Just like the broken windows hadn't been the end of her fury.

The door had let them off too easy.

Doors were never that easy.

Maella screamed. "Klylup!"

She screamed it once more before the camp finally came into view and Harry looked up from his work. She screamed it again before everyone understood what she was saying and began to scatter.

Even though the Klylup was behind her, Sethlo and Claritsa ran out to meet her. She veered away from the ladder and they followed.

"Keep it away from the ladder!" Maella screamed.

But it was too late.

The butterflies flew around the Klylup's head like a moving crown. As if they knew right where to go, they led the Klylup to the ladder. The monster trumpeted and raged. It lashed out at the wood and bone and glue. Maella screamed to gain its attention even as Sethlo shouted for her to stop and bring herself to safety. None of it mattered to the Klylup. It smashed all their work to dust.

Her stomach heaved. She couldn't stop it, she couldn't hold it back. Throwing up the last of the gray water, she watched it form a small puddle in front of her.

Acid burned her throat and tears burned her eyes. She had done this.

Sethlo grabbed Maella's hand.

Maella shook her head. She had turned over a stone and let out a handful of butterflies and some ants. She had broken the family rule and she had destroyed their best chance. *What did you expect would happen, girl?* Her grandmother's voice, compassionate in her rebuke, which made the guilt only cut deeper. Grandmother would love her anyway, no matter how many things Maella destroyed.

And that made everything worse.

The butterflies continued to swarm. Harry and Aretha tried to loop back around. Dedion and his followers looped the other way. They kept wide to maintain distance between them and the Klylup. The monster continued to trumpet its rage.

Claritsa grabbed Maella's shoulder and pointed behind her, hair in disarray, eyes wide and frantic. "Something is coming. It's like black tar on the rocks. It's coming this way."

Maella wanted to throw up again. This wasn't over. "The ants. They're ants."

"What happened?" Sethlo said.

But Maella didn't need to say anything. Claritsa knew.

"You opened a door."

"Is it still open?" Sethlo said, eyes widening. "Can we make it through?"

Maella shook her head. "The Klylup closed it. And it wasn't big enough and…the butterflies and the ants came from it."

A horn sounded again in the distance. It stilled the Klylup's frantic rage, but only for a moment. Everyone turned to face the sound.

Now the Klylup led the charge and the butterflies followed.

So that was it.

Ladder destroyed. Food gone. Gray water used up.

Those on the Thrae side of the door had gotten what they wanted. Maella and her friends had walked the rocks and would die because of it. She could sit on the stones and rest and once she was ready, she would turn over her last remaining doors until everything was destroyed.

She had already destroyed so much, she might as well finish it.

So she sat.

"What are you doing?" Sethlo said.

Harry, Aretha, Dedion and his followers rushed up at almost the same moment.

"Is there anything left?" Harry said.

Sethlo shook his head.

"We can't last out here," Aretha said.

"We must find a way to close the door in the sky," Dedion said.

"I am a doormaker," Maella said finally.

They stared at her like she was a zoo animal.

She was a monster, just like the Klylup. It made sense that they stared at her like that.

"I have four doors left to open before I die. I will open them now. Maybe one of them—"

Pain erupted on the left side of her head. Dedion had punched her and knocked her over. The sky, the rocks, the people, they blurred, and she closed her eyes because everything was spinning.

There was shouting so loud she could hear it over the ringing in her ears. She blinked open her eyes and saw fighting. Sethlo, Aretha, and Harry held back Dedion and the other two. Dedion lunged for Maella again. Claritsa shouted at him.

She saw it all sideways while her head spun. The door was far away, hanging in the sky like an ornament. The Klylup raged in the direction of the door in the sky, the butterflies following and forming a colorful moving crown. The ladder snaked out from the door in the sky and down to the ground, little more than a splinter from this distance.

Dedion shouted something in Thrae. He and his followers broke free and ran away, in the same direction as the Klylup.

"You can't give up, Maella."

Claritsa's voice.

Maella ignored her. Everything she touched, she destroyed.

Claritsa made her sit upright.

Aretha held her jaw like she'd been punched. Harry bent over, taking in deep, gulping breaths like he'd gotten the air knocked out of him.

Sethlo looked at her with the same shining eyes as Claritsa.

*You can't give up.*

The ladder continued its path down from the sky to the ground. Newcomers.

Aretha and Harry argued.

"Who will find your father, or your brother?" Claritsa said. "Who will get us home?"

"Who will find the One Door?" Sethlo said. "Who will help me make the worlds right again?"

"I can't," Maella said.

"You can," Sethlo said.

Claritsa sat next to her. "Don't kill us now. Don't give up."

Claritsa's words burned shame deep into Maella's heart. She faced a choice. Not giving up—that would mean standing up. But she didn't think she could. She was so tired. She was so tired of the emptiness of stone, of the monster that lived inside of her, of the way each time she tried to make things right, it seemed only to make things worse. So much worse.

She wanted to die. Her rage at the Klylup had spun out of control and destroyed their ladder.

Their best chance.

Sethlo and Claritsa watched her. Waited for her.

They looked at her like she wasn't some monster. They looked at her like they believed in her.

The world stopped spinning. She wanted to be worthy of that look, so she stood up.

She wasn't worthy of that look. Not yet.

But she wanted to be.

And then she saw it, because she was standing up, because the world had stopped spinning, because they looked at her and really saw her, and this allowed *her* to see—

Written in the sky, stampeding across the stones, standing all around her.

Their chance.

# Chapter 34

"THIS IS OUR CHANCE." MAELLA turned to Claritsa. "Do you see it?"

Aretha and Harry stopped arguing.

"What are you talking about?" Sethlo said.

Dedion and the two others were small moving specks of darkness. The Klylup was even further away.

"See what?" Aretha said. "What do you see? The ladder is destroyed. We're out of food and water. I should never have come! I could have been next, like Jessuf. I could have—"

Maella only had eyes for her friend, for the one who had always stood by her side. Claritsa had kept her sane. Claritsa had always helped her see herself as more than a monster.

She held her breath and waited. It was a risk, a bigger risk than the ladder they had been building, but it was the only one left to them now. She would not sit on the stones and give up.

Claritsa's eyes widened. "I see it." She flipped her braids over her shoulder. Gray dust flew into the air. They hadn't worked in the mine for several days now, and the purple tint of their skin came through more strongly than ever.

"What are you talking about?" Harry said. "This is the opposite of what we planned. We can't just go over there—"

Aretha collapsed onto the stones and moaned into her hands. Harry crouched next to her. She pushed him away and shouted at him in another language. Harry's face paled.

"We have to go after them," Maella said, turning next to Sethlo. Needing him to see it, too. Needing him to know that she wasn't giving up after all. That he had helped bring her back. They were in this together. "We climb *their* ladder before they take it back up. The Klylup, Dedion, whoever the newcomers are—*they* are our distraction now."

"Yes," Sethlo said, eyes growing wide. "We have to go now."

Time was not on their side. The ladder hadn't reached the ground yet, but it would, and then the newcomer would climb down, and the Klylup would arrive, and they would have only seconds for their chance.

Sethlo ran for the ladder. Maella sprinted after him, watching each foot as she carefully planted it on the next stone. She had so few doors left. She would need them all. Claritsa soon passed her, racing after Sethlo.

"We've tried this before," Harry shouted after them. His voice echoed in the emptiness. "They all died."

"If we're already dead," Sethlo said, pivoting around to shout back, taking his uncle's words and making them his own, "what's left to lose?"

Maella ran across the stones like she had been born on them and caught up to Sethlo and Claritsa. They ran on either side of her. They ran for as long as their bodies let them. They ran even though they had not eaten in days.

As they drew close enough to the door to make out the details, Maella puzzled out what she was seeing.

The ladder was down, its feet touching stone. The Klylup stumbled onward, zigzagging as the butterflies tormented it and slowed down its pace. Dedion and his two followers had caught even to the Klylup, taking a direct route to the ladder while keeping a safe distance away from the monster.

Newcomers were climbing down the ladder.

A lot of newcomers.

These newcomers wore uniforms. They had gear strapped to their bodies. They didn't look like Dedion or Sethlo or anyone else in camp. When they reached the bottom of the ladder, they formed a line in front of it, like a wall. The prisoners of Rock Heaven, barely twenty of them, stood randomly around, holding their hammers and small mining tools. The newcomers faced the prisoners of Rock Heaven, arms rigid at their sides, swords strapped at the waist.

The butterflies brought the Klylup into sight of the door. The newcomers carried weapons, but didn't look like soldiers to Maella. They seemed to be more like guards. They turned toward the monster. Someone shouted and the guards began to scatter. They did not look prepared for the Klylup even though they should have known the Klylup always came when they opened the door and sounded the horn.

Some of the guards and prisoners ran, others tried to fight the Klylup and each other. Still others dashed for the ladder. All sight and sound faded as Maella's focus narrowed on Dedion at the base of the ladder.

Maella, Claritsa, and Sethlo were still hundreds of yards away. The ladder was a dark slash in the gray sky and Dedion was grabbing onto the first rung.

There were shouts, screams, clashing metal, the roar of the Klylup as it plowed into the scattering crowd of prisoners and guards.

Dedion began to climb the ladder. There was someone with him. Maella almost recognized—

Daniel.

She waited for Daniel to try to stop Dedion. Instead, he followed up behind him.

Sethlo pulled ahead of her and practically flew to the base of the ladder. He jumped, launching off the bottom rung and grabbed Daniel around the ankles. Daniel lost his grip and they both crashed to the ground.

Daniel and Sethlo each leapt onto their feet. Sethlo's robes were in tatters, Daniel's cutoff jean shorts and plaid shirt were almost unrecognizable under the grime of gray dust. Their faces were hard and angry and mean as they stared each other down.

"Traitor," Sethlo shouted.

"You don't know me," Daniel shouted back. "You don't know me!"

They went for each other, punching, kicking, tumbling.

All around her was chaos, blood, swords, running, screaming.

Maella could not let Dedion get to the door first. Everything would be lost.

Daniel shouted at her as he punched Sethlo in the stomach and then the face. Sethlo crouched and swept his leg out, slamming Daniel onto his back.

One of the new guards appeared and used his sword to bar her way. The deadly metal was already covered in blood.

Maella's mind screamed at her to stop, but her momentum was so great, she knew there wasn't time. She couldn't pivot or slow down. The blade would cut into her flesh and pour her blood onto the stones.

At the last moment, the guard lifted his sword and backhanded her across the cheek. She fell to the stones as her face stung with pain.

Scrambling back up, she cowered, bracing for the next blow, as the guard's shadow fell across her. But the blow did not come.

She looked up. Another guard held the first one back. He shouted in Thrae.

"I don't understand!" Maella said.

The guard switched to English. "Do you not see the hair and the face? She is a Botron!"

The guard who had already hit her once paled. "I did not see it. Forgive me."

"There's someone on the ladder. He's going to close the door!" Maella screamed, unable to process what happened.

How did they know who she was? But none of it mattered if Dedion got away with closing the door.

Both guards looked up and sprinted for the ladder at the same time.

The Klylup rushed by and tossed aside the two guards before they made it to the ladder's base. Their bodies flew through the air and then landed with thumps on the stone, unmoving. The Klylup snapped at the butterflies flying around its head, trumpeted its rage, and barreled on.

Everyone was fighting. The Klylup was distracted. Dedion was climbing the ladder.

Maella had to go after him.

She was five rungs up when she chanced a glance down. The Klylup trumpeted and tore into three more guards, gulping one down like a gull eating fish. The orange and black little bodies of the butterflies scattered around her from a fresh wind that blew in. Some of the prisoners scattered back toward camp and the safety of the boulders. Others fought with the guards. Still others joined the guards against the Klylup, even though they only had mining tools for weapons.

Maella looked up and climbed as fast as she could. A storm was rolling in. It whistled through the stones and dampened the shouts of pain below. Dedion was halfway up, the wind pinning his clothes to his body and him to the ladder.

They could not let him get to the door first. He would close the door and trap them all on Rock Heaven. She and the other prisoners would be at the mercy of the guards and their swords. If the prisoners didn't kill her first, she didn't know what the guards would do. Her doormaker powers would not be enough to save them. Claritsa would never go home again. Maella would never see her family again. Sethlo would never make the worlds right again. Dedion and his hatred of her and all her family of doormakers would win.

She would not let him win.

The first rain drops hit Maella on the forehead. Then the water poured out like from a faucet. She reached for the next rung. Her hands slipped.

No.

She scrambled for a hold but couldn't find one. She slid down the ladder, losing everything she had climbed. Her stomach flipped and her hands burned trying to catch herself. Suddenly, when she had almost reached the ground again, she lost her grip completely and fell backward.

She landed on the stones, the breath knocked out of her, the rain coming down in sheets.

Trying to catch her breath, she forced herself onto her side. Rain quickly soaked her clothes. Sethlo leapt over her and climbed onto the ladder to go after his uncle. Daniel lay next to her, hunched in the fetal position, hands clapped around his chest.

"You did this to us," Daniel said, his voice empty of emotion. "I should have never helped you. I should have never helped either of you."

"You're probably right," Maella said simply.

But that changed nothing about what she needed to do.

She pushed herself to her feet. She had to get back to the ladder.

Daniel slapped his hand against his bare ankle and cried out. Claritsa rushed up and knelt next to him. Maella was relieved to see that she was still okay. Now Claritsa slapped at her arms like they'd been lit on fire.

Little black dots swarmed the rocks. Maella felt a sharp, stinging bite on her foot and slapped it without thinking.

The ants.

There were more screams. Cursing. People shouting, slapping their skin.

Those fending off the Klylup with their swords and hammers became distracted by the ants trying to eat them alive. The Klylup darted in and grabbed one of the guards, tossing him like a rag.

Daniel's feet were covered in ants—the writhing mass looking like terrible, shifting socks. He kept brushing them off, and then yelling out in pain.

"Dan—" But Maella's cry was cut off by the red hot bites that threatened to rip her skin into pieces. With great effort, she ignored the pain and went again for the ladder. The ants flowed across the rocks like a wave, trapping the people between them and the Klylup.

The wind whipped her hair and blew some of the ants into the air. The first lightning strike stirred up licorice smells. Thunder shook the ladder. Gray-green clouds boiled across the sky, blocking the sun. Rain blurred her eyes. The Klylup raged. People ran.

She began to climb the ladder again.

"Maella!" Claritsa screamed below her, but the wind tore her name to shreds.

Claritsa screamed again, but Maella couldn't understand it. She kept climbing, her hands and feet slipping on the wet wood as rain blurred her vision and her muscles trembled in protest. Every ant bite flared like someone had taken a lit cigarette to her skin.

She looked up once, but the rain blurred her vision. Sethlo and Dedion were two dark smears on the ladder above her. She could not tell their distance.

Wrapping an arm around the ladder, she used her other hand to wipe her eyes. She looked down at the same time that five lightning bolts struck the ground, forming a messy circle around the ladder.

Someone shouted her name. The rain slacked off for a brief moment and she looked up. Sethlo was pointing at her. No. Sethlo was pointing at something next to her.

"Stop him, Sethlo!" Maella shouted back.

Instead, Sethlo held onto either side of the ladder, taking his feet off the rungs. He slid down and screamed her name.

"No, Sethlo, you have to—"

She felt hot air caress her back. Slowly, so slowly, she looked behind her.

The Klylup stood at eye level with her. It opened its mouth wide, white teeth stained red, rot and licorice smells making her gag. Flesh was stuck in between its teeth.

No.

The Klylup roared.

Sethlo crashed into her and she was thrown off the ladder and back onto the stones—the breath knocked out of her again. She wanted to throw up. This fall hurt worse than the

last. She had been higher up. High enough to be eye level
with the Klylup.

Keeping her eyes closed against the pain that roared
through her body like a wave, she waited for teeth and a foul
licorice smell to overtake her.

Her eyes opened to a spinning world. Sethlo was still on
the ladder, racing back up to meet his uncle in time. From
the corner of her vision, she saw people running around—
away from the ants, away from the Klylup, away from each
other—some to camp, some for the ladder, others for the
stones. Ants blotted out an entire section of the ground. They
were a black, moving swamp. Sheets of rain began again,
blurring everything.

The Klylup slid into view, its one green eye fixed upon her,
its mouth open, gore hanging from its teeth.

Claritsa suddenly appeared. She stood in front of Maella
and began throwing stones at the Klylup.

Maella gulped down air for the first time in what felt like
minutes. Her lungs burned and her head spun from
dizziness. Daniel dragged her backwards across the stones.
With its massive feet, the Klylup pulverized the rock as it
followed them.

The Klylup tossed its head around in a great roar. Claritsa
was still there, far too close to the Klylup, throwing rocks at
it, screaming bloody murder.

"No!" Maella screamed into the rain.

Lightning lit up the stones like an endless field of broken
teeth.

Daniel forced her onto her feet and shouted. "Come on!" Rain soaked his hair, his face, his clothes. His lips were blue from the cold.

Claritsa darted away, but the Klylup was too close. It had locked onto her. Daniel suddenly was throwing stones at the Klylup's head now too, screaming at it to draw its attention away from Claritsa. Some of the guards, maybe a quarter of those who had first come down, moved in with their swords, stabbing and slashing at the monster. Blood dripped from the monster's mouth, its ears, its neck and shoulders and sides. The Klylup raised itself onto its hind legs and raged at the storm as if daring the whole world to a fight.

Then the Klylup came down on all fours, blocking Claritsa from view.

There was a scream.

She knew that scream.

She knew.

The surrounding air was made out of some kind of gel. It caught in her throat and nose and eyes. Water streamed down her clothes.

The Klylup tossed something into the air and it disappeared into the Klylup's gaping mouth.

Maella moaned.

No, no, no, no.

Maella could not see any sign of Claritsa.

The world fell out from under her feet.

# Chapter 35

THE KLYLUP SWIVELED ITS HEAD, searching, and then it locked onto Maella.

That great big glowing green eye saw her, knew her as the one who had gotten away.

That wasn't okay.

You didn't escape from a Klylup.

It was a monster out of bedtime stories. It was a monster in three worlds. She and Claritsa had woken it. No, Maella had woken the monster when she'd opened her first door. She'd woken the monster inside herself and the Klylup was the real-life version of what was inside her.

The Klylup pounded across the stones. Under its strength, water and stone flew into the air.

Maella scrambled to her feet, scraping her knees and hands.

Claritsa.

Maella's mind broke on her name.

There was no one left to hurt. Maella had destroyed everyone she loved. She had thought Claritsa was safe somehow. Safe because Claritsa was a survivor. Claritsa had always been better at it than Maella. It was Claritsa who had taught Maella how to survive.

*Don't be stupid.*

Claritsa's voice.

But it wasn't real. It was only in Maella's head. Words Claritsa had said to her a million times over when the two of them were bickering. She tried to make herself believe it had been someone else caught in the Klylup's jaws. She hadn't seen Claritsa. She hadn't actually seen her.

*Don't give up.*

Claritsa had said that right after Maella's father had gone through the door. Right after Maella had broken all the windows in the house.

Claritsa had placed a hand on her shoulder and looked at her with dark brown eyes. Maella could tell by the way Claritsa's collarbone stuck out through her skin and the way her arms were too thin that Claritsa hadn't been eating much.

That's all Claritsa had said. *Don't be stupid. Don't give up.*

Maella didn't deserve Claritsa as a friend. She never had.

She would keep trying to deserve her until the day Maella died.

But that day wasn't going to be today.

The rain smeared the Klylup's body as it barreled toward her. Maella threw herself out of the way. The monster rushed by, spraying her with water and stone fragments that cut her skin.

She ran for the ladder and saw how the Klylup had destroyed the last few rungs. Jumping for the splintered ends, she caught them, and pulled herself up. She climbed quickly, letting the door's vibrations echo inside of her black hole of a heart until it drowned out the ringing world around her.

The ladder swung in the rain and wind, attached only by whatever held it to the door. They had lost so much time, but Dedion must have slipped too, because Maella saw he hadn't yet reached the top. There was another person next to him about halfway up. They were fighting to pull the other off. Sethlo fighting his uncle.

There was a cry and one of the figures fell away from the ladder into the sky.

Her stomach flipped.

Sethlo.

She locked her legs around the ladder and threw the upper half of her body away. "Please. Please."

Snagging Sethlo's clothes, she held with everything she had as his weight slammed into her, almost ripping her off the ladder. She angled their fall to hit the ladder rungs. He gasped for air even as he grabbed on. His skin was tinted purple, slick with rain, and spattered with bruises and blood. Muscles bulged along his shoulders and arms as he shuddered from the near miss. He looked at her with wide eyes as rain fell off him in a dozen mini waterfalls. She could feel his heat, his closeness, how he had almost died.

"Stop him," Sethlo said between gasps. "Go."

Maella placed her hands over his and made sure each one firmly held the ladder. "Hold on. Just hold on."

Then she let go and climbed up. Looking down once to make sure Sethlo still clung to the ladder, she saw guards and prisoners still battled the Klylup—

No. She couldn't think about what was happening down there.

She looked up. Dedion had climbed two-thirds of the way now. Already her height made her dizzy. If this had been a building, she might have climbed many stories by now and she was only halfway. The door was outlined above him, orange against the storming sky. Somehow, the lightning didn't like the door. It struck multiple times across the landscape but did not touch the ladder or the door.

Dedion hugged the ladder again while thunder shook the air. She climbed through the thunder and made up some of the distance between them.

She could not think of Claritsa right now. She could not think of Sethlo. She could not think of Daniel or Harry or Aretha, or her mother and grandmother and brother. Or even Barth and how he had followed her up a different set of stairs and paid with his life.

Dedion's steps sent vibrations down the ladder, but she could feel the louder, deeper call of the door's vibrations and she gained speed. The storm sounds seemed to disappear.

One, two, three, four. One, two, three, four. She had turned into an animal chasing her prey. He was almost to the top, but she was gaining on him. She was faster.

She pushed herself harder. It was like scrambling on the rocks, only up.

One, two, three, four.

Dedion reached the top.

Maella grabbed for his foot. She dug her nails into the bare flesh above his ankle. Wrapping herself around the ladder, she squeezed it with her legs and pulled. He slipped a step. She held on. The storm's rage returned. Lightning arced from the sky in a dozen places and struck the ground in sync, like it was some sort of light show. Now the people on the ground looked like ants.

Dedion's clothes whipped in the wind and water streamed off him. The door filled her entire vision. It creaked, like its hinges needed oiling. The metal bar that propped it all open screeched as wind slammed the door against it.

Dedion kicked at her at the same time as he reached up and unhooked the metal bar. She twisted, trying to unbalance him. He slipped, letting go of the door and grabbing the top of the ladder. He looked down at her. His skin had deepened into a gray-purple flush of rage and the light in his eyes reflected the lightning that charged the air all around them with electricity. His face was filled with hate.

"I know you are a doormaker," Dedion said. "I know what you are."

With a rough hand, he peeled away Maella's fingers one by one. She tried to hold on, but cried out in pain when he bent one finger back so far she felt a pop. Her stomach flipped.

She was so high. Stretching out for endless miles was gray stone, gray sky, barren, lifeless earth. She could let go and the wind battering against her was so strong she might really be able to fly.

She looked up, pushing away that sick, breathless feeling. The rain splattered onto her face, into her eyes. Dedion went for the door again. His arm stretched out, brown skin, dark hair, hands covered in callouses, but not from mining. He hadn't been here long enough for it to be from mining. Blisters, scratches, skin not yet turned purple.

He pushed on the door, trying to close it.

A part of her wanted to see it closed.

A part of her *knew* it should be closed.

She climbed up the ladder and when she reached him, she used him as part of the ladder, climbing over him, and launched herself into the door's gap. She fell onto the edge, the bottom frame of the door cutting across her stomach. Her legs hung down on the stone side, kicking at Dedion trying to pull her out of his way even as he pressed the door closed, pinching her. Her upper half rested on the ground in Thrae, on—

Her brain couldn't understand what she was seeing.

She was hot, the rain drops evaporating on her skin and replaced with an intense warmth, like someone shined a heat lamp on her. At first, the brightness made it impossible to see anything through the door. Everything was orange, white, green. The light blinded her, but more than that, she couldn't understand the colors. Something rust red crackled under her hands.

It was ground, she realized.

Leaves on the ground.

Fall.

Her eyes adjusted.

A stone archway created a dark crescent shape above her head, but this fact only registered in the back of her mind. Her eyes drank in the colors, the sun, the warped tree that stood leafless a few yards away from her, almost leaning against a stone wall. Sunlight streamed over everything because there was no roof.

It was the oddest sensation—the upper half of her was warm, no rain fell, and she was in a landscape on Thrae that actually felt alive. Her lower half was wet, bogged down, the ladder swaying underneath her feet, pinned in place by the door with only a stone field waiting to become her grave.

A yank on her foot almost made her lose her grip. She slid backwards through the leaves, back through the door.

No, not yet.

She held onto the door frame and kicked back at Dedion. Her ankle was released, and she was able to pull herself halfway through the door again.

Vibrations made her eyes swim, but in spite of this she could see Thrae was like Dedion had said—a courtyard, walling off the open door. Bigger than she had expected. Old, ruined, open to the sky. The sky was bluish green with puffy clouds moving across it. Moss and vines grew along the stones, forming a green cover that shined in the sunlight so bright it made her eyes hurt. It was empty, but there was movement at a far wall, at a gate. She took in a breath and the air tasted different. Like she could taste the life that grew here—the insects that must live in the ground that was inches from her nose, the plants and animals that were almost within reach. She wanted to climb into this world and throw herself into the soft bed of leaves and just breathe in the life that was here.

This was Thrae. This was where she had come from.

There was a rectangular indent in the ground that marked a sort of platform where she thought they must stage the supply drop. A quiet little breeze played through the leaves before everything settled back into their piles. Then her eyes caught on the wood framing for the door.

Someone had carved a symbol.

She drew in a sharp breath. The carving looked done by a shaky hand, almost as if the person had been in a rush, and the symbol hadn't been finished. But she knew what it was supposed to be—her family's symbol.

She reached out to feel its grooves. *A curved quarter moon, its points sharp like knives. Three links, both separate and attached, pierced by the moon.*

Hope struck her heart like lightning. Her father or brother had been through here. This message *must* have been left behind by one of them. But which one, and when?

And then another thought bubbled to the surface. They could be alive here, in Thrae, at this very moment.

Her hands crunched against the leaves as she clawed her way through.

Movement at the far end of the courtyard became shapes that turned into marching men. These men looked different from the guards that had come down the ladder and were even now still fighting the Klylup. These people looked like soldiers. She didn't know who they belonged to, or, for that matter, who the guards in Rock Heaven belonged to, but none of them looked friendly.

*Politics.* Her father would say sometimes, as if the word tasted like bitter lemon. She didn't know why her mind brought that word out now, only that the guards below had opened the door sooner than they should have, they had not expected the Klylup to come, and they did dress anything like the soldiers now in front of her.

Maella knew the exact moment she had been spotted. One of the soldiers shouted and the front line broke into a run for her.

She climbed further through onto the Thrae side, into the leaves, making sure to keep her legs wedged in the door. She could not let Dedion close the door. If it did close, the portal to Rock Heaven would be lost—everyone trapped on the other side of it forever. Once it closed, even if she opened it again, it would open to a new place, not to Rock Heaven. That's what Keeper Shaul had told her—the pattern was breaking. Doors didn't go where they were supposed to go anymore, even if it was the same doormaker opening the same door. But she needed some relief. The door wanted to rip her apart. She could feel it in her bones—being halfway between worlds like this was building up pressure inside of her that threatened to burst. The door wanted her to choose and if she didn't choose quickly enough, it would kill her.

And if the door didn't kill her, she feared the soldiers might.

She looked back through to Rock Heaven. The storm raged, splashing rain into Thrae. Suddenly Dedion's face loomed into view. He threw open the door wide with one hand, letting in more of the storm. Lightning struck, lighting up the sky behind him. He grabbed her and pulled her back through the door. She fought him, but she wasn't nearly strong enough. The vibrations increased until she couldn't think.

Leaves were tossed into her face as the soldiers with swords reached the door. They were screaming at her. The smells of oil and musk and sweat and violence overwhelmed her.

One of the soldiers raised a sword over his head. A ray of sunlight hit the face of the man behind him.

Maella sucked in her breath.

The face. She knew that face.

It was her father.

But it wasn't her father.

She continued to fight, but Dedion was too strong. He dragged her back into Rock Heaven. She slipped through the frame of the door even as she kicked out, but he wrapped his arms around her legs, pinning them to his chest. She used her nails to scratch at his face and grabbed the wood frame.

More figures swarmed the door on the Thrae side. One of them looked an awful lot like—Barth?

Now she *knew* she was hallucinating.

The man she almost recognized shouted orders in Thrae. One of the soldiers dove for her, as if to grab her, before she slipped away for good. She reached out for him, letting go of the door frame. But the soldier had miscalculated. He slipped on the leaves, showering her with dirt as he flew into Rock Heaven's sky, screaming as he fell to the stones.

It was only Dedion's death-like grip on her legs that kept Maella from falling to her death after the soldier.

As if Dedion realized this fact as well, he let go. Maella's heart threatened to leap out of her chest even as she grabbed the ladder rungs in time. Now she was eye level with Dedion, at the bottom threshold of the door, their heads even with the top rung of the ladder. His expression twisted purplish-red with rage. He ripped her hands off the ladder and she slipped. Away from Thrae. Away from the face she knew. Dedion shouted something and stepped up. He reached for the door that swung wildly in the wind on Rock Heaven's side of the worlds.

That same familiar face appeared in the door's opening.

She *knew* that face. It tickled memories in the back of her mind. Memories of fountains and laughter and fire.

He spoke in Thrae and his voice boomed. Her brain tried to make sense of the words. She was on the edge of remembering this language she must have known once, but didn't understand a word of it except for *licatherin*. This man shook with anger and brought his sword down, the metal flashing bright silver as the blade embedded in Dedion's shoulder. Now blood rained over Maella. She wiped her eyes and saw Dedion press himself up, forcing the sword deeper. This threw the man backward into Thrae, the sword wrenching out of Dedion's flesh.

Blood streamed down Dedion's side and made the ladder slick under Maella's hands. In horror, unable to move, unable to stop it from happening, she watched as Dedion grabbed the door with both hands, swung it around, and used his weight against it.

The door in the sky closed with a click.

# Chapter 36

THE OUTER EDGE OF THE door began to crumble. Its warm light disappeared.

Dedion let go and fell. The expression on his face could only be described as—peaceful. The ladder began to shake. She watched, newly horrified, while everything that held up the ladder began to disappear.

She would fall to her death on the stones. Those below who survived today would die a slow and painful death. There was nothing in Rock Heaven except rock and *li-catherin* for as far as the eye could see. And now, guards. And now, no food.

Dedion had killed them. He had closed the door.

*It's not closed yet.*

She didn't know whose voice said the words. It could have been her mother, her grandmother, Claritsa.

The vibrations were still there—fading. The door's handle was crumbling, but not yet gone. It was still there, ready for her.

She forced herself up the last rungs of the ladder, her hands slipping in Dedion's blood. Reaching for the handle, she saw the rusted metal flaking off like powder.

But it didn't matter.

There was enough.

She fought against the vibrations and the handle and wrenched open the door.

The door zinged her with a bolt of electricity. Vibrations came back, stronger, different. Like notes from a strange song. Something smelled like smoke.

Before she allowed herself to look, she positioned the metal bar to keep the door from accidentally closing. Only then did she search the other side for the soldiers and the familiar face. She looked for Barth, captured by Foster, dead for all she knew, but she had seen him. He wasn't a hallucination, right?

Maella blinked.

The courtyard was gone. The leaves were gone. The tree was gone. The people were gone.

This couldn't be.

Everything was yellow. A dry wind blew from the other side of the door across her wet skin. Dirt stretched for miles —flat, empty. The sun shined so intensely, so big in the sky, it turned the whole sky a yellowish brown. Scrub grass dotted the ground.

It was a mirror image of the stones beneath her, washed in yellow dust, heat, desolation.

Maella's heart constricted. She lost her balance on the ladder and slipped down, caught herself, then slipped even more until her shirt caught on a broken piece of the ladder and hung her from it like she was a jacket thrown onto a hook.

She looked down. Guards and prisoners clustered around the Klylup, which lay on its side, its huge chest heaving with labored breaths. So many people had turned up their faces. Some of them began trying to climb the ladder, but two guards held them back with swords.

But she didn't have eyes for them.

She saw—

"Claritsa?"

# Chapter 37

MAELLA RACED DOWN THE LADDER.

"Maella, are you okay?" Claritsa's voice reached Maella and it sounded like her favorite song.

Claritsa wasn't dead.

A lot of people lay on the ground, not moving. The Klylup heaved ragged breaths. Low moans of pain ended each breath. The guards had fought instead of run—many of them had died. Only a half dozen were left of the original parade of newcomers who had come down from Thrae. One of them was the bald man with rings on his fingers. His clothes were soaked with rain but otherwise clean, like he had stayed out of the fighting.

The prisoners of Rock Heaven knew the Klylup drill and those who could looked like they had made a run for the protection of camp. Some of them returned from the boulders now that the Klylup was no longer a threat. Many of them carried swords taken from the dead guards.

Sethlo held a sword in his hand, pointing it at his uncle. He carried the weapon like he had been trained on how to use it. Dedion was covered in blood, sitting down, hunched over and holding his wounded shoulder. He should have been dead from a fall like that. He looked like he wished he had died and that it was a curse to find himself still alive.

Maella dropped to the stones and ran for Claritsa. They hugged each other like they thought they would never see each other again. The rain fell steadily. Joy burst into Maella's heart. Her best friend was alive and there was a door above them that would take them away from Rock Heaven once and for all.

Claritsa put a hand on her arm and motioned to the stones. "Maella, look."

The rain had driven away the ants and butterflies. No one saw where they went, only that they were gone, and that was enough.

"Lirella Chestent," the bald man with the rings called out.

"Ambassador Utheril." Lirella stepped out from the group of prisoners that had come back from camp. She inclined her head in his direction.

The sky cleared and turned blue and the water became mirrored pools between the rocks. The two leaders looked at each other like they were old adversaries. There was both a deep hatred and a hint of grudging respect in their expressions.

The two leaders spoke to each other in Thrae. Maella looked to Sethlo for help. It was important to understand what was happening here. *Politics*, her father's words came back to mind. The rush of battle and being so high in the air left her heart beating wildly, but everything was about to change now that they could escape Rock Heaven. She needed to be ready.

Sethlo blinked as if coming back to himself. Blood had dried dark red rivers down his lavender-skinned arms. He looked at his injured uncle and dropped the sword to his side.

"Are you okay?" Maella asked, not sure how to reconcile this warrior with the one who had wept out on the stones over his mother and sister.

"I'll be okay." Sethlo began to translate, even as he stayed near his uncle and kept his sword ready.

Daniel appeared and sat on a nearby rock, not looking at any of them. His shirt was torn, his face scraped up, and he held a heavy water sack in his arms.

The Klylup whined, like a puppy in pain. Maella steeled her heart against those sounds. Bodies lay everywhere because of the Klylup.

"Get your guards to put it down," Lirella said. Blood coated one side of her, running from a wound on her left bicep.

"Let the beast die in its own time. There is no—"

"Put it out of its misery, Ambassador. Do not be cruel to an animal that knows no better than what it has been taught. Save your cruelty for the humans who can understand it."

Utheril turned grave. "Very well, Lirella." He motioned to his people. "Put the beast down."

Two guards approached with their swords. They were dressed differently than the soldiers she had seen in Thrae, and she had time now to wonder what that meant. Did the different uniforms mean they were enemies? Or all on the same side, but with different jobs, like police officers and prison guards? She would have to ask Sethlo later.

The guards made quick work of the Klylup. The sounds of its death made Maella dizzy. Its chest stopped moving first. The great Klylup's head made a final lurch up from the stone, then settled into a pool of blood that curled into the surrounding pools of water. The broken wing with the bones that stuck out like flutes twitched a handful of times before going still. It looked lost and alone and little more than a baby.

Maella turned away because she didn't want to remember the Klylup this way. They had killed the monster because it had deserved death for the destruction it had caused.

"We are here to ensure the *licatherin* production continues," Utheril said.

"I think not," Lirella said. "That is not for you to say any longer." Lirella nodded.

Erentia, Radovan, Miall. They all had swords taken from dead guards and now pointed the blades at Utheril and the surviving guards.

Harry and a few others were there too, alive and unarmed, surrounded by bodies.

"The *licatherin* production—"

"Is over, Ambassador. That door has been closed."

Utheril paled. "The door is open. Doormaker Tain will send reinforcements."

Lirella laughed.

Utheril twisted one of his thumb rings. Then, as if he realized he was giving away his nervousness, he brought his hands behind his back and spread his feet wider on the stones. "The door is open."

"Because this…this *doormaker* opened a new door." Lirella said the Thrae word for doormaker like it was the most vile word she knew. She put all of her venom and disgust and hardship from her Rock Heaven imprisonment into the word.

Sethlo glanced at Maella. Claritsa grew still. Daniel's skin flushed as if from embarrassment.

"You have a doormaker?" Ambassador Utheril said. "Who is it?"

Maella sunk into the stones to make herself as small as possible, but of course there was nowhere to hide.

A crazy light entered Lirella's eyes. "Surely you must know who? You sent her to walk the rocks."

"A girl?" Confusion crossed the Ambassador's face. "Doormaker Tain sensed the disturbances here. He has been searching for the doormaker who can find the One Door."

Lirella laughed again. "You still believe in that old legend?"

"Yes," Utheril said simply. "And so does Doormaker Tain."

Lirella sighed. "I see. But it is not a girl you need."

"No," Utheril said, bowing his head in acknowledgment. "No, but still, Doormaker Tain will want to know of this girl."

"The door to Thrae has closed, Ambassador. When will you understand this?"

Shock covered Utheril's face as he did, finally, understand. He coughed. His people looked at him in confusion, their skin pale brown, almost yellowish. It was shocking to see their natural skin color against the sea of rain-washed purple on everyone else. He searched the landscape as if looking for answers, but the only answers he got were dead bodies and *licatherin*-infused stones that went on for an eternity.

"Which one is the doormaker?" Utheril said finally.

Lirella pointed at Maella.

Utheril turned to Maella. She shrunk into Sethlo and he held an arm around her shoulders protectively. The warmth comforted her, but did nothing to lessen the severity of Utheril's gaze or the disgust in Lirella's.

"Where does the door go?"

Maella shook her head. "I don't know. I have not seen the place before."

Utheril nodded to one of the guards. "Go take a look."

The guard returned the sword to his hip and stepped around the Klylup. Erentia got in his way, sword drawn.

"Lirella," Utheril said.

"We are not stupid, Ambassador Utheril. We will not let you anywhere near the door. Nor will we let this doormaker anywhere near any other door again." Now Lirella drew out her own sword. "Stand up, girl. Stand up and keep your hands in the air. Step away from everyone. You do not belong here."

Maella did as she was told.

Claritsa stood up as if to move with her.

"Stay. Daniel, Sethlo. Make her stay," Maella said urgently.

Daniel grabbed Claritsa's wrist. She shook him off.

Sethlo whispered in Claritsa's ear. Her eyes blazed first at Maella and then at Lirella. Lirella met her gaze with a frown. Aretha and Miall stepped forward as if to stop Claritsa.

It was enough.

Ambassador Utheril used their moment of distraction to motion to his guards.

Suddenly, there were swords at Erentia's and Miall's throats.

Maella gasped as Utheril drew his own sword, jeweled at the hilt, and held it to Lirella's neck.

"We have you outnumbered," Lirella said.

"We are dead to those on Thrae," Utheril said. "We will die if we stay here. We are sworn to protect the doormakers. We are the Hestroth. There is no choice for us."

Dedion staggered to his feet. He held his arm at an awkward angle. A sneer appeared on his face. "You are worse than dead. The Hestroth are worse than even her *tenbl*."

Utheril inclined his head. "I remember your case. You are Sechnel, are you not?" Utheril held up a hand. "Do not bother. I already know this and much more about each of you." He turned to each of the battered survivors, including his own guards. His gaze skipped over Maella, Claritsa, Daniel, and settled on Sethlo for a moment too long.

"I know each and every one of you. I have cared for you."

Erentia opened her mouth to argue.

Utheril held his hands up in surrender. "I have been your advocate, your voice to Doormaker Tain, even as I have been a sort of warden. I have taken care of you the best I was allowed to do."

"They were freeing us," Erentia said, turning on Maella. "We were giving them what they wanted and they had freed Jessuf. They were going to free more of us."

"You can't believe that," Harry said.

"I believe it!" Erentia said, her eyes flashing. "Is that the truth, Ambassador? Tell us here and now."

Ambassador Utheril pressed his lips together for a long moment. "This is true."

"You ruined our chances," Erentia said, turning back to Maella. "You've been sabotaging our efforts for a long time. I believe you closed the door on purpose."

"I didn't close the door," Maella said, shocked. "Dedion did."

"She didn't do anything wrong!" Claritsa shouted. "Dedion was trying to trap us here. He wanted us all dead. She helped stop him."

"Don't be a fool," Dedion said, not looking up.

"That's what happened," Sethlo said. His eyes were red-rimmed. His face hard, unreadable.

Dedion finally looked up at his nephew. "I do not care what you saw. You have allied yourself with the doormaker, have you not?"

Sethlo inclined his head. "She saved us. When the door closed, she opened it. We would all be faced with a slow, painful death without her."

"So you see, we cannot trust you." Dedion turned to Lirella. "I left camp to follow them and learn their plans. As you had asked, Lirella. As you had commanded." He said this in the most reasonable, logical voice. He said it without fear, he said it with surety. And yet a muscle along his forehead pulsed. But Lirella did not see it. Or if she did, she did not care.

"But he is Sechnel," Sethlo said. "He thinks we are all dead. He wants us all to die. You cannot trust—"

"A doormaker cannot be trusted," Lirella said. "Your uncle has become more flexible in his beliefs than he has shared with you. Even so, I will always trust a Sechnel believer over a doormaker. A doormaker cannot be trusted or tolerated to live."

Others joined in. Angry voices, angry faces.

Maella listened to them shouting for her death as she felt every part of her throb from pain. She had killed today. There was so much blood on her hands. She did not know that she would ever be able to get rid of the stain. She did not think such things were possible.

Let them punish her and then be done with it.

"Do not touch her," Sethlo said, raising his sword. He stood in front of her. Ambassador Utheril's guards flanked him.

This stunned her. What were they doing?

"You ally yourself with this...this doormaker?" Dedion said, disgust in his voice.

"I do," Sethlo said.

"Then it is done," Lirella said. "We see you no more. We grant you no more welcome. Anyone who allies with the doormaker marks themselves for death."

Claritsa grabbed Maella's hands. Her braids, clean of the gray stone dust, now back to the dark brown Maella had always known, flipped over her shoulder. She told Maella without needing to speak a word that they were in this together until the end.

"We can't kill each other," Harry said in English, stepping forward. He held up his hands in surrender. "Surely, we can agree that no one can stay here. Surely, we can agree that everyone must go through the door, wherever it leads."

Maella pictured the never-ending sand and wondered if it would be better on that side, or if Harry would regret his words. They had fought against the weather, starvation, the Klylup, each other, and here they were fighting over who got to go through the door. They were all alive, but they were ready to kill each other over the *licatherin*, over doormakers, and explanations, and patterns, and the One Door.

"We must go through the door," Harry said, grave and composed. He did not push imaginary glasses up his nose. His eyes seemed dull, as if he weren't really there with them.

That's when Maella noticed Aretha lay at his feet, her neck twisted too far, a peaceful look on her face in spite of everything.

"We must all go through the door," Harry continued. "We have water, but no food. We have no one to trade the *licatherin* with. Anyone left behind will be as if we had murdered them. There has been enough murder today. There has been enough death today. Let us leave this place. Let us go through the door and then go our separate ways. "

Lirella slowly nodded. "Everyone but the doormaker."

"We will die first," one of the Hestroth said, Erentia's sword still at his throat.

"I can arrange that," Erentia said.

"Stop," Utheril said. "Remember, we do not know what is on the other side. Have the doormaker and her followers go first to test the door. Send one of your people along to make sure the door does not close. We will then all go. We will take turns. One by one."

They held each other's gaze for a long time—Lirella and the Rock Heaven prisoners loyal to her, Utheril and the Hestroth guards. Maella and her friends were chess pieces in a much larger game she hadn't known existed until now.

*Politics.*

She refused to play their game or allow them to use her as a pawn. Yet she did not know the rules or even the scope of this game.

Why had her family left her so completely in the dark?

There must be a reason.

She held that little stone of love and belief in her family close to her heart.

She stepped forward, drawing everyone's attention.

The swords held against the Hestroth guards' throats tightened, as if expecting a certain answer in the tense silence.

The Rock Heaven prisoners saw Maella as they saw the Klylup. As a monster. She spoke into that tense silence, even as she feared her words would bring about a blood bath. If they could only see her as more than a monster—

She spoke about home and how the grass was so tall when she last saw it, the juice had stained her knees green. She spoke about blooming flowers and buzzing insects and gurgling water. She did not speak about her family—afraid it would remind them all of the monster they wanted to see in her, though her family was there in her heart and her eyes and her every word if you listened closely enough. She spoke about crossing the creek using the stones Claritsa had laid out for them so they might play with their friend who had brain problems. She spoke about eating peanut butter and how she wanted to taste peanut butter once more before she died because she didn't know how much she had loved it until now.

And she spoke about the way the prisoners had stood against the Klylup and the door and Rock Heaven itself.

Sethlo and Claritsa stood on either side of her. She warmed at their loyalty, even as a part of her whispered that she didn't deserve it. She would try to deserve it.

It took Daniel a long time to come to her side. He had helped her and Claritsa escape Barth and then Foster. She didn't know who he was deep down. Maybe Sethlo was right and Daniel didn't know who he was, either.

Finally, when she ran out of words, she was left deflated and silent. Erentia and the others still held their swords against Utheril and the guards.

She was a monster. What had she expected?

Lirella broke Utheril's stare and glanced at the Klylup's still form. Did Lirella think about how they had saved the

Klylup from death and how such a monster repaid them in the end? If she did, then Maella knew all hope was lost for her.

Lirella nodded at Erentia. Erentia hesitated, but then lowered her sword, glaring at Maella the entire time. The other Rock Heaven prisoners followed.

Dedion spoke in Thrae. Something sharp. He cut Maella down with a severe look even as he held his bleeding shoulder and hunched over from pain.

Lirella responded back with something equally sharp. Switching to English, she said, "Let it be as Harry said. There has been enough death today and I will not add to it. We go through the door and then go our separate ways."

"Go then, doormaker," Erentia said, spitting out the label. "Before we change our minds and slit your throat, after all."

Daniel took a step toward camp. He carried a full water pouch with him. "Allow us some food."

Lirella held up a hand. "Go now or condemn yourself forever to this place."

Dedion pushed to his feet, his shoulder bleeding through his fingers.

Sethlo stepped away from Maella's side and raised his sword.

"We have nothing for you or those who would side with you." Dedion spit on the ground. His saliva left a dark gray stain on the rock. "Your kind deserves nothing."

Maella placed a hand on Sethlo's arm. "It doesn't matter. Let it go." She had opened the door to save them all from a horrible death by starvation. They would blame her for that

—no matter what. So she took it in. She accepted their con-
demnation like it was normal, because it *was* normal.

Sethlo's bloodshot eyes pierced her soul. He was his own
dark storm.

"Let's go," she said. "Let's just go."

# Chapter 38

MAELLA NOW HAD THREE DOORS left before she died.

She didn't care if Keeper Shaul could be trusted. She knew maybe he couldn't. She believed him.

The Rock Heaven prisoners stared at her as she headed for the ladder. In those looks, they threw all their nervousness, their fear, their hatred at her. The door hung in the sky above her like it always had. A rectangular outline of light, swaying in the breeze.

In the heat of battle, she had lost herself while straddling both worlds—Earth and Thrae. She had felt the power of the door fill her blood, her soul, her mind. She had seen her family's symbol carved in its frame by a crude hand. She had felt the door's terrible wrongness. She had wanted to close it even as she had forced it back open.

Lirella and Utheril each sent one of their people up the ladder. They waited near the top rung, still on the Rock Heaven side of the door, both with swords.

They would make her go first through the door as they had threatened. The bottom few rungs were gone, the wood splintered where the Klylup had bitten at it. She would need to jump for her hold. She just needed to get this over with.

Sethlo stepped up. "No, Maella. I will go first." Blood had spattered and dried dark red across his face. He held the sword to his side. Dark purple circled his eyes and his scruffy facial hair made him look much older.

She shivered under his piercing gaze and remembered being held in his arms during the cold night. "I did this to us," Maella said. "The least I can do is go first."

She jumped, missed, and then Sethlo's hands were on her hips, helping her into the air. She caught the ladder with his help and pulled herself up, muscles quivering. She climbed slowly and carefully into the air.

As she passed the section of ladder where the Hestroth guard and Erentia waited, swords held at their sides, acting like they really would duel in the air if they needed to, the guard mumbled something Maella didn't quite catch. The words at least sounded kind and she realized with a shock that this guard was actually a woman.

Erentia shuddered and her hand twitched on the sword as Maella went by.

At the last moment, before Maella climbed through the door in the sky and into the world on the other side, she looked down.

Now that the storm had ended, puffy white clouds floated through a blue sky. The hulk of the Klylup's body below sucked in all light. From this height, the camp of boulders and the mining pit looked small and meaningless. The field of stones that extended endlessly into the horizon was both beautiful and harsh, peaceful and disturbing.

She turned away from all of it and noticed dark red flakes coming off the ladder where her hands touched.

Dried blood. Most likely Dedion's.

The hum took hold of Maella as she climbed through the door. Its wrongness, its darkness, shook her differently than when this door had connected to Thrae.

If there were only three worlds—then this feeling meant the world on the other side was Rathe. And she thought that sounded right, because it felt a little bit like that first door had felt. The door in the field. The door she had opened an eternity ago.

Remembering the Thrae soldier and how he had slipped through the door to his death in Rock Heaven, she pulled herself across the ground until she could stand without risking a fall backwards. Intense, scorching heat hit her. Yellow dust kicked up by her movements made her cough. The purple skin of her arms looked like terrible bruises against the yellow of the ground.

The air here pressed down on her, heavy, thick. She thought that must mean this place was at a much lower elevation than Rock Heaven. The air didn't smell clean either

—not like Rock Heaven's air. And there wasn't a hint of licorice to it.

Her hands shook as she pressed herself up to standing. She looked around, turning a full circle. Sand, dirt, sun. A desert. Hints of scrub grass created little dots across the landscape.

Eventually, everyone alive on the Rock Heaven side climbed the ladder and passed through the door.

When Lirella came through, Maella said, "I think this must be Rathe."

"You have no idea where this is," Lirella said.

"It feels different."

"Do not blaspheme any more than you have already," Lirella said.

Rock Heaven purple-skinned prisoners came through with pouches of water and armfuls of supplies. And of course the swords they had taken from the fallen guards. At least they allowed Utheril and the guards their own swords. And Sethlo also had his.

Daniel handed Claritsa the sack of water he had been carrying. "It's gray water. You need the energy."

Claritsa drank and handed the water back. Daniel offered it to Maella next.

She looked at him for a long time before taking the sack. He had destroyed their first chance at a ladder, but she didn't think he'd quite believed how deep the hatred for doormakers ran. She didn't know what to think of him, actually.

He had saved her and Claritsa more than a handful of times.

He had been kind to them, like he was being kind to her right now.

He was Barth's friend and he had betrayed her to Lirella and the other prisoners.

But she had also done him great wrong. If she were to weigh each of their wrongs on a scale, hers would break it.

So she took the gray water and drew out a long sip and let the *licatherin* soothe her shaking muscles. Daniel passed the water next to Sethlo, even as the two boys looked at each other with something close to hate.

"We go our separate ways now," Lirella said.

"We should stick together," Harry said. "Strength in numbers."

Lirella shook her head. "No."

"Let them go," Maella said, that angry knot inside of her growing bright like the sun. "If we stay with them, they might decide to murder us while we sleep."

"That is something only a doormaker would think," Lirella said.

They formed two groups in the sand.

Lirella's people.

Maella's people.

The guards and Ambassador Utheril were in Maella's group. They kept their swords drawn and pointed in the general direction of Lirella's people.

Sethlo and Claritsa were with Maella, of course, but that left Harry and Daniel. They held the middle ground on the sand and looked at each other, surprised that they were in the same position as the other.

"Come with us," Claritsa said.

Maella thought for all that Daniel was from home, and for all of his kindnesses, that he would go with Lirella.

But he did not.

He came to Maella's group. He looked at Maella as if asking permission. She thought of those scales and nodded.

But Harry was the surprise. After the way he had helped them build the ladder of bones and the way he had defended her and spoken about death—she thought he would come with her.

But he went to Lirella's group.

Lirella led her people through the sand. Those with swords walked backwards for a time to guard themselves. That was how Erentia and Miall and Radovan said goodbye to her. With swords drawn.

When they became dark specks on the yellow sand no bigger than the ants that had swarmed the stones on Rock Heaven, Utheril's guards lowered their blades. She would need to learn their names. They were going to spend a great deal of time together surviving this new place.

She walked over to the open door.

"Doormaker..." one of the Hestroth said.

She leaned through, back into Rock Heaven. The height made her dizzy. Someone grabbed her by the waist.

"Careful, Maella."

She let Sethlo's strong hands steady her. She reached out a little further, trusting he wouldn't let her go. Or maybe not caring if he did. She didn't think about it too hard.

She grabbed the door's handle and held on as its vibrations made the wood jump just a little in her hands.

She closed the door.

The door clicked shut and disintegrated until it was a pile of sand on top of the sand that surrounded them.

She felt both relief and fear. No stone, no wood, no cloth, no cabinet—nothing. She could touch the dirt, she could accidentally fall on it, she could move it all around. It would not open.

The vibrations that had thrummed in Maella stilled.

There were no doors here to open.

The wrongness left her.

No, that wasn't right.

The wrongness was still there, but muffled. She had to look for it, but when she did, she was able to find it. The vibrations sat in the pit of her chest and if she didn't think about it carefully, it might as well be the grumbling of an empty stomach.

She licked her dry lips, breathed out.

Ambassador Utheril didn't say anything for the longest time, like he understood somehow what she was feeling at that moment—the moment she closed the door and realized there wasn't another.

They had escaped Rock Heaven. They had escaped the *licatherin* mine. There should have been joy. There should have been a sense of freedom. But reality set in. They had faced a slow death by starvation in Rock Heaven, but here, death would come fast if all they had was Daniel's small sack of water to split.

Maella's muscles shook with exhaustion and hunger. Claritsa's hands also shook. Little earthquakes rolled along Sethlo's and Daniel's arms. Only Utheril and his guards did not shake.

It had been a long time since they had gotten a strong dose of *licatherin.*

She had not yet found the answers she needed about her family. She had not yet gotten her friends home safely. She had not yet brought her brother and father home. Three doors remained until she could test Keeper Shaul's prediction about her death. There were no doors here to open. They would find food and water or they would die.

They walked out onto the sand, in the opposite direction from Lirella's group.

They searched for water.

The *licatherin* withdrawals shook them.

And Maella led them.

If they should die out here, she deserved to be first, as payment for all of the terrible things done by her own hands.

Find out what happens next inside…

# Tower of Shadows (Book 2)

~~~~

# Doormaker Series

# Special Book Offer

The complete series (with exclusive bonus content) is available now in ebook, paperback, and audio-book formats.

**Learn more at:**
Books.JamieThornton.com/Doormaker

*Three worlds are falling apart...*

*...but making portals is forbidden.*

*Can an untrained Doormaker save her family, and Earth, in time?*

This complete epic fantasy series includes over a 1000 pages of ancient magic, first love, found family, hunting powerful relics, modern family curses, a crumbling empire, portals to other worlds, and more.

**4 novels, 1 short novel, 1 short story, and exclusive bonus content not available anywhere else...**

## Check out the book bundle at:
Books.JamieThornton.com/Doormaker

# About the Author

Jamie Thornton is a New York Times bestselling author of science fiction. While growing up, she was allowed to check out ALL the books from the public library, so whenever the real world turned too complicated, she escaped into other worlds full of zombies, apocalypses, portals, arcane mysteries, and quests for relics. An anthropology major in college, she then taught middle school science for a really long time while writing her own stories.

Known for the Doormaker portal fantasy series, and the Zombies Are Human apocalypse series, her work has recently been optioned for TV. In addition to writing, she enjoys talking to her animals, pretending she's a good gardener, and falling into research wormholes. She lives in Northern California with her husband in an old brick house that may or may not be haunted.

Join the newsletter for exclusive bonus content, new book release information, and lots of memes.

## Sign up at www.JamieThornton.com

Made in the USA
Monee, IL
14 January 2024